I0738956

DEADSIZING

A COUGAR-HANSEN MYSTERY

LORI HUGHES

Hughes, Lori, author
Deadsizing: A Cougar Hansen Mystery/
Lori Hughes

ISBN (pbk): 978-0-9938196-2-9
ISBN (ebook): 978-0-9938196-3-6

Design by OneBigMachine.com

Sexcess.org
info@sexcess.org

Sexcess.org is a division of
YAANTM Inc.
2704-628 Fleet Street
Toronto, ON
M5V 1A8

*Dedicated to everyone one who loves a good mystery
… the mystery of good cops and bad guys, the intrigue of
good sex and great sex, and the secrets in erotic and
happy-ever-after romance.*

Author's note

Nancy Drew addicted me to mystery and I've been reading and writing mystery stories ever since. My early writings were traditional, proper and prude because I ignored my adolescent sexual urges until well into adulthood, despite having read the sexual adventures in Portnoy's Complaint, The Dying Animal, Lady Chatterley's Lover, Lolita and Tropic of Cancer. But that was then, and now is now. In the intervening years, our culture has gone from prude to crude to the clashing confusion between consent and #MeToo criminality. That's why the sexual truth embed in fiction is so important. It's the one place we are free to explore sexual aspiration, honesty and reality, the heart and soul of life – and great story telling. This is the genre I love to explore.

Enjoy!

Lori Hughes

A PEEK INSIDE TO WHET YOUR DESIRE

She stepped around the butcher-block island, never letting go of his hand. He turned, and she walked into his arms.

He stopped breathing, absorbing the imprint of her body.

In that moment, there was more than a physical awareness, it was an undeniable connection across a forbidden divide. She felt his arousal … and the power of his embrace, the intensity of his body, the hunger in his hands. Her innermost, sexual yearning rushed to his needs.

"Shit," slipped between his lips like a hiss of steam. He inhaled. On the third exhale his pulse slowed and he circled the bed as instincts strained for the slightest sense of what might have happened before death erupted in this extravagant sanctuary.

His thoughts followed her long strides, down the hall. The last thing he remembered was the mesmerizing motion of her holstered Glock 9mm riding on her perfectly shaped hip, in sync with her perfectly undulating butt.

He called out. "See you in the morning."

She said. "Night." *See you in my dreams.*

LOVE & SEXCESS™

'Once upon a time' lasts forever, and we create stories of unabashed romance and intriguing mystery to nourish your unadulterated desires and seduce your limitless imagination.

If you like *Deadsizing*, try *Conflict of Interest*, and *Sacred Corruption*, plus our monthly short stories and serial novellas.

Visit: **Sexcess.org**

CHAPTER ONE

Her skin was pale, void, yet shaded, like the inside of an oyster shell, purple shadows marring her fading beauty. He couldn't push his eyes away. She was staring at the ceiling fan sluggishly beating the air, oblivious to his presence. The damp hair on his neck quivered, maybe from the draft of the incessant fan, more likely from the permanent scream just behind her eye. The horrific dread that locked in the moment she died, actually just before that moment, when the fear, not the emotionless bullet, sucked the life out of every pore of her body.

"Get everybody the hell outta here. Don't touch a thing. I want absolute security," said Sheriff Mike Cougar.

"It's secure." Chief Deputy, Gritt Hansen, swept her arm through the air, introducing her boss to a bedroom draped in opulence, every inch a fabricated fantasy in the mind of some pretentious decorator. She spoke in a hushed tone. "Taped up sir. Tighter than a can."

Mike Cougar wasn't buying his chief deputy's butchered clichés – usually funny, now annoying. "I don't give a shit if it's tighter than a drum, I want everybody, except you and the witness, out of the house, now."

"Kept everybody downstairs. Til you got here."

"And off the property."

"Off the property?"

"You deaf? Put a deputy outside the front door, that's it. Start canvassing the neighborhood."

She respectfully touched the brim of her Stetson, sheathed in plastic as a futile defense against the morning rain. The boss was agitated, not his usual, composed self. He hadn't waited for staff investigators to arrive, he'd taken charge of the crime scene. But barking out the obvious SOPs (standard operating procedures) wasn't like him. Normally, he was as somber as any cop can be when investigating the disgusting underside of human existence. He was quiet and all business, and his deep brown eyes never wavered. Focused. Intent. Taking in everything and everyone. And everyone noticed him, his presence … hell, he was a physical specimen, tall, dark and powerful, and with a great demeanor. He was seldom angry and never showed it. This morning he was showing it. Maybe it's the weather. Been pissin' down rain for three days.

Mike Cougar's gaze held the ashen corpse in a comforting crucible of respect as he clipped out more instructions. "And keep the maid in the front hall 'til I come down."

"Roger that." She left but wasn't completely comfortable leaving him alone. He's not himself.

He snapped on latex gloves and moved reluctantly, as if approaching a treacherous ice-patch. He took a step toward the violently ruffled bed. The lace-trimmed duvet had been yanked from the foot of the mattress, exposing pristine sheets with peach flowers that traced their way up under her dead nakedness. Her torso was already purplish, lividity setting in. The cover had been pulled hard and at the top-end it was scrunched in her clenched fists, drawn up as a protective shield over her chest. It hadn't helped. Her beauty vanished in a thundering blink, gone wherever life goes, as the bullet entered just over the right eye, cruelly dropping her back against the headboard – some really, expensive black wood. The flower petals now shared the sheets with spit-dots of splattered blood, except under her head where it had soaked itself into a red-black coagulum. He was within touching distance. His hesitancy – more a frozen-in-the-headlights disbelief – would have been unacceptable if anyone was watching, but alone in the room, his feelings were allowed a momentary freedom. He dropped his stoicism and let his gut push black bile into the back of his throat as the shrieking, dead stare of Chrystine Goodall seared a permanent scar deep inside him.

He mentally ran a first-pass checklist. Probably a .22 caliber, solid point. No sign of a struggle. No sign of rape. No sign of force. Other than the screaming bullet. Bedroom was messed up. The perp was maybe looking for cash and jewelry. But it looked staged. Killing her was the objective.

"Shit," slipped between his lips like a hiss of steam. He inhaled. On the third exhale his pulse slowed and he circled the bed as instincts strained for the slightest sense of what might have happened before death erupted in this extravagant sanctuary of … a strange thought crossed his mind. *Not of love, more like hedonistic excess.* He never relinquished the very beautiful, very dead woman from his eyes. He knew her. Most people in Westhaven did. Chrystine Goodall. She is – was – the wife of Alexander Goodall, Chief Executive Officer at Syntex. This homicide was different, even though he'd seen it all before: bodies broken by baseball bats and two-by-fours, ripped open by hunting knives and shotgun blasts, wasted on drugs or decomposed beyond recognition. But this one, in the shallow end of high society's gene pool, would rip away the veneer of gossip and expose a truth that would tear the heart and guts out of his hometown.

This was the second murder connected to a big-wheel executive at Syntex. Six months ago, Alan P. Douglas had been shot one night while walking his dog. A case that was going nowhere. Douglas, an arrogant ass was the CEO at Syntex until someone left his brains on the sidewalk for his dog to lick. Whoever did it, planned it. And left the small, 2 1/2" barrel, Ruger.357 Magnum at the scene. Untraceable. Typical of a professional hit. Three months ago, Goodall replaced Douglas. Now, his wife was headed for the county morgue. And a year prior to Douglas, the CEO at the time, Lawrence Weiss, was found dead in his bathtub after decomposing for three days. ME's report said, 'No anatomic cause' and 'Apparent aspiration,' neither of which was conclusive enough for Mike. But the caseload was heavy, so death had been accepted and filed as 'natural causes.' *Is Syntex cursed? Or am I? Are these CEOs going to be my personal Antichrist? And Chrystine … why, why, why?*

CHAPTER TWO

Gritt appeared in the doorway, her lithe, athletic body standing tall, ready for action. "Perimeter secure. Everybody outside the gate. Huddled like a bunch of ducks. What is it they say? Ducks in bad weather, flock together…. somethin' like that." She half smiled. He didn't.

"Interview the witness. No holes in the witness report."

There he goes again, spouting a blinding glimpse of the obvious. Something's bugging him. She did reports with no holes, even though she'd rather eat her gun than fill out a report.

"You're the boss." She departed, slipping under the yellow tape. He was the reason she was here. That, and the fact she'd always wanted to play cops and robbers and chase murderers, drug dealers and car jackers. She'd been running after something all her life, not always sure where she was going, but running head-strong toward something. But more than once, she'd wondered about her decision to be a cop, and more than once had thought of trading in her gun for a pair of rollerblades and a job as an instructor at the local fitness club. Aerobics and a good workout would be a hell of a lot healthier than the grind of paperwork and isolation of night patrol. She was still young. Hell, less than ten years ago, she'd stood tall on the Olympic podium with a bronze medal around her neck. And she could still compete, train and excel – if she wanted to. That was the big question, *want?* What was it about police work that she seemed to want? Why had she joined Mike and his small town, sheriff's department after six years with the FBI? Why not treat her healthy body to a healthy life instead of risking her life catching bad guys?

When she met with Mike two months ago she was running again, from the FBI. Not because she didn't want to be an FBI agent but because her superior was a bully and sexual abuser. And it wasn't about just the one asshole, two of her superiors had his back. When she reported him; they covered for him. The abuse was his grabbing her ass while on all-night surveillance – for which he got her fist in the chops. But reporting the incident created serious obstacles for her career. So she contacted Mike. She'd met him while she was in university and dating his younger brother, Emerson. One weekend when she came home with Emerson, he happened to be there. At the time, he was an FBI special agent and she'd never forgotten her first impression. A hunk – then and now. She'd experienced a sexually powerful attraction to him and basked in his attention, despite Emerson's discomfort. She was sure it wasn't the first-time, big brother had swept one of his dates off their feet. He was gracious, attentive, charming – mesmerizing. The epitome of still waters run deep. Not to mention a physical specimen. He told fascinating stories, particularly about the FBI and that might have been when she fell in love with the idea of going after bad guys. She was infatuated but not on his radar. To him it was flirting. Besides, Emerson was hot too. But the visceral attraction and sexual fantasies stayed with her for a long time. It was flirting on his part, fantasy on hers. Then two months ago, she'd wanted out of the FBI so contacted him. It was fortuitous that he was looking for a new Chief Deputy and agreed to meet her. Five-minutes into their lunch she was sold on him, ten-minutes in she wanted the job.

They'd formed a close partnership, working side by side through the drudgery of reports, minor crimes and a couple of murders. And now this one. She had the highest regard for him and characterized their relationship – and her attraction to him – as mutual respect. He was as charming as ever but curtailed it, keeping it professional, even though she was well aware of his caring for her – it was in his eyes, voice and periodic touch. On numerous occasions, she had to summon all her self-discipline to suppress her natural desires. It was more than his good looks, it was his warmth, love of laughter, brilliant mind and tough, take-no-shit attitude. But underneath the surface there was a struggle, a hidden pain that he religiously controlled.

CHAPTER THREE

Mike stepped forward, lifting the eiderdown. His heart whispered, *she looks cold.* He watched her nakedness with no connection to her non-existence, trying to paint some color back into her. His heart told him what his mind would not. She would haunt his days and ravage his nights far beyond any homicide he'd ever investigated.

He pulled the duvet back, leaving the waxen-like body exposed. His latex finger hovered over her ankle then softly pressed an indentation into the purplish tissue. An inner wish asked her to move, to live again … then sank into a vacuum and detached. The color blanched, then returned; lividity was three to six hours. That put death between two and five a.m. Rigor was moving into her neck and jaw but he couldn't touch her face, not with that dread-filled eye crying out, Why? He fumbled in his evidence kit then robotically went through the routine he'd done so many times before.

Five minutes later, Gritt ducked under the tape. "Techs on their way. ME here in an hour."

"What about the maid?"

She opened her notebook. "Came in as usual, seven a.m. Has access code. Disarmed alarm. Found victim twenty minutes later. I spoke to alarm people. There was an odd sequence of settings last night." She flipped pages. "At eleven fifty-two pm, entry through terrace door. System deactivated eighteen seconds later. No alarm. One forty-seven a.m., entry from garage. Shut off in six seconds. Both legit entries. Get this. At two-thirty, alarm turned off. Reset. Exit through terrace door." She added, "Oh yeah, there's a broken window. Terrace door. Smashed from outside." She reached into her pocket, pulled out a roll of money, smiled and snapped the elastic band off the wad. "Got a hundred says it's our perp entering."

Mike claimed she was the only deputy in the country worth robbing – carried almost a thousand dollars in cash, all the time. She explained that she liked to be prepared if a little wager came along on the ponies, basketball or football. She considered a little betting as a supplement to her 401K. But her habit had gotten her into a couple tight spots – especially as an off-duty deputy – and once he had to cover for her at the casino when she'd consumed too much drink and lost too much money. She admitted going to excess sometimes, but rationalized it as an occasional problem, not an addiction.

She said, "Perp had to know the code."

Mike half whispered. "Fuckin' bastard."

She raised an eyebrow. He seldom used foul language on the job, always controlled the emotion, particularly at a murder scene. Under his steely toughness was a sense of reverence for victims and he handled investigations in a subdued, methodical manner, giving no more of himself than required. Normally, he was easy going and laughed a lot but recently had been preoccupied and mad about something. And when he got mad, three things happened. First, he started yelling out orders – trying to control things. Then he'd go quiet and crack his knuckles. Then he'd eat – a lot. He ate twice as much as she did, but was just as slim, trim and hard. Those full-of-life eyes had gone gray. *Maybe I should take him out for wings and beer, and a few laughs? Soon. He needs a distraction. Maybe me?*

Mike usually made sense of death but here, in this bedroom, the cruel contrast between life and death, between beauty and carnage, between what-is and what-might-have-been made no sense. The loss of life had never left him so hollow. Gutted. But he had to get this case in perspective, get Gritt more involved, but not too much. She was good. Smart as a whip. Reliable. Single-minded. Emotionally restrained, and a reassuring presence in the toxic swamp of death. Hiring her was the best thing he'd ever done. Here she was standing across from him in her crisp-cut uniform, looking the spitting image of the day she stood on the Olympic podium, tall, statuesque, self-assured and a beaming beauty. Except today, she wasn't beaming. "Can we get some damn food? Coffee and doughnuts. And where the hell are the techs? I'll talk to the maid … is she the only witness?" He didn't wait for an answer. Picked up his evidence kit and was gone.

Gritt puzzled. *Why the switch?* She'd already talked to the maid and he said he was doing the bedroom? *He was certainly checking the body when I came in. And if he's eating, he's pissed.* She stood in the bedroom doorway. Almost seven years playing cops and robbers and she still hated being around dead bodies – bodies pulled from rivers covered in bloodsuckers, bodies dangling from rafters, bodies stuffed in freezers, bodies in basements, stairwells, cribs and … king-size beds. She'd learned to transform the act of bearing witness to the dead by forcing it through the mechanical brain, the part that didn't feel. *If he's being emotional – god knows why? – I gotta be extra cool.*

Mike went to the kitchen looking for doughnuts and didn't go back upstairs until the medical examiner came, just after ten. While the ME examined the body, Mike, uncharacteristically, stood back, just inside the bedroom door. And he was cracking his knuckles.

"Not a lot of unanswered questions here," was the first utterance from old Doc Wemyss. Mary Wemyss reminded Gritt of her always-grouchy Aunt Polly, real and unvarnished. "Probably 'round two or three am. Air conditioning and the fan," she nodded at the thumping rotator, "probably slowed the process. I'd say, dead six to eight hours."

Those eight hours held the secret to this murder, a freeze-frame of life and death that would have to be painstakingly disemboweled, without committing hara-kiri.

Doc rattled on. "No rape. Maybe recent sex, but no force." She turned to Mike "You can take her outta here, I'll do the rest downtown."

He reacted. "Yeah … okay." He motioned to Gritt, touched her arm and dropped his voice. "Handle her carefully."

After ushering the body bag into the morgue van, she found him in the kitchen working on his third doughnut and complaining that he liked chocolate, not plain. "And I hate cinnamon."

She said. "I lov'em. Ya' know the ol'sayin'. If ya' can't eat 'em, leave 'em for me." She laughed. He didn't.

Through a slurp of coffee, he asked, "So deputy, you got this solved yet?"

She ignored the sarcasm. "On first pass, the evidence – and my hundred bucks – says perp broke in, had alarm code. Either a pro or knows someone. Points to a hit. But the secret lies with her. If she – "

His eyes shot up. "Enough with the bad puns … your sense of humor isn't needed here."

Where did that come from? "No pun intended … I'd never – "

"Never mind. Never mind about her … need more evidence, less speculation."

"Apparently the husband is out of town – trying to contact him. Means he could have an alibi. So gotta look at potential love-triangle and if – "

"Leave that to me. You stick to the husband and crime scene. Leave no stones, hairs or shards of glass unexamined." He strode out of the room.

She didn't have to be a detective to see how quickly he dismissed the idea of an affair. *Stick with it girl.*

CHAPTER FOUR

"Your wife is dead," reverberated in Alexander Goodall's head for a couple of seconds. Then he relegated it to a mental compartment where all distractions went and responded to the policeman. "Thank you officer."

The policeman seemed unsure what to do next. Usually a victim's family needed to talk or ask a few questions, but this man spoke as if he was now dismissed. "Sir … if you have any questions, you can contact your local sheriff's department, Sheriff Mike Cougar, Here's his number." He handed him a piece of paper and left.

Goodall, standing like a solitary tree in the paneled corporate offices, fiddled with his cuff link, cinched his tie and returned to the boardroom where he was holding a meeting.

From the end of the over-sized, boardroom table a stiff-and-starched, gray-haired, blue-suited executive inquired. "Everything okay Alex?"

Goodall's flash-smile – a plastic product developed from years of practice – masked the moment. "I'll take care of it later…. Where were we?" His flip-switch charm put the meeting back on track and the half-dozen people at the table continued as if the 'urgent message' for the visiting CEO had never happened. Goodall knew the importance of Mr. Stiff-and-Starched, he was a big customer – eight percent of sales, twelve percent of profits, high-margin, repeat business. The customer was concerned about the massive downsizing he'd executed at Syntex and he'd flown in to alleviate the concerns. The customer's focus was on quality and he was here to assure them that quality will, in fact, improve, not diminish, due to his downsizing strategy. He'd told his board of directors there was nothing better than a sense of urgency, triggered by layoffs, to motivate people and he'd used one of his favorite Machiavellian quotes, 'It is far safer to be feared than loved.'

This morning, as his Vice-President outlined their plans, his mind toyed with the compartmentalized thought, *Chrystine is dead.* Then, from somewhere inside his head rose a question, like a whisper behind a closed door, *Are you sad?* His thoughts rolled over like wet cement, trying to congeal into something firm. *Somewhat.* She was a hell of a woman, a trophy, and an asset in his business and social life. Her resume was impressive: Swathmore, Harvard Law, six years at American Express and four at Goldman Sachs, that's where he'd met her. She'd hated law so after they married she went into charity work. She was good at it and it was more suited to her because she really didn't have what it takes to survive at the top – long on nice, short on guts. Sometimes she was a little too nice around the opposite sex; god could she flirt, turn an entire room of hard-ass executives into fawning sheep. But she gave him great profile. She was often in the press and had recently had a feature article in Cosmopolitan – about both of them – although Vogue would have been better. No question, she was talented, hell, she was even writing a novel. But that was history. More recently, she'd become a problem. A couple of months ago, she'd announced she wanted a divorce. He'd laughed at her, the gall. Divorce was out of the question at this stage of his career. He told her she would not get a divorce or anything close to her ridiculous demand for a forty-million-dollar settlement. Since then, he'd practically ignored her, traveling extensively and when at home, sleeping in a guestroom. He didn't care; he got laid whenever he wanted, beautiful chicks, models, all of them. And he hadn't kidded himself, he was pretty sure she'd been sleeping with someone. Last week, a business contact of his had seen her leaving the Hilton late one night. But all that was part of their tawdry secrets. To the outside world, they were one of Corporate America's most stylish couples. He loved the image and had kept it intact by telling her that if they ever did divorce and she expected to get a big settlement, then she'd better fulfill the obligation of maintaining his public image. And she would because she loved all the bobbles and bangles that his money could buy. Now, she was gone, blown away, and everything was about to explode in a media frenzy. But that didn't have to be a bad thing. He could envision the widower becoming a sympathetic, respected, tower of strength, fighting on, alone, committed to saving the company, rescuing the sorrowful, hick town and being an example for all to admire. Maybe he'd make the cover of Forbes.

That afternoon, in the whispering luxury of his private jet, he scanned his iPhone and called his secretary. "Brook, notify the sheriff I'm on my way. On the ground by three-thirty, house by four. What do you know?"

"Very little sir. Police aren't saying much. They simply said there'd been an accident and …" She struggled for control. "I, I'm so sorry sir. I don't – "

"Just let them know." A poke of the screen and she was terminated.

Alone, ensconced in one of nine leather seats, he looked like an emotionless mannequin. Peering into the blue that cradled his forty-million-dollar toy, he pondered life without Chrystine. Then he called his lawyer.

CHAPTER FIVE

Mike was waiting in the foyer when Goodall came through the front door with Chief Deputy Hansen standing behind him. The contrast between the two struck at his sense of proportion. Gritt exuded more presence and respect than this self-inflated piece of aggression. Her eyes were relaxed, waiting to see what happened next and her black uniform, soaked from the rain, made her look like a purebred, black labrador returning with her quarry. Goodall, at least two inches shorter, was quintessential business. Impatient. Aggressive. With a stone-cold demeanor. He was a clone of what the boardrooms of Wall Street must be full of, and despite evidence of too much good food and drink, he was full of energy, ready to take on all comers. His face reflected a synthetic charm and his eyes were ever-alert, searching for what was next, before it happened. He looked like he was born wearing his custom-tailored suit, blue shirt, gold cuff links and designer tie. Even his hair, with a touch of black coloring, wasn't out of place. Obviously, Hansen had held the umbrella for this ego-dick.

"What the hell's going on Sheriff? Nobody's telling me anything. Your deputy here might as well be a deaf mute. Her communications skills need upgrading. All she says is, 'you'll have to ask the sheriff.' Well, I'm asking!" He looked like he was going to push past but he saw what everyone sees in Mike Cougar, a don't-even-try-it, rock-like presence. Even this domineering chief executive felt the opposing authority.

"Mr. Goodall, your wife is dead. Murdered." He said it as well as it could be said. Direct, no hesitation, with compassion.

Gritt heard another emotion in his voice. Compassion, yes, but there was pain, a palpable sadness. More than she expected. And his eyes dropped from Goodall's gaze.

"Murdered?" Goodall moved toward the stairs.

"Sorry sir, this is a crime scene. You can't go there. Not until we're finished."

"For god's sake. This is my house. Where's your sense of decency? Your warrant?"

Mike knew that anyone worried about his murdered wife didn't worry about a warrant. "Chief Deputy Hansen will show you the warrant sir. House has been secured since early morning and your wife's body was taken to the county morgue at ten fifty-five. If you disturb anything it could impede our investigation." He turned. "I have a few questions, let's sit in here." Not waiting for an answer, he walked into a living room drowning in affluence.

Goodall sank into a chair. "Anything missing?"

Usually Mike empathized with the anguish of a victim but something about this man hardened his feelings. Maybe it was the arrogance or maybe it was the talk around town that had preconditioned him. People called him 'Ax Goodall.' He might be popular in the social columns but in the bar and coffee shop-talk, he was a hated or feared man. He even made Mike uneasy, not in a bullying way, more like a blackjack dealer makes a new player feel when first sitting down at the table, worried that his emotions will show. His emotions must never be exposed to this man, regardless of how tough it might be.

Gritt sat in one of the sofas, crossed her long legs and leaned back to observe her boss in action. She'd seen him in similar situations and he was good at penetrating the pretense of a witness.

Mike remained standing. "We don't think it's about theft, even though some things may have been taken. We'll need you to confirm what's missing."

"What about, what do you call it? Forced entry?"

"Maybe," said Mike.

"Maybe?"

"I understand you were in Scranton, Pennsylvania last night?"

"Maybe?

Mike frowned. "Maybe you were in Scranton?"

"Uh … no. Maybe forced entry? Of course I was in Scranton."

Mike asked, "When did you last talk to Mrs. Goodall?"

"You don't know if there was forced entry or not?"

"When did you last talk to your wife?"

"Last night. She called me at my hotel, about two."

"Is that normal? At that hour?"

"She'd just gotten in."

"Why'd she call?"

"We often speak when I'm out of town."

"Did you call her last night?"

"Earlier."

"What time?"

"I don't recall."

"How long did you talk?"

"Couple of minutes."

"Did she seem upset? Frightened? Anything unusual?"

"What are you looking for sheriff?"

Goodall appeared truthful, but his words were clipped, measured, saying only what was required. He was controlled, as if he was holding a business meeting, not discussing his wife's murder. *Cold-hearted bastard.* He continued the questioning, establishing Goodall's whereabouts and garnering information pertaining to events prior to the murder. "Do you know where she was last night?"

"Attending some charity event at the Hilton."

"When did it end?"

"Sheriff, please – "

"Do you know?"

"I'm not my wife's keeper. She had a busy schedule, much of which I knew nothing about. Was she found upstairs?" He rose from the chair, moved toward the window then turned back. "Was she sexually attacked?"

"Why do you ask?"

"Was she?"

"Any reason to believe she might've been?"

"My wife's a beautiful woman. Alone in this house … a rapist could've stalked her, got in somehow … forced entry. What the hell do I know? Maybe someone came home with her, just innocent socializing that got out of hand."

"Someone with a gun?"

"I don't know! Trying to reason this out."

"Do you own a gun sir?"

"Was she shot?"

"Does Mrs. Goodall own a gun?"

"No.... How the hell would I know?" Goodall stepped closer and faced him square up. "Let me ask you sheriff, do you have any idea who could have done this? Any clues? Anything?"

For the first time, Mike sensed real emotion in Goodall, a skin flush, a quivering behind a purplish vein in his right cheek. Anger? Anxiety? He remained silent.

"Was she sexually assaulted?"

Mike turned to Gritt. "Give us a minute."

"Sure." As she closed the French doors behind her she thought. *Dismissed? That's not like him. Always wants my take on interviews. He looked unsettled about the rape question – and earlier in the bedroom he had his rape kit out. Is he keeping something from me?*

Mike moved behind a wingback chair, a barrier to prevent him from punching this smug-ass in the nose. "Sir, I can't give you details on our investigation at this time. And I don't want the media knowing too much. It's for your protection – "

"Who the hell do you think you're dealing with? Some whimpering widower? I don't need your protection. And if anyone knows the importance of confidentiality, I do. Corporate deals, the kind I make, don't happen if someone talks too much. Trust me, you can trust me. For Christsake, this is my wife we're talking about."

"I understand but – "

"I don't think you do. I'm not about to place all my bets on your sheriff's department. I want the full weight of the law brought down on this. I want this bastard found. I'll spend whatever it takes. That's what you need to understand."

Usually Mike had no trouble remaining calm when people behaved irrationally but today he felt as if he was either going to hit Goodall or walk out. He tried to sound composed. "We'll know more after the autopsy. Crime scene should be cleared by tomorrow. In the meantime, I suggest you stay with friends or at a hotel, this property is off limits."

"You do what you have to. But mark my words, I'll do what I have to." He looked at the sheriff as he would a subordinate.

Mike's eyes dismissed the attempt at intimidation. "We'll want to talk tomorrow. Anything you can think of will be important."

There was a deliberate change in tone. "Of course." He pulled out his mobile phone and headed for the foyer. "I'll be at the Marriott."

Mike wasn't sure which of his feelings were stronger, suspicion or revulsion. But he was looking at the backside of a formidable adversary. Gritt came in. "What do you think of mister bigshot?"

"Smoke and mirrors. He's trouble. We're gonna get a lot of 'don't recalls' and 'ask my lawyer.'" He shrugged. "Better get our shit together." He used to relish going after the likes of Goodall and trimming their bloated-ass lives down to some measure of reality. Because there was no reality in their gold-coated fortresses, built on power, greed and a sociopathic view of what was important in life – themselves. All of it motive enough for murder. But during this, his second term as sheriff, his interest in justice had faded as he experienced more political and bureaucratic bullshit. Constantly frustrated – if one more dick-head politician called him one more time about one of more dick-head friend in trouble, he was going to quit on the spot. He was losing his appetite for the task at hand and had considered resigning – until Gritt. She'd changed everything. She was his saving grace, in more ways than one.

CHAPTER SIX

Seven months ago, Mike had gone through the process of interviewing Gritt and had come face to face with his own truth. She had been more than just another applicant for Chief Deputy. For that first interview, he'd flown to meet her for lunch in Washington DC, and as she sat opposite him, he couldn't dispel the image of her as Emerson's ex-girlfriend. It had been ten years and yet, it seemed like yesterday, and although he'd told Emerson she was beautiful, he hadn't told him about his sexual fantasies. She was nineteen then and now she was a special agent with the FBI – and even more stunning. Before all of that, she'd been an Olympian, bringing home a bronze medal in the women's 1,500 meters. In that first interview, he went through all the standard questions, but he'd already made his decision.

She displayed a maturity beyond her years and looked like she did on the Olympic podium – proud, confident and exuding an inner strength that was as poised as her sculpted-to-perfection body. When he asked if the name Gritt was a nickname, she'd explained it was Danish. Her mom and dad were born in Denmark and now naturalized US citizens. She was born in Rochester, New York. He'd thought, *Danish explains so much.* Tall, maybe five-ten, natural blonde hair, kept short, and brilliant blue eyes that took everything in, like her Viking ancestors must have scanned the horizon when exploring the world. The only thing more impressive than her beauty was her command, command of self and command of the moment. She was also a young woman searching for something.

Back in Westhaven, he'd put her through more interviews and tests to make sure there were no rumors that he'd hired her because of her looks, not her talent. Of course, both were true. Her work at the FBI more than qualified her and before leaving the Bureau she'd been getting perk assignments because she was tough and good.

Working alongside her had re-ignited his passion for catching bad guys, and no bad guy was more of a diabolical sociopath than the bastard who'd killed Chrystine. It demanded his full commitment – and hers. Anything less, and the dead Chrystine Goodall would unravel everything.

• • •

It was after eight and Mike was staring at the words, no longer reading them. The witness reports were burning through the back of his eyes and the bulging disc in his neck numbing his shoulder. He'd given up on chiropractors, but the disc hadn't given up on him – after too much reading it relished delivering a searing headache. He said to the empty office, "tomorrow ... tomorrow." Dropping his feet off the desk, he pulled out his phone. "Gritt ... question for you?"

"Sure."

"Who ordered the lousy coffee and doughnuts this morning? ... just kidding." He chuckled.

She was so damn tired she didn't laugh. But she was glad he was getting his sense of humor back. She attempted humor "See no evil, hear no evil, speak no evil about bad coffee and doughnuts."

"I read the witness reports – twice – can't find inconsistencies, which doesn't make sense. There's always inconsistency. The maid – "

"Agree. It's as if Goodall is rehearsed."

"Yeah. Been rehearsing all his life, maybe hiding something. Alibi is tight." He continued talking about Goodall's statement, but it was more musing than asking for input.

She was on the eastside, filling up with gas and heading for home, looking forward to a veggie burger out of the freezer, a glass of wine out of the refrigerator and a weary body in bed. He often called after hours but there didn't seem to be any specific reason for this call. *Maybe he's just lonely?* She thought about his recent dark moods.

"Where you at?"

"What?"

"Just getting gas. Wanna talk about this?"

"Just leaving the office," he said.

"What say I drop by. Two tired heads are better than one." It was her heart talking, not her head. Her head was saying get your ass home and in bed, but Mike's out-of-sorts, grouchiness had been troubling her. Getting her tired ass over to his place was important.

He said. "I'll pick up a pizza. Maybe we'll come up with something over great pizza and cheap wine?"

"See ya' there."

He worked late, a lot, and when he went home he was alone. Except for his cat, Mercedes, who he claimed would be the only Mercedes he'd ever own, and his first love, Billy, an amazing old spirit in a Border Collie's body. This dog was like no other. Gritt swore Billy was either reincarnated from one of the three wise men or Einstein. He could turn doorknobs, mute the remote when he wanted attention, fetch anything and with a combination of barks, whines and big brown eyes, communicate better than most people. Billy was sixteen and showing his age. Had a lot of arthritis. But there was nothing wrong with his brain. Billy and Mercedes were Mike's only real companions – and Gritt. Two at home, one at work. His dad, a retired cop, lived in town but he wasn't what anyone would consider a companion. *I wonder if the loneliness is getting to him? Or was his ex-wife sticking it to him, again.* A few months back, over a few beers, he'd said, 'You'd think the bitch – after a brief marriage and almost nine years divorced – would leave me alone?' That's all he'd ever said.

Mike drained his coffee and reached for one more chocolate-chip cookie … *these are like sawdust, nothing like mom's.* She'd made the best – always special for him. His ol'man didn't like chocolate-chips so she made banana bread for him. He remembered how the damn, frozen bananas would fall out of the jam-packed freezer every time he opened the door; god forbid that mom might run out of bananas and the ol'man would be deprived of his precious staple. His mother had constantly done for them. Even tonight, when his workload was a cement block on his head, he would talk to her. It wasn't any mystic crap – communing with the dead – he just liked to have someone to talk to and Billy was at home. Probably why he called Gritt.

Whenever he spoke to his mom, he sensed what she would have said if she were alive. He only needed to close his eyes and she was there, not in a definitive, physical outline, more a drifting presence – her smell and voice, as real as the day she'd said good-bye. It had been one of those freeze-your-ass-off days in February and she'd been more worried about him wearing a hat to school than the long drive she and his father had to take. They were going to Syracuse to attend the Police Association's annual ball. They went every year, but on that day the weather was bad, and every weather report warned staying off the roads unless absolutely necessary. Well, according to grandfather Cougar, the original cop in the family, it was necessary. He was Chair of the Police Association and his son had better be there for the biggest fundraiser of the year. Mike remembered his father hanging up the phone and looking like a big, old dog who'd just been scolded into submission, his usual scowl sagging like melted wax, as it did whenever Cougar Senior pounded on him with his domineering attitude. His father had said, 'He says anyone worth their salt can drive in winter weather.' His mother's reassurance that they'd be fine didn't help her husband's inner storm, knowing they shouldn't go. But he had to try, had to live up to his father's expectation.

Mike's mother had pulled his hat snug on his head, hugged him a little longer than usual and kissed both cheeks, she usually kissed just one. To this very day, he felt the warmth, the life, the love in her kiss. At sixteen, he was busy being tough and independent and hadn't been big on all the mushy stuff but, secretly, she made him feel special. That day, as he joyously leapt off the back steps into the drifting snow, she'd called after him, 'Young man, keep that hat on your head, I don't want you catching your death of cold.' She didn't see him take it off the minute he was out of sight. And he never saw her again.

Before locking the office, he watered the plants and as he watched the water give life to his African violets he saw the dead Chrystine Goodall and Alan Douglas. Their indelible images were like Siamese twins lying in two pools of blood, and his gut was yelling, *they're connected.* And yet, the evidence said these murders were as separate as life and death. Chrystine was killed in her home; maybe by someone she knew because the scene showed no signs of a struggle. Or she'd been surprised at the last moment. Douglas, on the other hand, appeared to have been shot by a pro, maybe robbery. Watch, ring, money had been taken. But it was also possible a pro could have killed Chrystine. But why? What ripped at Mike was the fact that Douglas' dog, a Doberman, had been useless during the attack. That's what had sent him back to reread the witness file of Mrs. Douglas' statement, the part where she'd said:

> *Shiner (the dog) was a good watchdog ...*
> *would've protected Alan. Attacked anyone*
> *bothering him. Even in the house, people*
> *stood back when Shiner was at his side. Alan*
> *would have had to tell him to stand down. If*
> *not, they would have had to shoot Shiner.*

According to the first officer on the scene, the dog hadn't let him near the body. It took a dogcatcher ten-minutes to get him under control. Douglas had been shot at close range. So why had the dog allowed the assailant to get close? Had Douglas known him? Had the dog known him? The proximity of the shooter was the only similarity to Chrystine Goodall's murder. On a first pass, he considered it a coincidence that Douglas and Goodall had both been CEOs at Syntex. It wasn't as if she was the CEO. He was certain that her only crime was being married to him. Nine times out of ten the prime suspect is the husband. But what would be his motive? Or was it intended for the husband but took her instead? Or was he trying to convince himself of that because the alternative was too damn frightening – the killing of corporate executives by some nut bar.

He ordered the pizza and headed home.

The kitchen light was on. It kept Billy comfortable after dark. Whenever he came home late, Billy waited in the kitchen and despite the pain in his back joints, hobbled to the side door before Mike unlocked it. Their greeting was preordained. Mike would cup his hand under Billy's chin, smile into his wanting eyes and say three "I luv yous." Then Billy flicked three licks across Mike's face and Mike kissed his forehead. Then the rest of life continued.

Billy's aching limp loaded old memories into Mike's mind. Up until a couple of years ago, he would drive home from a workout at the YMCA and Billy would run home instead of riding. He loved to run. As sheepherders, Border Collies run for miles. He would race along the sidewalks, cross at corners and if the light was red run parallel to the street until he could safely J-walk. Backyards, fences and weather were no problem. In the winter, as he pounded along he would let his tongue hang out and slurp up a little snow so as not to dehydrate. Stopping was out of the question. He usually beat Mike home.

Sally, his ex-wife, had never understood the man and his dog. She'd claimed that not only was dog man's best friend, but this dog had it better than she did – no mortgage, no debts, no sex-on-demand and an unlimited supply of food, water and shelter, plus more TLC than any woman could ever hope for. During their brief marriage, he'd compartmentalized his emotions, but they couldn't survive the grind and grime of his FBI work as he became more attached to the job and detached from her. She bitched, he worked late. Soon they gave up trying to make it work. He divorced her before their first anniversary. Even though that was ten years ago, she still showed up in his life, periodically. Her mother, Doris Planck lived in Westhaven and she came to visit, infrequently, but enough to remind him of her latent anger ... *hell hath no fury like a woman scorned.*

CHAPTER SEVEN

Mike greeted Billy with their ritual, put the pizza in the oven and opened a bottle of wine. Gritt arrived fifteen minutes later. As she strode down the hall, he admired the long, limber legs that had covered 1,500 meters in just a few seconds over four-minutes. And as she unbuckled her gun belt, he admired the rest of her. He felt better.

"What's up boss?" She dropped her belt on one of the two chairs and plopped onto the sofa. She felt comfortable in his house, decorated in early American sparse. Typical male domicile even if he was the farthest thing from typical, which she'd known from the minute they'd met, and even though she dumped his brother for Olympic training, she'd never forgotten the taller, handsomer, more intriguing, older brother.

After opening a couple of beers, she muttered through a mouth full of pizza, "There's no way I should be eating this crap. I was heading home to a healthy veggie burger and a good night sleep and then, as usual … work."

"Are you filing a complaint. If so, paperwork on my desk by seven, sharp."

"I ain't doing more paperwork. Only thing I'm doing at seven is sleeping. Not on 'til nine tomorrow, in case – "

"Banker's hours? Or just a hangover from FBI days?"

"Some good days back then. You?"

"Yeah. Some good, some not so good. No regrets."

"None?"

"Regrets are like putting rocks in your socks and trying to run a mile … of course, you should know what it's like to run a mile."

"Used to run ten, with a fifty-pound backpack."

"I used to run a mile when I was eighteen, just to get a beer."

"Speaking of beer – "

"Who me?"

"What say I buy you a beer over at Frankie's one-night?"

"What? Like a date?"

"Nah, no date. Just an off-duty chat." She saw the spark in his eye. She liked that. She wanted to see more of his fun side. Get past the sheriff shit. *Wonder what the real Michael Cougar is like?*

He grinned at her reclining on the sofa. "You know what they say about dating?" His eyes filled with mischief, like a teenage boy asking a knock-knock joke.

"What do they say about dating?"

"A date is just an interview for sex?"

His eyes dropped. Was he being an embarrassed teenager? Or her boss, avoiding her gaze as he skated too close to his adult-only thoughts? It was playful. She liked it. "Sure. But how many interviews does it take? One? Three? Ten?"

He smiled. "Seriously. Think about it. If you go back over all your dates, I'll bet you can count the number of interviews – and they're different for different guys."

"Depends on a lot of things. If – "

"The thing is. The woman is always the interviewer, the guy the interviewee and – "

"Not necessarily. I'll bet you've been the interviewer on many a date. I'll bet there's been dozens of women applying for a job – sex – with you. Hell, if – "

"Not really."

She saw a melancholy in his eyes. A memory? A good one? A bad one? "Come'on Mike. Divorced as long as you've been, the line-up has gotta be around the block … a good-lookin', gun-toting, handsome catch like you? Hell, Billy can't fill all your needs. If I was betting – "

"Yeah, but you're not betting. And you sure as hell wouldn't want to bet on me. The only catching going on in my life is criminals. And right now, I ain't doing so hot on that end either."

"You telling me you're not doing so hot on the woman front?" She said it lightly, watching his eyes. With his looks, brains, build, he could have any woman who'd want him – and who the hell wouldn't want him? If she didn't work for him … *OMG.* Ever since that first lunch, she'd struggled to relegate her sexual fantasies of him and lock them up in a corner of her mind. And as the police work had intensified, she replaced them with a mantra of 'mutual respect' – to dampen her desires.

"There is no woman front. I'm not shopping, not buying. It's a fool's game." As much as he didn't want to sound cynical about women, the curiosity in her blue eyes urged him on. "After a stupid, empty marriage, you'd think I'd have learned a thing or two. No, not mister hot-shot sheriff, mister mystery solver. Hell, if ever there was a mystery that can't be solved, it's women – no offense."

"No offense taken."

"I'm done. Had it. There's a lot to be said for being single. I can't fathom ever again being … wanting to be – "

She stood up. "I need another beer – you?"

"Uh … sure."

She'd interrupted him. It was a reflex action. Did she do it on purpose? Didn't want to hear his proclamation? "Keep talking. I can hear you."

He watched her walk – stride – into the kitchen … so graceful, supple, sensuous, sexual. *Even in that less-than-complimentary uniform her Olympic goddess body is so obvious.* "No more women. No more dates. But I'll take you up on the free beer."

She was back holding two, cold Genesees, standing next to his leather recliner. "This free beer. Or the one I'm offering at Frankie's?"

"Both."

She curled up in the corner of the sofa, long legs tucked under her. "I hear a lot of cynicism … for a single guy who I assume has not been in a serious relationship for … how long?" He wasn't looking at her, just staring into the beer can. "Actually, you sound more like a guy who just got dumped."

"You know what I can't figure out? What's missing…. Motive. There's no goddamn, fuckin' good reason for someone to kill her." His eyes turned from the beer to her.

She saw the pain, the questioning. She went to him. Sat on the arm of the chair and put her arm around his shoulder. "We'll get the bastard."

He leaned into her. Felt her warmth. Almost rested his head against her. But didn't. Instead, placed his hand on her knee.

Geez. She suppressed her involuntary reaction.

He gently patted her leg. "I know, I know … we'll get him. But that's not going to help her much. One of your silly clichés would work here … too little, too late."

He was sad, heavy sad. She wanted to run her hand through his hair, pull him close, ease the ache. Instead, she squeezed his shoulder. Just once.

He looked up and pressed his fingers into her leg. "I trust you Gritt."

She brushed her hand across the back of his neck. "Always … you always can." She pulled on his shoulder.

He put his beer down and put his other hand on her hip. "We must trust each other … or this case will eat us up."

She stood up. She needed separation. Didn't want it, but needed it.

He saw strength and determination as she rose, it was as if she was stepping up on the Olympic podium. He stood to face her, taking her hands. "I know the sheriff isn't supposed to hold hands with his chief deputy but … just for a moment. Think of it as a double handshake."

"Yes sir." Addressing him formally didn't subdue her rising flush. She wasn't sure if it was obvious in her face, but it was racing through her body. *I never should've sat next to him, touched his neck … I just care about the state he's in.* "What can I do?"

"This case … Goodall. It's going to get worse before it gets better – much worse. I need you – us – to be focused, in sync … on the same page." He took a deep breath. "And the death of Chrystine is going to get very complicated and – "

"I understand." She didn't, but felt his grip tighten and his eyes soften as he mentioned Chrystine Goodall. She squeezed his hands. The urge to pull him in was almost uncontrollable. She stretched up and kissed his cheek. It was more than a peck, but less than she wanted. "I do, I do understand." She saw warmth and strength in his eyes – and vulnerability.

He let go of her hands, but not her eyes. "You're the best thing that ever happened to me … to this department. I'm counting on you … to help me nail this bastard, no matter what."

It was a plea.

His intensity filled her, shutting everything out. It was as if she was on the podium, an overwhelming sense-of-strength and happiness coming together, except it wasn't a podium, it was his living room and he was standing next to her. She liked it. Very much.

He blinked. "Another beer?"

She almost said yes. "Nah, I should get home. Can't be late tomorrow. Damn boss is always in early."

He headed to the kitchen. "He won't give a damn. You could walk in at noon and he wouldn't care. He knows you need downtime, some fun." He looked back over his shoulder, *I'm not your boss, I'm not a sheriff, I'm just a guy who wants to be with you, who needs some downtime, some fun … with you.*

To avoid a complete collapse of self-discipline, she buckled on her gun belt, hoping it would help restore a sense of professional conduct and stop her from straying any further into personal fantasy.

"I'm exhausted. Love to stay … but – "

He stopped, one hand on the refrigerator door. "Why is there always a but? Life has too many buts. But ... maybe your right. I've got an early morning meeting with a big pain in the butt, my ol'man.

"Sorry about that." Any meeting with his dad could be agonizing. "We'll do it again, soon. At Frankie's." She walked toward the front hall, distancing herself from her undeniable desire. His lean frame, silhouetted against the white kitchen, plus the disappointment in his tired eyes, were begging for a hug.

His thoughts followed her long strides, down the hall. The last thing he remembered was the mesmerizing motion of her holstered Glock 9mm riding on her perfectly shaped hip, in sync with her perfectly undulating butt.

He called out. "See you in the morning."

"Night." *See you in my dreams.*

For him, sleep didn't come easily and with Billy curled up in a snoring bundle on the bed, Chrystine Goodall's ghost drifted across the room.

• • •

Gritt never had trouble sleeping, could sleep anywhere, anytime. Except tonight. On the drive home from Mike's she'd been operating on autopilot, just concerned with getting her tired, frustrated ass home. It wasn't until she hit the bed that reality and fantasy clashed.

The reality was her obvious denial, the fantasy her runaway imagination. Alone, wrapped in her duvet, the voice in her head kept saying, *be disciplined, disciplined, disciplined,* but her feelings whispered, *I want him, want him, want him.* This wasn't the first time she'd allowed her sexual fantasies of Michael – she liked to call him Michael in her mind – to overtake her, but this evening at his place had been too much. Toss. Turn. Discipline. Want. Conflict. Sweat. He was there with her, holding, kissing, touching, filling her ... and then he wasn't. She got up, changed her wet night-shirt, drank Ovaltine, and tried again.

Staring at the ceiling, she focused on Michael the professional instead of Michael the fantasy. Because he wasn't in a good place and that wasn't good for the case. And the fact that he was meeting his ol'man in the morning would exacerbate the tension. Hell, his dad, Jack, was also a cop. He'd retired from the city police force a couple years ago but played cop every time they got together, always haranguing about this or that case. He just couldn't leave it, or his son, alone. His nickname was Jackhammer, but for her, and others, it was Jackass. He was a hothead, a know-it-all and acted as if his life was a huge, angry knot. The day he handed in his badge was a good day for everybody who'd dealt with him, especially Mike. Unfortunately, it had the reverse effect on Jackhammer as he tried to reconcile his loss of power and authority. No badge, no gun and no respect had made him an irritated, unemployed malcontent. Mike never denied his father's shortcomings and once in a quiet moment with her, had talked about the conflict between trying to show respect for his father and wanting to throw a large building at him. He'd said, 'the ol'man always wants to be the hero, has to be right, no matter who he runs over.' Then he shrugged, 'What are you gonna do? He is who he is. And his father is who he is. Maybe it's in the genes?' She didn't know the grandfather, other than he was also called Jack, also a retired cop, and living in an old folks' home in Syracuse. Of course, she'd known Emerson, the youngest son … *what a tragic story.*

In the morning, she would try and be Michael's sounding board and help him put some distance between he and Jackass. The pang of emotion pushed her back into fantasy and somewhere between sexual forays, she slipped into sleep. Until the neighbor's barking dog woke her.

CHAPTER EIGHT

The sun was just kick-starting the day when Mike, with four coffees in hand, kicked his car door shut and walked to the back of the house. It was one of those veterans' houses, a three-bedroom box with clapboard siding and a seen-better-days picket fence propped up by unkempt grass and flourishing goldenrod. A nineteen fifties, green and a used-to-be white aluminum awning hung over the back stoop. Jack hadn't spent much time on upkeep since he retired. For the longest time, he hadn't been interested in anything and hadn't done any crossword puzzles, the one thing he labored over for hours as the self-crowned, crossword king – as long as the definition of his kingdom didn't reach beyond the boundaries of *True Crime* magazine. But he seemed better now that he was cruising the streets driving a taxi, part time. It got him out of the house.

Jackhammer was a tough son-of-bitch to get along with. Always in charge, always right. Always talking about how it was and how he'd done it in the streets or in Vietnam. How he was a hero. For Mike, he was more of a pain in the ass and if he had his druthers they wouldn't talk shop at all. But it just might help Mike on this case and keep the old man away from brooding with his best friend, Jack Daniels. The only way to find any redeeming qualities in their relationship was to keep communications open. He'd been trying for years, to no avail. But here he was again, ready to take the heat in search of something, knowing there was probably nothing. Despite the aggravation, he'd involved him in the Douglas case, and now Goodall, with the faint hope he might get some extra smarts from one of the better beat cops in Westhaven history. Beyond the obvious father-son confrontations, he suspected he hadn't forgiven his father for his mother's death, just as his father hadn't forgiven *his* father or the truck driver. It no longer mattered to

Mike, but it did to Jackhammer, who still had to win, always.

The screen door banged open. "Well, well. The prodigal son returns."

"Pops. What's new?"

"You here."

"Don't start." He passed him two coffees. "Here's a peace offering, two black, no sugar. And another one." He held up a third Styrofoam cup. His father was a coffee addict.

"What's with you? Never wear your uniform anymore?" Jack backed into the blue and yellowed-white kitchen, flipped the top off a cup and spilt it. "Shit…. Collar the bastard yet?"

"Yeah. Taking the rest of the week off."

Jack knew the kid was a good cop. But too much by the book, too political. He didn't get that the system didn't work. Sure, as sheriff, he had to get re-elected, but a real cop had to write his own book because the scum made their own rules. But the kid went to college so was supposed to know more – what a crock. It was disappointing that he hadn't joined a police force instead of the sheriff's department, but what the hell, at least he came around for experienced input. None of the kids came by much. The eldest, Don, an engineer at Syntex, only dropped by on obligatory occasions like Christmas and Father's Day, and Emily, his daughter, hadn't spoken to him for years. She was a police officer in Syracuse – at least she was keeping the lineage intact. And perpetuating his personal curse, the youngest, Emerson, a US Army Ranger, had been killed in Afghanistan.

Juggling the coffees, Jack asked, "What's the crime scene tell ya'?"

"Got any cookies?"

He nodded at the cupboard.

Mike said. "Somebody knew what they were doing. One shot … to the head."

Jack heard it in the voice; the kid sounded soft. *You gotta be tougher than that. It's just another dead body.* He asked, "Burglary?"

"Jewelry box emptied. But not convinced. Looks like a cover.

Place is loaded with stuff for the taking. Wasn't touched. They've got antiques, electronics, toys and an original Wyeth. And a Picasso."

Jack had no idea what a Wyeth was – he'd heard of Picasso – but knew the kid wasn't focusing on what mattered. "All those rich Johns are the same. Making millions just so they can accumulate a whole bunch of crap they don't need. Somebody ought'a take it all away from them. See how they feel."

Mike watched his father wiping the coffee off the linoleum, which was a haphazard pattern of gray and white splotches on deep blue. He'd always thought it looked like pigeons had shit all over the floor. Suddenly, he saw the image of his mother on hands and knees washing the floor, like she always had. When he was little, she never stopped working, doing everything while her husband tracked down bad guys. Then she died. But that was something the family never talked about, ever – a Jackonian edict. "I'm thinking it was a professional hit. Ordered by the husband."

Jack, still rubbing the pigeon-shit spots on the floor, barked without looking up. "Where the hell did ya' get that idea?"

He heard the unspoken … *stupid.* He wanted help, not criticism. But there was always the implication that he wasn't up to his father's expectation. He'd lettered in three sports at Syracuse University, made Dean's list and had been elected sheriff of Haven County at the age of thirty-three. *What the hell else do you expect of me?* But it would be eternally so because Jackhammer needed lesser men around him to help reinforce his façade of importance and distance himself from his father's expectations. Mike had discovered the best way to deal with him was to go along, let him think he was king of the walk and try to glean the smarts from the shit he served up.

Jack said, "I don't think their glamorous marriage was what it appeared to be. Apparently, she wasn't happy and – "

"How the hell would you know?" Mike pulled a chair up to the table.

"Talk."

"Bullshit. You're not on the force anymore."

"This town will always be mine. I know it better than anyone. Thirty-two years in the streets and twenty-seven growin' up here. I smell things before they happen. Did hear somethin' about a bad marriage. Could be she was fooling around. In those circles, marriage don't mean shit. Maybe – "

"Could be you got it backwards. Could be he was fooling around." He rummaged in the box of chocolate-chips.

"Could be a hit intended for the husband. A mistake. What about drugs? Those rich people are into a shit load of weed and dope."

"No way."

"Never rule out drugs. The black plague. Where there's money there's drugs."

"No way."

"You'll learn kid. Scum acts the same whether it's a two-bit hooker or a rich set of tits and ass."

"You're sick. You don't know shit about this case and already you're spouting crap. I came here to tell you what I know. Least you could do is wait 'til you got something to go on." He chomped on a chocolate-chip.

Jack Cougar read people like a blind man reads Braille. His son's anger was defensive. "Just throwing out possibilities."

Much to Mike's surprise, Jack listened for a while. So he filled him in and emphasized that Goodall was the prime suspect.

Jack waded in. "You don't think it's drugs, but I'm not ruling them out. You said Goodall had recently come back from Indonesia. Over there it's as easy to get China white as it is to get laid in a massage parlor. And up there on *The Hill*, in those fancy-ass estates, they don't deal in fifty-cent bags. Don't discount anything. Too early." He slurped on his second coffee. "From where I sit, the bopper theory makes some sense. The heater and a solid point .22 is a pro's MO. Could be someone she knew. Like a lover. In those circles, they sleep around as often as they play bridge. Who wouldn't want to sleep with her?"

"You're repeating yourself." Mike hated the know-it-all attitude. "This isn't a lover's quarrel, besides – "

"What about sex?"

"I'm waiting for the ME."

"Shit, while you're waiting on Doc Wemyss the leads will dry up. Should'a done vaginal swab."

"My money is on a hit. Wanted to ask you if there might be any typicals in the city's old files. Hit men who might've worked in upstate New York?"

"I'll call Captain Hyll in Rochester. He'll get you the chief of detectives. They might have something on a known bopper. But …"

Here it comes from the oracle on high.

"… if a hit man is involved, it's likely some guy on the fringe. A wanna-be, some guy hoping to make the big time."

How dare he suggest this murder wasn't big time. "What's Captain Hyll's number?"

"Said I'd call him."

"You're retired. I'll use your name as reference. I'll – "

"Harry and I go way back. Leave it with me."

"Can't do. Needs to be official. And my father, ex-cop is not official. If I – "

"Bullshit. It'll be unofficial, ol'buds. I'm telling ya', cut right through the red tape shit. Even though you hotshots are all about bullshit and red tape. Tellin' ya', it's about cops workin' with cops, cops who've walked the streets. And I walked a lot of streets with Harry." He took a breath. "Look, if ya' don't want me to call him, I won't. Do it your way … What's new?"

He stopped priming the pump. By no means had they exhausted the discussion about the case but the discussion was exhausting. He dipped his cookie in the coffee and watched a chocolate chip melt into the black liquid. He was relieved when his father started talking about his older brother Don. Emerson was never discussed. He wasn't just buried next to his mother, he was buried deep inside Jack's pain.

"Ya' know Don isn't too fussed about all these layoffs. But he's more scared than he's admittin.' Says it's the way of the future. I think he's full of shit. Course he don't listen to me. Says it's all necessary if companies are to compete in a global world. Necessary my ass. Ya' know it was just two weeks after that asshole Douglas laid-off three-thousand people, including my huntin' buddy Archie Sims, that Arch committed suicide. Don's got his head up his ass."

Jack droned on about Don explaining away the never-ending downsizing. "Don spouts the technology bullshit and uses the word lean like it was right outta the Bible, the gospel according to Saint Don. Ya' know he's been going to night school and just spent a couple thousand on the latest, stupid computer. Says he's not about to go the way of the rest of 'em." He started on his third coffee. "But they gotta do more than dump people overboard. It's run aground thanks to them but that don't justify throwing crew overboard. There's a fuckin' obligation here. Somebody has to take care of these people." He flipped his palms up. "But know-it-all Don doesn't see it that way. He's blind. But ya' can't tell him that."

"He'll be fine Pops."

Jack grunted.

The small talk rattled on as Jack told stories about the old days. "I remember this small-time hit-man I rousted. Saw him hangin' in front of Mancari's Hardware. Thought it kinda strange. When I get outta the patrol car he runs. I put it on the radio, grab the twelve-gauge and take out after him. Couple blocks later, I come on him in a parking lot. He's got a piece in his hand, looked like a nine-millimeter. Pointed right at me. I level the shotgun at him. For a few seconds, it's a Mexican standoff. I'm thinkin', fuck … hope he's not dumb as he looks. I'd just run what felt like three miles and am ready to puke, 'cept I gotta hold the twelve-gage steady. Finally, the guy drops his piece. I keep him down 'till back up arrives. When I get back to my cruiser, I start gettin' the shakes, so decide I better get the round out of the gun. I rack it back … guess what? There ain't no fuckin' round in the chamber. I'd never racked one in. Then I really got the shakes." Next, he started in about his Marine buddies and 'Nam.

It was time to leave. The old man loved to carry on about his heroics. His diatribe served two purposes; pumped his aging ego and confirmed his son's accomplishments were a notch below his. "Gotta go Pops."

"Yeah, yeah. Like to stay close on this one, ya' know."

He didn't know. "See you."

As the unmarked car pulled away, Jack watched from the shadows of the living room, as if he was on a stakeout. His son didn't realize how much help he was going to be. He pulled the drapes, poured a bourbon, neat, and attacked the next crossword.

CHAPTER NINE

Gritt was learning how Mike thought on the job, but last night, off the job, was a different story and she had no idea what he was thinking. When it came to the job, he was on top of everything, doing whatever was necessary, but it wasn't what he *was* doing that was odd, it was what he was *not* doing. He wasn't asking for background on Chrystine Goodall and was adamant that Doc Wemyss deliver the autopsy results directly to him.

She popped into his office where the flora was getting its daily watering – the place looked like a greenhouse. "Hey.... How's it goin'?

"It's going."

He was more interested in the swirls of water seeping into his plants than her. Or maybe the discomfort of last night was still bothering him, which wasn't good for these murders. They were a load. Called them 'red balls' – big cases, big ramifications and big trouble if they weren't solved. The noise from the DA and local politicians was becoming a din, but nothing they couldn't handle as long as he was a hundred percent. Right now, he wasn't.

She said. "Ya' know what they say. Good thing about bangin' yer head against a brick wall is when ya' stop the bricks don't know the difference."

He turned around. There was a sliver of a smile – could be a wince. "When you stop, it feels good."

"That too."

"Get everybody in the patrol room in an hour. Make sure the board is up to date and witness reports all in. And evidence submission slips done. No mistakes. DA wants an indictment ... soon."

"That guy's a shark." She got no response. "Know why sharks don't attack lawyers?" She paused. "Professional courtesy." She laughed, alone.

He put down the watering can.

She kept poking at his depression. "Yer trapped in an elevator with a lion, tiger and lawyer. Yer gun only has two bullets. What do ya' do?"

He looked at her as if to say, this isn't going to work.

"Shoot the lawyer twice. Just to make sure he's dead."

"We'll be dead if these cases don't get solved. Patrol room, one hour." He turned to his computer. "And Gritt ... thanks."

She smiled. "Look on the bright side. We coulda' been lawyers."

He wasn't trying to mislead her, he just couldn't come clean, yet. Too much at stake. He needed time to sort things out and if that meant she thought he was holding back or angry or depressed, so be it. His father was a problem, but he wasn't the half of it. He could handle him, it was the other half that scared the shit out of him. And last night was risky. And stupid. He shouldn't have given into her allure – actually his hunger. Except he wasn't sure he had a choice, his self-control was missing in action.

"How'd the chat with Jack go?"

"It went."

She let her eyes linger on his. "That's it?"

He looked away. "Pretty much."

"Com'on?"

"Usual Jack shit. About him ... and Don and Emily."

She ventured into what might be forbidden territory. *We only talked about this once, during one of my interviews.* "Does he ever talk about ..." her heart skipped ... "Emerson?"

He sat on the edge of his desk. Mister-tough-guy slipped away and he looked like he did last night, vulnerable. She pressed – Emerson's death had left a stain inside her too. "I know it was a while ago, but I knew him too, you know. If you ever need to talk about him, I'm here. Actually, I'd like to ... sometime. Not now. But sometime."

"I know."

"Maybe over a beer at Frankie's."

His brown eyes reached out to her. "I should to … with you, not the ol'man. Hell, he'll never talk about him. Never." He stood up. "I'd take your hands, again. But not a good idea in the office … know what I mean?"

She smiled, "Got it."

He winked. And smiled.

That's good. "We'll cover it all at Frankie's."

"Might take more than one beer."

"I got the time."

"I'll try and find it," he said.

"We need to find it. Soon." She got the connection she wanted. He winked and smiled again.

Damn she's irresistible … those eyes. "Soon."

"I'm holding you to it." She left, sounding more certain than she was.

CHAPTER TEN

Dick Ryder tossed the newspaper on the floor and it joined a week's pile of old news. He picked up the remote, hit volume and went back to The View. He glanced at the newspaper staring up at him. *That Chrystine Goodall was a looker. Real shame someone that gorgeous is now a cold, piece of meat … what a piece of meat.* His mind fell into its daily cesspool of shame and his thoughts free-roamed. He was glad the asshole Goodall was getting a little of what he deserved. It was time for him to find out what it's like to lose, lose something important, like a wife. Although he hadn't lost Irene, she sure no longer respected him, even though she said she did. How could she? Shit, he hadn't done a fuckin' thing – except drink – for five hundred and eighty-nine days since getting downsized. Counting the days had become a habit.

He couldn't feel any worse. Actually, wallowing in the shit and self-pity helped. It was a place to hide. He was at home in it. No one could get to him when hiding in his own shit and he could think about whatever he wanted.

I'm glad Goodall lost his wife. Just imagine that gorgeous body in bed. Bet she was raped. For sure, no man's gonna pass up something like that when he knows no one will ever find out. I'd never have done such a thing a couple of years ago. Shit, I had everything going for me then. Beautiful wife – Irene is no Chrystine Goodall mind you – and two great kids. Good job. And I was good at it. No one put anything over on me. No sir. I knew my stuff. Lot more than that asshole Goodall will ever know. Marketing was my baby. Couldn't fool old Dick. Seventeen years paying attention to every detail and running the show like clockwork. Then Weiss screwed me, canned me. Yeah, I'd have a go at a gorgeous woman like that if I knew she couldn't tell anybody. Why not? You just point the gun at her and tell her to do it.

He spun around the dial and stopped on an Oprah rerun. The phone rang, once, twice, three times. Irene and the kids were out so they wouldn't be answering it. He stared at Oprah as if he expected her to answer it. The machine clicked on. It was the old kind because they'd cancelled the telephone company service to save a few bucks. Shit, they'd canceled everything and were still short every month. He left the TV on because Oprah was about to give some bastard with six kids, thousands of dollars in gifts. *I got two kids and no fuckin' job, how about giving me something.* He leaned over and turned up the answering machine.

"Dick, it's Sid. I'm goin' over to Frankie's. Com' on down, it's on me. Wanna talk to you."

Sid Leavens had become a sort of comrade-in-arms. He'd been vice-president of sales at Syntex until asshole Douglas cut a thousand more poor bastards. Funny, during all the years working together Dick hadn't liked Sid. They were opposites. Dick a buttoned-down guy who believed sales was under marketing; Sid, on the other hand, proclaimed far and wide that sales was the lifeline of the company without which there was no need for anybody else. He wasn't a Willie Loman, but could've played the part as well as Brian Dennehy. He'd probably been on the first list of cuts but because of his connections with big customers the chainsaw-touting CEO had kept him on longer than they'd liked. He got his pink slip – actually they're green – seven months ago, just a week before Allan Douglas got his pink brains blown out. Douglas was a pussycat compared to this Visigoth Goodall. Sid had become a rumbling crank.

Dick found solace in their drinking and bitch sessions as they groveled along the bottom of their depressed lives. Except Sid didn't have near as much to be sick about, hell he had a decent pension from twenty-one years at Texas Instruments before coming to Syntex. And his wife had inherited a tidy sum. He never complained about money problems because he didn't have any. He railed about the egotistical, holier-than-thou CEOs who thought they were saviors, and he called them purveyors of death, making a gazillion bucks for shareholders on the backs of millions of good, ordinary Americans. And Dick didn't disagree; hell, he was the living – and dying – proof.

He decided to go to Frankie's Diner. What the hell, free dinner and drinks would leave more food for the kids. And it was a chance to dump some of the depressed shit from his head. They'd talk about who might have done the murder? Who would want to kill that gorgeous woman?

CHAPTER ELEVEN

The hand reached through the dark as it had hundreds of times before, catching the phone before the second ring. The woman stirred as the man's voice broke in a husky whisper. "Hello."

"Mel."

Mel Ebe looked at the clock, 1:52 a.m. He was not surprised. Alex Goodall called him anytime, anywhere. And didn't give a damn. Ebe dragged up onto an elbow. "What's the problem?" He was careful not to use Alex's name; the less the woman knew the better.

Goodall said. "Need to talk about Chrystine. I want the bastard who did this. Get a private investigator on it."

"Okay." They could have covered that in the morning, but Goodall spent millions with Ebe's law firm. That paid for a lot of aggravation.

"You alone?"

"No."

"Geez Mel, do you ever wear out from all that young stuff?"

"I'll take this in the den." He shuffled down the hall.

Goodall said. "I don't have a good feeling about this two-bit sheriff. I want to know what he's doing, what he's thinking. If he's making any progress. I want a private investigator."

"First thing."

"I've scheduled the funeral for Saturday – need to get it behind me. Next week's board meeting is expecting my annual estimates. Schodenhauer wouldn't consider a death in the family enough reason not to be ready. Need to cut another two hundred million. That's twenty-four hundred jobs. The timing might be good, what with the funeral and all. Sympathy might mitigate some of the anger."

Ebe listened as the widower went on in what sounded like anger but lacked sincerity. He figured Goodall was laying groundwork, forming a plan and not too worried about his wife's killer.

"Sheriff's coming by in the morning. I'll let you know what he knows. I want you as point person. But we should get a local lawyer, reporting to you? You know the attitude in this hick town towards high-priced Park Avenue lawyers."

Ebe stifled a yawn. "Anybody in mind?"

"Try Solomon, Hoffman, Hinton. Big name in town. Sleepy bunch."

"I'll call in the morning." Mel was used to Goodall's arrogance but underestimating small town law enforcement and lawyers was a mistake. Pitbulls weren't big but they could be dangerous.

Goodall turned upbeat. "Now that I've got you up Mel you might as well take advantage of that sweet, young thing you're hiding in your pied-à-terre."

"Talk to you at ten." As he slipped back into bed, long, soft fingers slipped inside his boxers and pulled him into his world of sexual escape, away from the turmoil of Goodall's world. He considered his mistresses and sexual perversions part of the job, not an addiction, just a necessity in the blackness of endless money. As his bedmate's warm, wet lips moved across his torso and down his abdomen, he could still hear Goodall's distracting voice in his head but when she took him, Goodall was gone. And he went into the darkness, the only place he could find peace.

CHAPTER TWELVE

Frankie's was right out of the fifties. Red vinyl booths with yellowing, arborite tables along the windows and fifteen or more with chrome chairs filling-in the middle, all the way back to the kick-worn kitchen doors. It was a home away from home for a lot of Westhaven regulars, at least those who lived in the south-end, working class neighborhoods. It was more crowded over the past year, a kind of bitching-post for ex-employees of Syntex. But Dick figured Frankie wasn't making any more money because most of the clientele couldn't afford much. He was a prime example, drinking a beer instead of his usual martinis, nibbling pretzels and staking out a booth for a couple hours. But Helen, Frankie's wife, always made him feel welcome. She felt sorry for him, like she did all the other poor bastards. But tonight, she'd do better because Sid was buying. It was going to be a couple martinis, veal scaloppini, mashed potatoes, maybe lemon meringue pie and a Michelob or two, not his usual Genesee. The time with Sid was the only good thing left in his life.

He arrived before Sid and order a martini and reread the murder story. He was staring at Chrystine Goodall's picture – *can't believe she's been dead thirty-six hours* – when he heard Sid approaching.

"Dick. How are ya'?"

The big man crossed the restaurant like a cruise ship coming into dock and awkwardly squeezed his bulk in between the vinyl and arborite and extended a shovel-sized hand. Dick shook it, then quickly withdrew his hand, *this guy has hurt a lot of hands in his day.*

"Ya' feeling any better? Least you're not feeling as bad as that bastard Goodall. Too bad it was her, not him. What was her crime, other than being married to that asshole?" He was talking with no expectation of an answer. "He probably killed her. Had her killed. Or whoever killed her was actually gunning for him. Bet that's it. Lotta guys would like to kill that son-of-a-bitch, let me tell ya'. Including us, right Dicky?" His laughter rumbled above the restaurant chatter and brought a bleached smile to Dick's face. He didn't stop. "Yeah, given the chance, I'd do the guy. But I'd do it with my bare hands. Downsize his lung capacity by ripping out his throat, then restructure his head and lay it off on the floor, then as a bonus shove some stock options up his ass." Relishing his metaphors, he chuckled on. "Or I'd downsize him into Pike Lake with a large iron box full of pink slips tied to his neck. All in the interests of the shareholders mind you." His barrel chest and pot belly heaved from exertion. "Nah, I wouldn't shoot him, too quick, too easy. He needs to feel the pain, know it's coming, dread the ending. Just like he did to us, taking our lives away." Another deep breath. "Right?" His puffed-cheeks grinned and he looked to Dick for approval of either his sense of humor or his perverted imagination. "Right Dicky?"

"Right." Dick's lack of enthusiasm was no indication of the depth of satisfaction he would feel if Goodall were dead instead of Chrystine. But he'd do it differently. He hated getting anything yucky on his hands: leftover food, garbage, dirt, bird dung. He washed his hands a dozen times a day; it was just the way he was. He'd use a gun. Clean, detached. A rifle. Take him down at a board meeting when he was spewing bullshit. Have him go face down in front of all those contemptuous, wealthy bastards that decide the fate of hundreds of thousands of people. Not just the ones let go, but their families, relatives, friends and the dozens of shop-keepers and restaurants, all bleeding because of a bunch of rich bastards trying to get richer. This downsizing was a wave of misery that never ended. Yeah, Goodall should be ended. Dead.

"Come on Dick. Let's look on the bright side. Have another drink." He waved at Helen. "Two of the usual, beautiful." That meant a martini and double Cutty on the rocks.

Sid liked his scotch and could suck down half a bottle in the time Dick sipped through two martinis. After a couple of doubles and a lot of commiserating, they were deep into analyzing the murder. Dick talked about it, but his interest was nothing compared to his boisterous companion. He was going on about how it might have happened, who might have done it, and how. And he had a lot of knowledge.

He chased a mouth full of apple pie with a swallow of scotch. "Yep, my instincts about people are seldom wrong. I'll bet ya' million bucks – chump change to that bastard – he did it. And his alibi won't hold up, wait and see. Mike Cougar will be all over him; he's nobody's fool. Lot better he's handling it than city police. If it hadn't been for Cougar they would never have caught that rape-murder sicko last year."

Dick looked past Sid toward the entrance. "Speaking of Cougar, here comes the elder."

Sid turned and stuck his shovel hand in the air. "Jack, over here."

Jackhammer Cougar, shrouded in his permanent frown, moved toward their booth with no indication that he'd heard the invitation. His stride was a little shorter than it used to be, but it hadn't lost its deliberateness. It was a swagger that he must have got from watching too many John Wayne movies. He arrived at the end of the table and stared down, barely acknowledging them.

Sid spoke, "Evenin' Jack. Join us?" Sid didn't budge, but like an obedient pup, Dick slid along the cracked vinyl to the window, emitting a sound that was either squishing vinyl or bad gas. "We've been discussing the murder. Could use your insight."

Cougar lowered himself in next to Dick. "Not much to think about."

"Why da' you say that? Hell, Dick and I've been dissecting it for an hour. I say the husband did it." No response, so Sid continued. "Who else? Dick says it was a burglary gone bad. Hates Goodall; wishes him dead. But doesn't think he did it."

Cougar looked sideways at the diminutive man in the corner of the booth. "Dick may be right. Could be a screwed-up break-in."

Dick stared at Sid, suppressing the urge to say, *I fuckin' told you so.* He heard his psychiatrist's voice in his head, warning him about his impulses. Calmly he said, "It would take a sophisticated burglar though. Security system in that place tough to disarm. Probably heard how rich Goodall was. Shit, he's been bragging about it in the media since the day he got here."

Jack said. "Pros don't work like that."

Dick sucked his low self-esteem back into the corner of the booth.

Sid hid his disappointment behind a gulp of scotch then jumped in. "Even if he didn't, he's still a murdering son-of-a-bitch. Guys like him kill people, a few thousand at a time, cutting off their livelihood, leaving them to rot in mass graves like this god-forsaken town. But he'll never get arrested for it, because it's legal. There's no law against it. Big business writes its own laws." Nobody was responding so he rolled on. "Look at what's happened since he came to town, better still, go back to when asshole Weiss and Douglas showed up. In less than three years they've lined up five thousand, eight hundred and seventy-one people on the firing line and as good as shot 'em. Criminal! Look at Dick here, living example. Look at Art Kinder, Irv Speigel, wrecked, and that Kane woman. And your buddy Archie Sims, dead. Suicide. Because they couldn't handle life after a lifetime of dedication to their company. What did it get 'em? What's it worth? Nothin.'" A trace of angry spit escaped his lips. "Nothin' to those wealthy bastards who ride in here on a horse named shareholders, chop off thousands of heads, then ride out of town with bags of money. Compare that to what our government does for a bunch of no-name, foreigners in places like Afghanistan and Iraq. Spent billions trying to stop atrocities. Yet here at home, they not only ignore, but praise the likes of Goodall and Douglas as great American titans. They're no better than that despot Assad. I tell you, those guys think nothin' of dropping a few hundred-billion in the name of foreign intervention but wouldn't spend a dime to stop Corporate America's genocide of good Americans. And now they want to save a million immigrant Dreamers. What about our dreams?

Our lives? That's the trouble with Trump. Wants to build a wall to keep criminals and rapists out but ain't doing shit to stop his rich buddies from raping us. He's as full of shit as the rest of them." Beads of angry sweat glistened on his forehead. "The likes of Goodall and Douglas are a bigger threat to us than any Mexico hombre or foreign dictator." His harangue was cut off by a gulp of scotch. He stared at Jack. "You don't think Goodall did it?"

Jack's tone changed as he talked to them like buddies, "Could've had it done. His kinda money can buy anything."

Sid started all over again, trashing the indulgent lifestyle of the rich then festered over horror stories of people wallowing in economic despair.

Dick just listened. It was as if he was watching reality TV – about him. Sid's litany of pain was *his* life. He felt the rumble in his gut and tasted the phlegm; he had to get out of there, get some cool air. Despite Jack's overbearing presence, he asked to be excused.

Jack was curt. "Gotta grab a coffee and hit the road. Dick, ya' got change for a buck?"

Dick dropped four quarters on the table. A minute later he climbed into his 2008 Ford Taurus – he'd lost his company Buick the day he was fired. Fighting to quash his anger, he crammed the key into the ignition, yanked the car into gear and slammed the accelerator. He didn't see the van. It was as black as the unlit street and moving fast. Then he saw it. Instinct jammed on the brakes and fear waited for the sickening crunch. The empty seconds were filled with a shrieking horn, screeching tires and devouring headlights. He didn't open his eyes. Silence. Then the horn screamed again. His eyes dilated. The van was sideways in the street, pointed directly at him, three feet away, headlights flooding the interior of his car. He smelled the stench of burning rubber. Someone was yelling.

"Fuckin' asshole. Where ya' goin?' Asshole!"

Through the fractured light Dick saw the driver get out of the van and a second guy open the passenger door. His mind rolled over with no thought. His foot slid off the brake and stomped the accelerator. He didn't hear the screams or breaking glass and folding metal. All he heard was an inner voice, *no more. Nobody's going to fuck with Dick Ryder any more. Nobody.* The Ford smashed the headlights, crumpled the grill, snapped off the plastic bug-deflector and bounced the van twenty feet. The guy in the passenger seat was hit by the open door and rolled under the front wheel. The other guy was frozen in fear, now standing behind the Ford. Dick eyed him in the rearview mirror, racked the car into reverse and took aim at the longhaired asshole.

There was a yell of disbelief. "Fuck…. " That was as far as he got. Dick felt a thud as the guy's head disappeared. He stopped, took a deep breath and shot past the van into the night. He never looked back. The voice invaded his head again. *What have you done Richard Roger Ryder? … what a stupid name. My mother was stupid to name me that.* Then there was a different image in his mind, the gorgeous Chrystine. He was with her, she was very much alive in a life that looked a whole lot better.

CHAPTER THIRTEEN

Gritt introduced herself to the urbane front-desk manager at the Hilton. "Chief Deputy Hansen."

"Tom Connor. How can I help?"

Gritt asked a few questions.

On the evening of the murder Connor had observed Ms. Goodall's comings and goings and said she'd come downstairs, alone, and entered the ballroom. Later, he saw her talking with two people on the far side of the lobby but couldn't identify them. She'd been registered in room seven-seventeen. Gritt queried the oddity of her having a room while not staying overnight and the manager explained people sometimes take a room for the evening to 'freshen up' before dinner or to entertain after the event.

Gritt asked. "When'd she check-in?"

"Just after five."

"Did she entertain after?"

"Don't know. Checked out at one-twenty-five."

"When did you see her with the others?"

"I was off at eleven … maybe ten-thirty."

"See her go upstairs?"

"No."

"See her after that?"

"As I said, I was off."

"Who was on at one-twenty-five?"

"Eddie and Eli, bellhops. One of them might have helped her. Toni was at the front."

"I'd like to talk to him," said Gritt.

"Her."

"What?"

"Toni's a her."

"What's with parents, giving girls names like Toni … *and Gritt?*" Tom didn't get it.

"She's not on 'til eleven."

"Got her home number?"

"She'd be sleeping now."

"Wake her. This is a homicide investigation."

The manager went to get the information and Gritt meandered across the lobby into *The Pinnacle Lounge.*

A twenty-something kid who looked like he should be in high school instead of bartending, greeted him. "Miss … what can I get you?"

I can't believe this guy thinks a deputy sheriff, in uniform, with a Glock strapped to her side would even consider a drink before lunch. "Few questions."

"Sure. Shoot." He threw up his hands in mock defense. "Just kidding."

"Know who Ms. Chrystine Goodall is?"

"Woman murdered?"

"You see her here? Two nights ago?"

"Hard to miss." His smile faded as Gritt's frown expanded. "'Round ten thirty or eleven. Her and another lady and some guy."

"'Member what they looked like?"

"Sure. And what they drank. She had a Manhattan, lady in the burgundy satin dress had – "

"Could you ID 'em. From a photo?"

"Sure."

"When'd they leave?"

"Women left first, then the guy."

"What'd he look like?"

"Not sure really."

"You said you could ID 'em."

"The women. I remember the women. Not the guy. With two

hot ladies, who's checkin' the guy?" He shrugged. "Left by himself, went out the front door. Saw the valet get his Lexus. Cool car ... black."

Gritt thanked him and left, not sure how much she'd learned. But would work on finding the black Lexus. The time gap of her whereabouts and who she was with had now been narrowed to between eleven-thirty and one-twenty-five, two hours. Enough time for almost anything.

From over her shoulder she heard the bartender. "Officer." He caught up. "I remember now. The lady also came into the bar around four that afternoon. Just walked in for a minute. The guy I told you about was sitting at the bar, drinking vodka martinis, straight up." He realized it was unwanted detail so hurried on. "He walked over to her. I remember 'cause she kissed him. I thought, lucky stiff."

"On the lips?"

"Uh?"

"Did she kiss him on the lips?"

"Nah, cheek."

"Other than his martinis, what d'ya' remember about him?

"He was a lawyer."

"Yeah?"

"Made two, three calls. Had a BlackBerry. Had to be a lawyer. One time asked for a Bill Hinton. It sounded like Bill Clinton, that's why I remember."

"Thanks. If you think of anything else, call me at the sheriff's office." She handed him a card. This was a positive lead – Solomon, Hoffman, Hinton was one of Westhaven's most prestigious law firms.

• • •

Gritt had just finished updating Mike on what she'd learned at the Hilton and he was furious. She was silent. *If I let him go on maybe he'll get the bug outta his ass. Geez, he needs a good enema.*

"I should yank you off the case. This investigation is in a critical window. Shit, it's barely forty-eight hours old. I won't have you, or anybody, out freelancing, chasing down your own damn theories. If you're going to follow something up, clear it with me, *first*."

She half apologized. "Just thought – "

"Start the background on the husband. Leave the rest to me."

She shrugged, "You're the boss." *He's erratic, not like him.* "What about the lawyer who called Solomon, Hoffman, Hinton?"

"Talk to Waggs and Gibson, do background on Goodall. That's it. I'll deal with the lawyer. Stay out of the hotel end of it. Understood?"

She didn't understand so she didn't reply. And she sure as hell wasn't going to let the homicide dicks, Waggs and Gibson, take this thing over. There was more to this than the boss was letting on. *Maybe Jackhammer has him all jacked up?*

She started making calls about Goodall. The Wall Street Journal, Fortune and Forbes had all covered his career and there was plenty of reading – memories of her FBI days. When Doc Wemyss called, Mike was out so they put her through.

Gritt realized she wasn't supposed to hear this report first but the Doc was yakking before she could stop her. The ME rattled off the highlights. "Cause of death, massive head trauma, single bullet wound to the right, temporal lobe. Time of death, between one and four a.m. Stomach contents well digested, maybe six hours. No trauma. No rape. But definitely sex that night. Small trace of semen, maybe a condom. I'll send the full report to the sheriff."

She thanked her and went back to her calls. But she kept going over the Doc's words, *I knew it, it's about sex … a dumped lover?*

CHAPTER FOURTEEN

Dick wanted to throw the knife, bury it like a vibrating tuning fork in the swinging door. His head screamed, *do it*! But his muscles strained like the chain on a junkyard dog as he fought to hold onto his sanity. Irene hadn't said a word, simply pushed through the door into the dining room. But she was yelling inside, shouting at him to go to hell. She would never say that out loud – her God would strike her down. *If there's a God, where the hell is he? Where has he been the last five hundred and eighty-nine days? Nowhere. That's where. There is no God. He's dead. Maybe he got downsized.* Then a second voice, *and somebody else is gonna be dead real fuckin' soon.* He stared at the wobbling door then lowered the carving knife. *The only bright thing in my life is this shiny, steel blade.*

Irene would be upstairs by now, crying herself through the reality. He should go to her. But couldn't. She'd have to cry on her own because he felt like a fish out of water, just flipping and flopping to nowhere. The only time he had strength was when he was angry, then the blood and piss flowed, and he could do anything, take on anybody. He used to be able to handle all his problems, but these days he was useless, a real dick-less Dick. All he did now was take it out on Irene, spewing his black emptiness in rising waves of rage. He'd just done it again, here in the kitchen. They'd argued about money and his drinking, as usual. He didn't need her telling him the obvious – too much booze and too little money. Fighting wasn't like them; hell, they were loving people, twenty-seven years married. It was the fucking situation. The economy. The company. Assholes like Goodall and Douglas and Weiss. And that bastard Schodenhauer on Syntex's board, he was the real, bleeding-ass, greed-monger. He was worth billions and still dismantled companies and annihilated peoples' lives to make another billion. *Asshole …*

somebody oughta' kill him.

His gloom rolled back in like a New England fog, momentarily smothering his torment. He ran a hand through his thinning hair and pulled it, just to hurt himself. It felt good. Physical pain was much easier than the mental crap. He rubbed the handle of the knife and noticed it said, *Cutco. Made in USA.* Soon, everything will be made in China or Korea. Nobody's gonna pay Americans to do what starving Asians will do for a buck an hour. Next, they'll be moving Syntex to a third world country. Ain't fuck-all anybody can do about it. He raised the knife, felt the madness race to his arm and plunge it into the loaf of bread. The steel jammed into the breadboard and his palm sliced down the blade. The only pain he felt was the drum beating behind his eyeballs. The blood on the kitchen counter was a small sacrifice, a small price to pay for the fleeting liberation from his imploding self. He knew it was the drinking – at times he had trouble remembering what he'd said or done. He was going crazy even though the psychiatrist said he wasn't. She gave him some gobbledygook about how it was an 'impulse disorder' and told his GP he had 'borderline psychosis.' Said, that's why he kept exploding. Like last week, when he took a baseball bat to the neighbor's fence. Stupid bastard out hammering on a Sunday morning. No respect. Just like those assholes in the van, blaming him when they were going too fast. Assholes deserved it. He ran the cut under cold water but couldn't stop the bleeding so mounted the stairs to ask for Irene's help. He needed her, he was the one down and out, thrown like garbage into the corporate dumpster.

Irene was brushing her hair in front of the vanity, the one with the folding mirrors. She'd always done that when she was unhappy and had been doing it a lot lately. He had a remote pain for Irene, an ache that he was aware of but didn't really feel. Hell, it wasn't her fault. It wasn't his fault. He knew whose fault it was, but that didn't help. What they needed was less pain, less anger and more love – and more money would sure as hell help.

"Sorry Hon. You know … what I said downstairs." He was

standing at the door waiting to be invited in. His Irene would forgive him, she always did. She was a gem, a tower of strength all wrapped up in a five-foot three, hundred-and-ten-pound package of compassion. They'd been through so much together: her brother's death, her sister's divorce, her niece's cancer and his father's death. It was funny how his father's death, at first, had been a relief, but now was like a black room that opened up once in a while and pulled him in, slamming the door behind him. Inside, he'd scream and swear at his dead father – who was somewhere in the darkness – and the only way out of the blackness was when he quieted down and asked his father to open the door. In there, his father was still in control, still fighting to tell him what to do and how to do it. And Dick couldn't get rid of the hope that his father had gone to hell because of the thousands of times he'd told him how inadequate he was compared to his brother. He hadn't been an abusive father to his twin boys, just a pain in the ass, especially to Dick, not so much Dan. Dan was better at almost everything, dad's shining expectation held high above his way-too-average Dick. T-ball, Little League, basketball, soccer, grades, science club, reading club, cubs, scouts; Dick never broke away from the middle of the pack and never got away from father's criticism. Dan did. His mother played buffer while father rationalized his incessant pushing of son number two with his much-repeated insistence, 'I just want the boy to do his best, exceed his grasp, reach for the brass ring.' The pushing of son number two stopped the day son number one died of an overdose. They were seventeen.

After Dan's death his father was silent for a year, but gradually got back to berating him about how important it was that he succeed in business and make a lot of money, so he could do better than him. Secretly, he suspected his father's real interest was in making sure his son could support his parents in old age. Well, that wasn't going to happen, even though two years ago he'd been confident he could help support them when he retired. Well, his old man didn't have to worry about it, he died of a heart attack, three months after Dick got "early retirement." His mother then had to climb on the back of her only surviving son. Ever since, he'd felt like a beast of burden, and in the black room his father yelled and called him a jackass, a drunk and a failure. Dick no longer disagreed.

Irene turned. He looked so pathetic, so lost. She held out her hands. "It's okay."

He reached for them like they were a pair of crutches, as if they would support his crumbling spirit. "It's not even the damn money that's the problem … you know. It sets me off. It's the depression. I can't control it. I'd never hurt you." He heard his sniffling appeal and let it drag him into the room.

"Let's take care of that cut. No need to talk right now."

"No, no, I want to. Dr. Borachi said it was best that when I can't see her I talk to someone who'll understand. I should call and see if I can get in tomorrow."

"I'm sure she'll see you if – "

"No she won't," he exclaimed. "That bitch is too damn busy to squeeze me in when I need her. You have to fit her schedule. She's more important than the patient. According to the egotistical doctor, we're damn lucky – " he heard, *fucking lucky*, in his head, but restrained himself. Irene abhorred swearing. " – to get in at all."

"Now Richard. She's done you a lot of good. Maybe she can prescribe some more Risperidone."

"Those drugs. They're for crazies. I don't need drugs, I need a job. Or win the lottery. You know what pisses me off. The lottery is fifty-seven-million this week and I can't afford to buy a ticket, not one f … lousy ticket."

Irene slipped her arms around his waist and rested her head on his chest. She didn't know what else to do. The sadness was suffocating.

He absorbed her quietness and the fire receded. But he would not forget her fear when he yanked the knife out of its wooden block and screamed. But he was a good husband, a good father, law-abiding – until now. Again, the voice, *maybe everyone would be better off if I was dead.*

CHAPTER FIFTEEN

That evening Mike crossed the threshold of his cookie-cutter, suburban home. It was early – for him – and Billy was waiting just inside the door. Mike was gently rubbing his rump when Gritt called.

"Got the ME's report. Bringing it over – "

"How the fuck did you get – "

"They put Doc through to me and she'd spewed it out before I could stop her. No big deal. Took notes."

"Just notes?"

"She's sending report tomorrow. Thought you'd want this much. I'm five minutes from your place."

"Okay."

Mike and Billy were lying in his extended recliner like two forlorn buddies watching a baseball game. Without getting up he said, "What did Doc say?"

She ran through her notes and at the end said, "Said no rape. But definitely sex that night. Few hours before death. Small trace of semen – "

"Small?"

"No problem getting DNA. Could be critical."

"Did she send it for testing?"

"Didn't ask."

"Good. Leave it to me."

She mused, "I'm thinking ... as much as you don't buy the love triangle, DNA can tell us for sure. If – "

"I said leave it to me."

"Boss, with all due respect, I think we need to talk this through ... like you always say, leave no stone unturned until we've looked under every rock. Cause that's where the bad guys live. And after my chat with the hotel bartender, this rock got a lot bigger."

"Ya' know what the rock is? … Your head. You're not listening." He flipped the recliner chair upright and put Billy on the floor. Billy looked pleadingly because he too heard the irritation in his voice. "How many times do I have to tell you to go after Goodall, not some fuckin' fantasy in your head."

"Excuse me … fuckin' fantasy?" She jammed her hands on her hips. "That's not only not true, it's insulting. Doc's evidence confirms – confirms – Chrystine Goodall had sex a few hours before she was murdered. And she is placed at the hotel – a typical venue for an affair. At the very least, we should be looking for witnesses, interviewing people." She stopped because he was not reacting. Just standing there, staring down at Billy. *Is he listening to me*? "Listen, you do whatever the hell you think best. I'll stay out of that. But, I'm tellin' you, somebody better start questioning hotel staff and guests who were there." She stopped again. Again, he said nothing. But he was looking at her. His rich, brown eyes, usually full of curiosity, were empty. "Mike … what's wrong?"

"Nothing … fuckin' nothing." He started to go to the kitchen.

Instinctively, she grabbed his arm. "Mike …?" He brushed past her. She would have reached for him again except Billy was between them. She followed. *Get out of here before things get out of hand.* But instinct said, *stay close to him.*

He wanted to tell her to fuck off and go home but he was also glad she was here. He went to the middle of the kitchen and stood on the opposite side of the butcher-block island. Billy slipped underneath and Gritt stopped a few feet away. The momentary quiet was calming.

She'd faced domestic disputes in kitchens, staring across an unknown space, watching for threatening signs. She saw the wooden block of knives just to his right, normally a potential danger. His hands were planted on the island but not in an angry grip. His face wasn't taut nor eyes narrow and the veins in his neck were not pulsing. He looked weary.

"I think you should go," he said.

"I don't."

"Shall I make that an order?"

"Won't change anything."

"What's with you? It's called insubordination."

"Not insubordination, sir. Just want to – "

"What's with the 'sir' shit?"

"Just want to make sure you're okay … before I leave."

"I'm fine … leave."

"You're not. And I'm not."

"Not okay? Or not leaving?"

"Both. I'm not leaving and won't be okay until I know you're okay." She stepped up and put her hands on the butcher-block and tried to reach beyond the hollow in his eyes.

He sensed her slipping inside him, warmth rising up under his skin, blood suffusing through his arms, legs, gut. An odd fusion of strength and weakness overtaking him. He was vulnerable. There was no 'sir,' no 'boss,' no 'sheriff,' no 'deputy sheriff,' just this. Whatever this was?

She saw it. In his eyes. A relinquishing. A letting go of something. She reached across and touched his hand. It stiffened.

The tension in his arms anchored him to the island, preventing him from pulling her into his isolation and feeding his need.

She stepped around the island, never letting go of his hand. He turned, and she walked into his arms.

He stopped breathing. He absorbed the imprint of her body.

In that moment, there was more than a physical awareness, an undeniable connection across a forbidden divide. She felt his arousal. And hers … then the power of his embrace, the intensity of his body, the hunger in his hands. Her innermost, sexual yearning rushed to his needs.

He reached to bury himself in her. His hands gripped her buttocks, lifted her.

His hardness pressed against her tummy and her legs opened to accept him … then her holstered gun bumped against the butcher-block. Her legs released him as she pulled her head from his neck. He let go. Not a word was said, their eyes said everything.

She whispered, "I'm sorry …"

"Oh my god … I never should have let – "

"It's okay … I just wanted to – "

"I didn't mean to drag you into this," he said. "It's my problem."

"Our problem. Your problems are mine, mine are yours. It's *our* case."

"Not this time. Not this part."

"No Michael. I came to you. I know you're hurting. You needed a hug. It's only natural that our respect for each other spills over and triggers natural instincts … you know, natural male-female stuff … our libidos got ahead of us … no big deal."

"You don't know the half of it." He went to the fridge and took out two beers. "Gritt … I'm truly sorry."

"No need. It's done. Over."

"No. It's not." He popped the cans and passed her one.

"It is … as far as I'm concerned." *Maybe it's not over for him … and that's okay too.* Her femininity stirred again.

He pointed between them. "We're over." Then put a finger to his temple like a pistol. "But I'm done."

She mimicked his pistol action. "What's with this?"

He blinked. "Aaah, nothing. If we don't solve this case – soon – I'm done."

He was scrambling. Didn't sound honest. *Whatever?*

He swigged the beer. "Let's start over in the morning – and thanks for putting up with me."

When she went to bed, she immersed herself in sexual satisfaction and escaped the on-the-job problems – for now.

Mike lifted Billy onto the bed and looked into his big brown eyes. "Billy, I damn near blew it tonight, in more ways than one. Almost lost my cool … she is one hot, deputy sheriff, right? … Billy? She's hot, don't you think? Come on Billy, agree with me … I mean irresistible. Right?" Billy blinked. "You know what happens when us guys get distracted by women? Of course, you're too old and I'm supposed to be too smart … but you know what's goin' on. It ain't an excuse, but it sure as hell has my brain bent outta shape." He stroked Billy's back. "I'm in a bad state. And tonight, damn near fucked everything up. You know what I almost told her? … I was on the verge of giving into my sappy pain, letting my heart get ahead of my brain. I mean … I like her. She's special, terrific woman … could share a lot with her. Trust her." He bent down and gently lifted Billy's chin toward him. "Personally, between you and me Billy, I have trouble controlling myself when alone with her … you know, she's fuckin' gorgeous. Smart. Tough. Sexxxxy." He shook his head and dropped his eyes from Billy's stare. "Billy … I almost told her … that I'd had a one-night stand with Chrystine Goodall."

CHAPTER SIXTEEN

Mike's stomach was not happy, and the eggs were floating like rubber mats in a cistern of bad coffee. He pulled out of the parking lot of a cafe called the Good Eat, on the eastside of town. He'd never stopped there before but wanted to avoid Frankie's and other regular spots. Because he felt like shit, looked like shit and wasn't up for the constant patronizing that people slurp on cops. After Billy fell asleep, he had climbed into the patrol car and driven aimlessly until dawn. He spent a couple of hours wandering the country roads and stayed away from The Hill and Goodall's palatial home.

His immediate problem was a meeting at nine with Alexander Goodall and Gritt, and he was about as alert as a mugged wino. After trying to rationalize his behavior with Gritt, he was even more pissed with himself. He'd seen internal affairs – the sex kind, not the investigative kind – destroy too many good cops and ruin too many good cases. And yet, he'd done it. Screwed up in the worst way. He was an elected, public official, *and an idiot*. All night he'd beaten himself up with *Why? Why? Why?* He had a dozen answers. He needed love to fill the hole his mother had left – and his father keeps digging deeper. And his relationship with women had been a wasteland. He thought he'd dealt with it, despite the constant stream of women who run through a cop's life, most of them on the wrong side of the tracks, with ex-husbands, no-good lovers and a hopeless need for one good thing in their life. The law, dressed up in uniform, was a beguiling beacon to which these women rushed for solace and sex. But he'd never been interested and always shielded himself from the discarded side of humanity. But that's not where Chrystine Goodall had come from. He wasn't sure exactly where she'd come from or how she so quickly enveloped his life, but he'd been irresistibly drawn to her, like a mirage, like a young boy's fantasy. Now a nightmare.

As the smoke-gray dawn brought the unwanted day into his crumbling career he reached for the ultimate rationalization, the one he'd shared with Billy, 'It only happened once.' Since Chrystine's murder, he'd tried to avoid talking to his mother about it but couldn't. Her response was clear. *Work must be your focus. Chrystine is gone, find her killer. She was an antidote for your sense of abandonment. Nothing more.* He didn't like the idea that Chrystine was *nothing more.*

• • •

Mike met Gritt in Syntex's corporate lobby and they were ushered into Goodall's extravagance on the top floor. An office that was wider, longer and filled with more furniture than his whole house.

"Have a seat." The wave of Goodall's hand seemed to indicate two of four chairs facing the floor to ceiling windows. Both hesitated. Goodall eased the uncertainty by sinking into a sofa that stretched along the windows and curved around in front of his desk like the Great Wall of China. He said. "I have thirty minutes. What have you got so far?"

Mike asked. "Have you thought of anything else? Or anyone who might have reason to kill your wife?"

"Nothing."

At this rate, it'll take thirty hours, not thirty minutes. He pressed, careful not to let his hostility toward this overbearing bastard show. Just a couple days after his wife's murder this ass was sitting in his office as if it was business as usual. Mike listened to his heart. *Bastard has no compassion, zilch. No wonder Chrystie – that's what she liked to be called – had needed someone's attention.*

"Nothing is too small to consider." He watched the eyes. No flutter.

"I know what I know. She had no enemies – that I know of. Maybe some from her past. I wouldn't know. Hell, she did nothing but good. Obviously, you're on the wrong track."

Mike didn't miss the subtle switching of Goodall's comments from maybe she had enemies to she was a saint. He was trying to lead, ever so artfully.

Gritt stiffened. "Mr. Goodall, do you use the law firm of Solomon, Hoffman, Hinton?" The question was like a clay pigeon, hanging in the air, everyone riveted to it, waiting.

"What's that got to do with anything?"

"Has your wife ever used them?"

Goodall hesitated. "No…. Actually, I don't know. So what?"

That's three answers in one. No. I don't know. And yes. He was still mad at Gritt for poking around at the hotel, but she was onto something here. Maybe a can of worms Goodall would like to keep a lid on. He decided to help pry it open. "Is it possible she might retain a lawyer without your knowledge?"

"She was involved in charities. Could need counsel? People with money, in the spotlight, have to protect themselves from all kinds of frivolous claims."

Gritt, like an Olympic runner with her sights fixed on the runner ahead of her, asked, "Ever heard of Wyatt Jones?"

"Should I …?"

"You spoke with Mrs. Goodall the night of her murder." She glanced at her notebook. "At two-ten a.m. After she got home. You'd called her earlier. Couldn't remember what time. Have you recalled the time of that call yet?"

"Haven't thought about it."

Gritt feigned ignorance. She'd received records from the hotel in Scranton. Goodall had called his home at twelve-thirteen a.m., nearly two hours before his wife returned the call. But that wasn't what interested her. She'd been considering the theory that Goodall might have spoken to his wife at two-ten, flown from Scranton to Westhaven, killed her and returned to Scranton before morning. She'd checked on the speed of his Citation jet and the possible turnaround time, and in order for him to do it, it put the murder close to five. Doc had said death was before four a.m. And she was alive at two-ten. But she'd found two other calls from Goodall, *after* two-ten. One at three a.m., on the dot. No answer. The next, one minute later. He'd left no message. She'd have to get the phone records but still wanted his explanation on the record. Why would he have called his wife twice, left no message and done nothing when he knew she was home alone? "Do you recall calling your wife any other time that night?"

"I make more than fifty calls a day, day and night, including a few calls to my wife. If you expect me to remember every call … well, I wouldn't expect you to understand the world of business."

"At three am?"

Mike saw Goodall fidget with his cuff link.

Goodall replied. "Yes … yes. I did call back. I wanted to ask her something."

"What did she say?"

"I didn't get an answer."

"Did you leave a message?"

"No."

"Why not?"

"She must have been asleep. Wasn't that important."

"But you called again, a minute later."

"I thought she might've been in the shower, so tried again."

"You weren't worried?"

"No."

Gritt stopped and let the suspicion hover like thickening smog.

Mike took a different angle. "Were you and your wife having any problems in your marriage?"

"Every marriage has ups and downs. Nothing out of the ordinary."

Mike's throat tried to suck everything out of his stomach. He couldn't get the next question out.

Goodall punctuated his point. "Not being married, you

wouldn't understand."

Gritt filled the silence. "Which law firm do you use?"

"The company has several."

"Personally."

"Taylor and Ebe, New York."

"Been in touch lately?"

"Deputy. I'm in touch with more lawyers and accountants than a call center."

"Who at Taylor and Ebe?"

"Mel Ebe."

Mike found his voice. "So your marriage was good?"

"Yes."

They were interrupted by a voice on the speakerphone. "Mr. Goodall, your overseas call is ready."

He abruptly stood up. "You'll have to excuse me." He didn't wait for a response. "If I think of anything, I'll call."

Gritt extended a handshake. Mike couldn't. But he got the lie he was looking for, *no marriage problems, 'nothing out of the ordinary.'* And he was curious about what Gritt was fishing for.

CHAPTER SEVENTEEN

The swirls on the dark surface of the coffee looked like tiny oil slicks and no amount of stirring dissipated them. And the clink, clink of the spoon was both irritating and mesmerizing. But Gritt sat patiently, letting the boss set the pace of the discussion, which was moving like a pregnant turtle. They had been in the *Dip & Sip* for ten minutes and he was still playing with his coffee and not saying anything. And he looked like shit. Said he'd been up all night, thinking about the case, driving around. Hadn't even gone home in time to give Billy his medication. That wasn't like him. She decided to start the conversation by sharing her thoughts on Goodall having flown back to town and killed his wife. Then she had to address the elephant in the room – the one in the coffee shop, in the case, in their lives.

She explained the timeline for Goodall's jet and the unlikelihood of that theory. Then she ventured into her second theory, a love triangle. He showed marginal interest in the first and immediately dismissed the second. But Gritt, with the doggedness of an Olympic athlete in training, laid out her suspicions about Mrs. Goodall's movements at the hotel. When she mentioned the lawyer in the bar there was renewed attention. She explained that the reason she'd asked about Wyatt Jones was because he was a lawyer at Solomon, Hoffman, Hinton and matched the description of the guy who met Mrs. Goodall in the lounge.

He asked. "What's Jones got to do with this?"

"Don't know. But from the bar Ms. Goodall went to her room and he went out the front door. Left in a Lexus. Could've gone home. Could've parked around the block. Gone back to her room."

"She could see a lawyer for any number of reasons. No reason to suspect an affair. Leave it. I'll follow up on Jones."

Gritt sipped her coffee. "Already did."

The clinking stopped.

"Didn't take much to track him down. Valet knew him. I called Solomon, Hinton. Confirmed he was partner. Handles family law."

"Family law?" He sipped his coffee. "That's divorce stuff."

"No shit." Gritt expected some heat but got nothing as he went back to spoon clinking. His face was sad, not angry. She went where she shouldn't. "Mike, might be none of my business. But somethings not right … with you. Case getting to you? We'll crack it. I'm – "

"Billy died."

"Nooo …." She touched his arm and squeezed until he looked up. *He needs a hug.* She held the squeeze until his eyes dropped back into the black coffee. She drained hers and ordered two more. Not until he started the spoon thing again did they talk. He explained how he went back around five am to give him meds and found him on the bed.

"At least he went peacefully." He rambled for five minutes, worrying about how the loss of Billy might affect his thoughts for the next few days – and how it can't. "Funny. Thought I would've sat with him. Boxed him up. Or whatever you do with a dog who has passed. I didn't. Had to leave. Get some space. Breath. So, I drove."

She took his hand. It was cold. She held it for the longest time as they sat in silence. Despite all the death and carnage that they often encountered, this was personal. Billy was probably the only love he'd had in his life since his mom died. Sad. But it partly explained his tough, I-can-handle-anything exterior that protected the real Michael from being touched by anything and anyone. *Wonder if I can get inside him?*

"Thanks." He withdrew his hand. "I'll be okay."

As they stood to leave, she glanced around the coffee shop. Maybe ten guzzlers, all preoccupied with their caffeine addiction. So, she took his hands, squeezed, and pulled him as close as she dared, searching the darkness in his deep brown eyes. *Oh god, his mouth …*

his lips. "Michael … you know I am here for you. Anything. You name it, you got it. I'll do anything for you…." Her legs tightened, restraining her feet from rising on her toes, *his lips* … "Anything."

"I know." He squeezed, hard. "And I am going to need you. More than you can imagine." He withdrew his hands.

He needs me. And he can't withdraw that connection. She was inside him, for an instant, maybe next to where Billy was?

In the parking lot, he booked off to go and take care of Billy. Alone in the car, the silence was stifling. *Chrystine.* Then replaced it, *Gritt.* Memories of Chrystine filled him with guilt, despair, emptiness, fear. The cop in him was struggling to control the black sludge rendering him almost useless, and now Billy on top of it. The anger rose like thunder clouds. He slowed the car and the traffic around him did the same. Were they staring at him? Yelling, *You stupid bastard, how could you?* He glared at the woman in the car alongside. She braked and fell back three lengths. He had to get hold of his emotions. Lock them up. Not allow Chrystine to visit – like now. She was standing in front of him, radiant. Her eyes lingered, like sunshine in a meadow, and he slipped back into the memories.

On the first day they'd met, he'd driven up the driveway as she was pruning a Japanese maple. The initial impression wasn't glamorous. She wore a droopy, straw hat with a white handkerchief around her neck and what he thought women called a frock – faded and frumpy. What he noticed most was her neck. She'd said, "Good morning Sheriff," then slipped the handkerchief from her neck and patted away tiny beads of perspiration. She missed one and he watched it run down her gleaming skin, wriggle over her collarbone and disappear beneath the frock. She was talking; he was staring. Later, he told her, 'I fell for your sweaty neck.' Her beauty was sexy, in an elegant way. Hypnotic. Even when she moved away from him, as she did that day, putting her hat and gloves on the patio, he was not able to deny his visceral attraction to her. So, he stepped over the boundaries he'd constructed to protect himself.

He discovered that she hadn't had much love in her life. Lots of counterfeit attention, spurious affection and all the excitement money could buy. But short on love. No truth, no trust. Just dishonest hope. She hadn't been able to wean herself from the indulgence, the instant gratification and the plastic reconfirmation that she was okay. He'd found her longing for some strength in her life, something other than the ever-shifting emotional ground she floated on. She'd been pushed by a mother ridden with social anxiety; the result being a reluctant figure skater, a failed prom queen, a Miss Photogenic Tulsa, and a runner up Miss Oklahoma. Her father left home when she was ten. For years, her spirit had yearned for stability and someone who wanted to be with her instead of seen with her. For reasons he had not had time to understand, she'd seen something in him. Even on that first day, he'd had trouble saying good-bye. She shook his hand and he held on to it, too long. She didn't seem to mind. After he climbed into his car, she stood by the open window, thanked him again and touched his forearm. Something switched inside him, like a weathervane in a thunderstorm, yanking his hidden hunger out of the past.

His ache returned. What if nothing had happened to her? Would they have settled for an affair? She'd said her marriage was easier to stay in than get out of. And maybe they just had temporary needs. He saw her in front of him, sitting on the bed at the Hilton, mesmerizing blues eyes pulling him in. That night, he realized she wanted him to fill an empty corner of her life and his defenses fell, his heart opened, a little, and she slipped in.

He pulled to the curb. The anger screamed, if only he could have been there for her. If, if … if only he'd stayed that night … she'd be here now. The feeling of abandonment exploded. His fist slammed at the pain. He hadn't been there when she needed him, too worried about what might happen if he got caught up in a relationship. So, he'd made a choice. He left. Left her alone. To go home alone. To be murdered. His fear of relationships had paid the ultimate price.

He yelled into the silence. "I'll get the fucking bastard!"

CHAPTER EIGHTEEN

At first Mike didn't hear the knock. He opened one eye and blinked at the sliver of sunlight streaming between the curtains. Again, the knock. He kicked the recliner upright. " Okay, okay … coming." His mobile was on the table and he grabbed it as he went to the door. It was 2:55.

Gritt didn't knock a third time. She knew he was there, the car was in the drive. She'd stopped by to see how he was doing but figured best not to force the issue. He deserved some time alone. Hell, he needed time off, but this case had him tied up in one big knot and he couldn't take time off. She wanted to help him through the knothole. *Billy sure picked a lousy time to leave.* She turned to leave.

"Hey … What the hell you doin' here?"

She glanced back. He looked like hell. "Just checking in, seeing – "

"Something up? A break?"

"You okay?" As out of sorts as he appeared, he was still a physical specimen. Standing there in a white T-shirt and blue jeans, she just wanted to hug him – for him. And her.

"Fell asleep. Came back after taking Billy to vet." He went back in the house, leaving the door open.

She followed and called in a ten-forty (off duty) because this is where she should be right now, for him, the case … herself. Since the Dip & Sip, she'd struggled with her conflicting feelings, wanting to support him while suppressing her undeniable need to go to him, to take his pain away. So she crossed the threshold of what was both a looming problem and an urgent need.

He was flinging the living room drapes open. "Here, let me do that." She put a hand on his back. "Go freshen up."

"Freshen up?" He grinned as if he was in pain. "Freshen up is something my mother always said in polite company when she really meant 'go to the bathroom.'"

She smiled. "That too."

"Do I look that bad?"

"Worse."

"Gotta snap out of it. Can't – "

"No you don't. Not right now. Just go with it. This is too much all at once. Losing Billy has got to be – "

"Sssshitty!" He slumped onto the arm of the sofa.

"Take some time. I've got your back. I'm all over Ryder. Just drop out for a while – at least the next twenty-four hours. You need rest. Why not – "

"It was best for Billy. Time to go." He looked up. "He wouldn't want me to tank … wouldn't let me. Be barking at my heels, tellin' me to get my ass moving." He stood up.

With no thought, she stepped up next to him, close, and put her hands on his chest. "I think your ass needs to rest, not get moving. Billy would suggest the two of you curl up on the bed for a nap and after – "

"Billy would first lick my face – three times – I'd lift his chin and kiss him three times, and then he'd lead me to the bedroom. And then – "

"Like this?" She gently ran her tongue across his lips. Three times. Slowly.

Everything rushed from warm to hot. He took her mouth as if it was his last breath. Desperation replaced thought.

She was aware of him lifting her in his arms, but her face was so buried in the heat of his neck and the smell of his skin that she felt nothing until the softness of the bed. And then, the most tumbling, erotic waves of sexual need. She was there for him, taking him, healing him. Filling his emptiness, his hunger, his pain, his unrelenting need.

She remembered parts of the physical. She had no idea where her gun belt, clothes or consciousness went. His mouth devoured every thought, every inch of her. She was wet before he got to her, and he made her so much wetter. His tongue was ravenous, probing, pressing, turning her inflamed lips and clitoris into erupting desire. His mouth, his hands, his fingers, took what they wanted, what they needed … and then he was deep inside her. Hard. Harsh. Magnificent. Unrelenting. Exploding.

He was insatiable. Unrestrained. Exacting. Soaring into her hot, glorious brilliance as she took every ounce of his hunger and pain, lifting him from the darkness, as he burst into blazing gratification … and momentary freedom.

The afternoon sun, flickering across the bedroom, was the first sign of consciousness. She dared not move. *Sex in the afternoon is extra special.*

He was reluctant to open his eyes, to return to reality. He pulled her close.

She had absorbed his fire. Taken his release. Honored his need. She drifted from erogenous exhaustion to wonderment, and then to wondering. Lying next to his strength, she felt strong. Tapping into his vulnerability, she felt vulnerable. Not knowing his feelings, she questioned her own.

As he watched the sunlight paint the ceiling, he heard his inner voice … *what have we done? What will we do?* He pulled her closer.

She never wanted to leave the silence, never let him go.

He had to release her.

His body shifted. His breathing changed. She pressed into his chest as his voice rose up thorough his body – a low, husky whisper.

"Wow …"

She kissed his chest.

He squeezed.

She pressed. "You can say that again."

"Wow."

"And again."

"Wow." He kissed her hair. The smell beckoned his visceral urge. His legs moved against her.

She pressed. She was ready.

He went motionless.

She glanced at him. He was staring up, at nothing. "What is it …?" She stroked his arm. Nothing.

He knew his next movements would determine their future, their relationship, his career … and hers. He swung his feet onto the floor.

"Michael …?"

What he wanted to say was stuck behind his heart somewhere, instead the words came from the pit of his stomach. "This was not good … I mean, it was good, very good … But it was not a good idea. I'm sorry. I should – "

"Michael, stop it. Stop with the sorry. There's nothing to be sorry for." She put a hand on his back. He stood up – in all his beautiful nakedness. Her femininity stirred. "This was us – just us. A moment in time. A much-needed moment. I needed …" She slid across the bed and touched him. "I needed you. Really … really."

He glanced down at her. *My god she's beautiful.* "I needed you…."

She saw the vulnerability, the want, swirling in his bottomless brown eyes. And then it was gone, shrouded by a stern gaze. "It was impulsive. You're a beautiful woman … was a rebound reaction … I'm struggling, shouldn't have – "

"Rebound?"

"I could blame it on Billy dying but that wouldn't be fair to him. Besides – "

"Not to mention, a lie."

He pulled on his underwear.

She stirred again … *red Jockeys.*

Picking up his jeans he said, "There's no excuse for weakness, I should never have – "

"Michael, please … stop it. Let's not spoil a beautiful thing – even if it's only once. It was – "

"It's only once. Neither of us can afford this. Or handle it."

She watched him button his fly. *Button flies are so sexy.* "Handle it? Of course we can. You said it the other night. We can handle anything. We trust each other, completely." She slipped out of bed, picked her gun belt up off the floor and began gathering her clothes.

He was speechless. Standing magnificently naked – a statuesque Olympic athlete – holding her gun belt in one hand and her underwear in the other, she was a perfect metaphor for his clashing emotions. Law and order on one hand, love and sex on the other. A train wreck or a love boat?

Fully clothed and cognizant of their dilemma, they sat over coffee in the kitchen and tried to talk it through. If it wasn't so serious, it would have been comical. Gritt watched him acting cool and rationale while sensing the irrationality of his feelings. Nothing he said rang true – not dishonest, just evasive, avoiding reality. She listened, nodded, sipped her coffee, and managed her own denial. Their relinquishing to desperation was not an accident, and not about to go away. She wasn't sure how he was going to 'handle it,' but she had to try and disconnect and wait and see. He kept repeating three things. He was sorry it happened … glad it happened … and it wouldn't happen again. She asked. "What did you mean by 'rebound?'"

He was stirring his coffee and clink-clinking his mug.

Who stirs black coffee?

"Rebound? I don't know."

"You said, 'a rebound reaction.'"

"I did?"

"Yep." She locked on his eyes. He gazed. Perhaps an impulse to be honest. He stopped the incessant clinking.

"Might have meant …" Then he lied. "Billy. Rebounding from his passing. Don't they say it's part of grieving?"

"Do they?" The honesty impulse disappeared, his eyes went back to the clinking spoon.

"I gotta decide where to bury him."

She swigged the last of her coffee. *So much for honesty and trust.*

CHAPTER NINETEEN

"I'm going to prescribe some new medication for you Mr. Ryder."

Dick gazed at Dr. Ivana Borachi sitting across from him. *She looks like a grinning Buddha, holding forth in her cozy little corner of the world where twice a week I come to rid myself of all that's wrong in my corner of the world. Plenty. She's overweight and ugly. Certainly by Chrystine's standards.* Today, he was considering telling the doctor some of his thoughts about Chrystine. Not too much. No one should know how much he thought about her, although there was quite a bit he couldn't remember. But he had to talk to someone. That's what a psychiatrist is for, right? It wouldn't be out of line because Chrystine's death was all over the news. And he needed to talk about the van. This doctor-patient confidentiality was good because she couldn't go to the police, as long as she didn't think he was a threat to anyone. Or himself. He wasn't about to tell her too much about his anger at Goodall, but he did want to talk about himself. And thoughts of suicide. It would be so easy. Everything would be over, in a snap. Everyone who'd made his life hell would be sorry. Sure, Irene and the kids would miss him, but they'd manage. He'd be gone and they'd all be sorry.

An hour later he was feeling better. He'd filled the prescription, taken the medication and pointed the Ford toward The Hill. He found it therapeutic to meander through the money-lined boulevards. Under normal conditions these filthy rich, shit-houses, rising over manicured lawns with garish gates to keep out the riffraff, pissed him off, but under the influence of the drugs, or a couple of drinks, he was okay. He could dream. One time, on his way past Chrystine's house, he'd seen Irv Liegerman, Syntex's financial guy, coming out the drive in a big-ass SUV and it was all he could do to control himself. His anger was within a heartbeat of red-lining as he imagined slamming his car into the bastard's vehicle. Could've killed him, right there. Should have.

As he drove along, he saw a tint-windowed Mercedes and mockingly addressed its unseen occupants. "Fuck you. I'm just a meaningless peon in a Ford, but I can drive up here too." He scrunched down as he turned into Upper Middle Drive, where Chrystine lived – had lived. His chest tingled, part excitement, part fear. He had more than once thought of blowing the house up, right off the map – with Goodall in it. But not Chrystine – like those suicide bombers in Afghanistan. He saw the yellow tape and the deputy standing at the gate. He wanted to look at the house but couldn't let the deputy see him gawking. Never know what the son-of-a-bitch might think. He kept his eyes forward, but after passing the driveway he peeked. Fear returned. He clenched the wheel and tramped the gas pedal. The roaring engine caught the attention of the sheriff's deputy as it veered around a curve and disappeared.

Dick didn't regain normal breathing until he pulled into the Home Plate – a noisy, sports bar full of loud, fat ex-jocks. But the best burgers and cheapest drinks in town. He had twenty bucks in his pocket and Buzz, the owner, had cut off his tab three months ago. Asshole. *Next I'll be begging for food.* After a burger and beer, he was on his way. He didn't notice the Crosstown taxi slip into traffic behind him; all he was thinking was, *next drive-by, Syntex.*

CHAPTER TWENTY

Stuffy wasn't the right description of Solomon, Hoffman, Hinton but it was definitely a crusty, old establishment. The thirty-foot expanse of stone steps, brass name plaques and boxes of red geraniums, hanging like military epaulets, suggested you were entering the halls of tradition. Apparently, back in the twenties, the building had belonged to an insurance company. Mike liked the grandeur of the architecture and the way the vaulted halls echoed his footsteps and then swallowed them up. The receptionist looked like she'd been there since the insurance company was founded and after she'd walked him to a second waiting room, he wondered if she'd have enough steam to make it back to her desk. Hell, he was the one in need of some steam, some energy, a break in this case before it crushed him, buried him.

"Sheriff Cougar. Mr. Solomon will see you now."

Maybe Nathan Solomon had been with the insurance company too. His corner office must have been the original library, and the books lining the walls were certainly older than the white-haired patriarch, but not by much. Neither he nor the surroundings were intimidating – more regal, like the chambers of government might be in England. This was class.

The portly lawyer's smile brimmed with hospitality. "Sheriff, Nathan Solomon. Coffee? Tea?"

"Tea would be nice." His stomach would revolt if it had to process another ounce of coffee.

They chatted, actually beat around the bush about the tragic murder until the secretary set the silver tea service down and departed as quietly as she'd entered. Solomon got to the point. "You mentioned on the phone your interest in Wyatt?"

"Following up on a few things. Apparently, he met with Ms.

Goodall the night she was murdered."

"I spoke with him. Trust this can be kept confidential?"

"I'll do what I can."

"Mrs. Goodall came to us, recently to discuss a divorce."

Mike willed his eyes void of emotion. He'd known Chrystine was unhappy in her marriage, even afraid, but she hadn't mentioned divorce. He had no idea she was ready to risk Goodall's wrath because she had seemed frightened of him. This meant she would have been single again. He saw her walking through his mind in that flowing grace of hers. Then, he saw her lying in her bed, dead. *Why hadn't she told me?*

Solomon's voice sounded like it was coming from inside a cave. "Do you think it's related?"

He reached for the tea. "Just gathering information."

"Wyatt told me he'd met her that evening. Assured me he knew nothing, other than what he'd discussed concerning her file."

"I'd like to meet with him."

"He's expecting you. I should point out our firm was retained by Ms. Goodall, and from a legal standpoint she's still our client. Anything we do must protect her interests. He'll fill you in."

Although Wyatt Jones was listed as a partner, his office, its size, decor and distance from Solomon's was like the difference between the butler's and master's quarters. Mike suppressed his initial feeling of jealousy, *he's good looking and Chrystine kissed him in the bar according to Gritt's report.* Jones was nervous but had no trouble answering questions. Mike's initial interest was on her request for divorce and he got more than expected.

Jones explained. "Seems Ms. Goodal had talked to her husband three months ago about a divorce and he was furious. Threatened her. Turned nasty. Said he'd see that she got absolutely nothing, even though she was due a tidy sum according to the prenuptial. Said he'd tie her up in court for years."

"Any physical abuse?"

"Said not."

That meant she'd lied to Jones because she'd told Mike that Goodall had shoved her over a couch one-time. That was the first time she called him. They'd talked on the phone, and since she didn't want to file a complaint, he gave her some advice and hadn't expected to hear from her again. She called three weeks later and asked if he'd come by in an unmarked car. He took his Chevy Blazer. After his embarrassing gawk at her neck, they'd chatted for an hour on the terrace. That's when his fantasies began. Watching her against a backdrop of red maples and pink dogwoods, he'd felt like a teenager in the presence of the prom queen. Her beauty was undeniable. But it was her zest for life that fascinated him as she talked about her ideas for helping others, and making a contribution through the generous and measured use of her wealth – his wealth. She loved the good works she was involved in and despite the acrimonious marriage, she had not wanted to give up on it. Because it would have jeopardized her opportunity for giving to the less privileged. She enjoyed giving away Goodall's millions. She said that he was worth over five hundred million and yet, only gave away a paltry ten million a year, saying 'that's a lot less than the interest he earns.' Despite Mike's infatuation, he'd thought her commitment to give Goodall's money away was misdirected, after all it was *his* money. But because she looked like she'd stepped off the cover of a Virginia Secrets' catalogue, the testosterone attached his loneliness to her unadulterated sexiness.

Again, they met at her home. Again, he went in his Blazer. Again, he was fantasizing. She opened up to him, as if they'd been friends for years, and she was worried that her husband had bought a gun. Perhaps his mistake was when he gave her a sympathetic hug at the end of that visit. Or maybe the evening he was off-duty and they shared a bottle of Chardonnay beside her secluded Koi pond. She'd cried that night and just inside the terrace door – the same one broken the night of her murder – she looked up at him, let her emerald eyes open wide and invited him into her life. He took her mouth. Everything after that had been inescapable. Not uncontrollable, just inevitable. He stayed away for a week, then she called. She was going out of town and wanted to see him before she left. They agreed to meet that night at the Hilton. He booked off at eleven, called her at eleven-thirty and was in her arms before midnight. That's when it became uncontrollable. Their needs blurred the senses, churning into torrents of passion, pulling them beyond reason into a brief time and space … of hope.

At twelve fifty-eight, he left the hotel by the service elevator. She checked out at one twenty-five and was dead an hour later. That morning his life became a putrid bog of rotten, stinking, black quicksand.

Wyatt Jones was talking about the conversation he'd had with Chrystine at the hotel. *Who cares? It's irrelevant. Nothing is going bring her back?* He reprimanded himself. *You owe it to her. Find the bastard.* The lawyer's next words hit him like a stun gun.

"The real reason she wanted a divorce was for the sake of her daughter."

"Excuse me?"

"A previous marriage. A well-kept secret, as dictated by Goodall. He wanted nothing to do with Chrystine's past. Or for it to infringe on his future. The quid pro quo for his support payments to the ex-husband and child was that no one know about the daughter." The sheriff wasn't responding so he continued. "She'd made a Faustian deal with the devil. She regretted it; despite the half-million a year paid to her Ex, who the daughter lived with. But she could no longer bear keeping her daughter out of her life. That's why she filed."

Mike asked. "What's her name?"

Jones scanned some papers. "Justine."

"Age?"

"Thirteen."

His voice went hollow. "Anyone told her?"

"We contacted the father."

As he walked down the arched hall, he heard the echo of his

footsteps, over and over, punctuating the names pounding in his head
– *Chrystine ... Justine.*

CHAPTER TWENTY-ONE

As Gritt pulled through the station parking lot, she could taste the dripping burger and cool, yellow suds over at Frankie's. It had been a long day and she was about to 10-7 (out-of-service). Then came the call.

"All units. Code-16 in progress. 3726 Ridge Road. Shots fired."

She yanked the cruiser through a one-eighty, ripped the tires into the pavement and hit the siren. "Unit 2-952. On my way. Four minutes away." Code 16 was an assault. It was at Syntex. She heard Mike respond.

"Unit 1-951. Ten minutes away. What've we got?"

Dispatch replied. "911 call. Reports shots fired. Fourth floor. A Mr. Liegerman. Apparently not hit. Couldn't keep him on the line."

Gritt was first on the scene. There were maybe sixty cars in the Syntex parking lot. She swung diagonally in front of the last row of cars, fifty feet short of the main entrance. She popped out, squatted behind the front fender, Glock drawn. There wasn't a sound. A lone security guard was sitting inside the main door reading a magazine. She'd assumed there would be pandemonium, people screaming, running. *Maybe it's a false alarm ... should wait for back up.* But the adrenaline was flowing. It had been several years since she'd been the lead on a shooting. And someone inside could be in jeopardy. She grabbed the radio. "Unit two, nine, five, two. Outside main entrance. No sign of shooter. Going in. She was up and moving, scrunching low to cross the expanse of asphalt, her sinewy body running like she was in the Olympics – fast, deliberate, under control. She strained to watch the night-black windows, *will they shoot? Would it hit her? What will it feel like?* The unknown ten seconds seemed longer than a four-minute mile. She made it, slapping her body flat against the glass door and exhaling. The security guard's white-haired head jerked up. She waved him towards the door. He didn't budge. She raised her Glock so he could see it. He moved like he'd forgotten his walker, crossing the lobby and unlocking the door.

She asked. "Where's the shooting?"

"Who are you?"

"Got a 911. Shots fired. Fourth floor. What's goin' on?"

"Beats me. Haven't heard a thing."

She led him back to the marble reception desk, gun on ready.

"Do you know a guy named Liegerman?"

"Be on the fourth."

"Can you call his office?"

"Guess so."

She saw Mike's car screech into the lot. "What's your name?"

"Charley."

"Charley. Unlock the door for the sheriff. Tell him I'm on my way to the fourth floor." She sprinted to the elevators, hit the button and hugged the wall. The doors opened. Nothing. She punched the third floor. She could've called Mike on the portable but knew he'd take over. She'd talk to him when she arrived on the fourth. At three, the doors glided open. She was startled by the lights – had expected darkness. It looked deserted. She found the stairs and climbed to the fourth floor and eased the door open. She hoped the silence was the only thing there. Could be an armed assailant, anywhere; plus, this Liegerman guy, dead, alive or hostage. She peered right. Two glass doors twenty-feet away and an empty hall beyond. Left, an open area with a circular reception desk, a dozen chairs and a glass table layered in magazines. Nothing out of place. She eased into reception. Behind the desk was a hall that she couldn't see down. For protection, she squatted next to the desk and regulated her breathing. *I hope this desk isn't cheap particle board.* She switched on her portable and whispered. "Mike. You hear me?"

"Where are you?"

"Fourth floor. Reception. Nothing so far."

"Stay put."

Mike's voice was a touch of security. It slowed her heart that was probably running well over what it did in the last 200 meters of a race. "There's a guy named Liegerman up here."

"Stay put. I'm with the guard. We're calling his office."

"Roger." The silence tightened around her emotions as she began to think instead of react, *you damn fool, even a cheetah doesn't go hunting alone.*

Mike was back. "Here's what we got. Liegerman is in his office. Unharmed. So far. Confirms a shot fired. Repeat, one shot fired. Fifteen minutes ago. Nothing since. He thinks it came through his window. No sign of shooter. Repeat, no sign of shooter. There are other people in the building. No one seems to know anything happened. I've called for SWAT. We'll clear the entire building. It'll take a while. In the meantime, I'll get a fix on where Liegerman's office is from your position. Stay put."

"Roger." She was sweating profusely and relaxed her grip on the gun, and took a few deep breaths.

Mike was back. "There's a hall off reception. At the far end, on the left, is a large corner office. Liegerman is in it. There are six or seven offices on the left before you get there. On the right, just before you get to his office there's an open secretarial area with four desks and an office supply room, copy machine and stuff. That's it. Stay put until SWAT gets here."

"Got it." She was more than ready to agree. She'd had her rush for the day, for the year.

Suddenly, there was a crash down the hall. As she shot out of her crouch she grazed her shoulder on the corner of the desk. But that didn't compare to the pounding in her head. In the FBI, she'd learned that fear has a way of either freezing or focusing the mind. It was all in the training – and the Glock in her hand. She clicked off the portable, not wanting to risk identifying her presence. Creeping down the hall, her gun leading the way, she saw the glassed-in offices along the hall. She peered into the first one, then the next, and the next … all empty. Then she checked behind the secretarial desk to the right. Nothing. The supply room door was open, but she couldn't see inside, only one end of a copy machine. She decided to head for Liegerman's closed door, now just ten feet away, *the supply room is too small for anyone to hide in.* At Liegerman's door, she steadied herself in a half-squat and turned the knob. The gun went in first, followed by dilated eyes. They swept the room. Nobody. She found her voice. "Liegerman?"

Nothing. Then from behind her … *Click.* Her heart hit her rib cage. She spun, ducking below the sight line of a desk. If there was someone in the supply room at least she had them isolated. And a clear shot if they came out. But an assailant can still cover a lot of ground, *after* being shot.

She shouted. "Come out. Hands where I can see 'em. Now!"

The silence was forever. Then there was another click.

"Throw out your weapon. Now!"

There was movement – from Liegerman's office. *Shit.* She twisted and leveled the gun into the office. A diminutive man was rising from behind a large desk. The fear in his face told her it was Liegerman.

"Don't shoot" was the feeble plea.

She stayed down, hidden from the supply room but totally exposed to anyone in the office with Liegerman. "You alone?"

"I'm okay."

"Get down. Stay put."

Again, the click from the supply room. Ten seconds and a hundred heartbeats later, she inched around the desk to get a better look inside. The only place someone could be hiding was behind the copy machine. She sucked in air, and a lot of courage, and jumped into the doorway. She was staring at a printer out of paper, clicking away. Her fear released in laughter.

From the safety of the Liegerman's office, she reported to Mike, "Clear."

"Sit tight until SWAT arrives."

"Roger." She was glad the race was over.

Three hours later, she and Mike had finished interviewing Liegerman, the security guards, a dozen people and SWAT had cleared the building. It was not a very complete picture, but based on what they had, it had frightening possibilities. It appeared that a single shot from a high-powered rifle had pierced the widow of Liegerman's office at approximately eleven-fifty p.m. He wasn't hurt. The bullet was imbedded in the far wall, ten feet from where he'd been working. The crash Gritt had heard was Liegerman knocking over his chair trying to crawl out from under the desk. Neither Gritt nor Mike discussed the unanswered question: Was this an attempt to kill a Senior Vice-president of Syntex? Or could it have been a wayward bullet from a gun discharged by accident, a gun in the hands of teenagers. Out here on the edge of town it was possible that some idiot, hunting at night, could have shot in the wrong direction. But none of the explanations sat well.

Gritt offered one of her pithy aphorisms. "This is too much of a coincidence to be a coincidence."

Mike said. "Profilers say criminal behavior is consistent even when it's inconsistent. There's always a pattern." He pulled her aside. "I want you to quietly leave and go up to Sentry Hill, Cedar Point Park."

"Cedar Point?"

"Take Thurm with you. Don't make a big deal of it. I'm wondering if the shot could've come from there. It's a clear sight line."

She looked over her shoulder at Sentry Hill rising in the night like a camel's hump. "That's two hundred yards. More."

"Just a hunch. Cedar Point would be empty this time of night. Somebody could walk in, fire a gun and walk back out with nobody the wiser."

"He'd be a helluva shot."

"This wasn't a hell of a shot. Missed by ten feet. Look for a vantage point and something the shooter might brace on: tree, post, fence.

Twenty minutes later she and Thurm were trudging through Cedar Point Park.

He asked. "What'er we lookin' for?"

"Something that might suggest someone was here with a rifle. Taking pot shots at a big-time executive. Maybe there'll be a note with his picture?"

Thurm tried his version of humor. "Maybe we'll find the smokin' gun with prints. Except it's darker than a well-digger's ass up here. Not gonna find much of anything."

She wasn't about to make fun of Mike's hunch, but as a betting woman, she knew the odds were slim of finding anything in the dark. Their flashlights danced among the trees as they pushed to where a chain link fence separating the park from a fifty-foot drop to railroad tracks.

"Thurm. Check along the fence. I'll poke around the picnic tables.

Fifteen minutes later she called Mike, "Unit one. Do you read?"

"Unit one."

"Got something."

"Roger. On my way."

He arrived twenty minutes later and she walked him to a picnic table where her flashlight illuminated several coins in the dirt under a picnic table.

"Could be nothing'" she shrugged. "Bet lots of people lose change out of their pockets, sitting here on the table. But fact that it's more or less in line with the window. You know what they say – "

Here comes another clever-assed cliché.

"Something always comes of nothing."

He smiled. "Actually, it's 'Nothing comes of nothing,' from Shakespeare … but I know you know that."

She smiled. His humor was coming back.

He said. "Tape off an area – in every direction."

Thurm headed for the gate. "I'll get the tape."

Mike yelled. "Not there idiot."

The deputy stopped and looked at the boss, half apologetically, half surprised. Even if he had forgotten, in his haste, that the area was a crime scene, it wasn't like Mike to call any deputy an idiot. *Sure lost his humor in a hurry.*

She was absorbed in the contents of a trashcan and shouted after Thrum. "Bring some gloves." Then to nobody said, "No self-respecting dog would dig in garbage."

As Thrum strung up the tape, Mike searched around the tables and she, latex-gloved her way through the trash. After numerous "yuks" and "shits," she was silent. Then a tight-lipped whistle echoed out of the trashcan.

Mike brought his flashlight up on his deputy. There in the glow was his grinning beauty with an empty shell casing sitting on the end of a pen. "Look what we got here."

They carefully bagged the coins and empty shell casing and sent Thrum to file them in evidence. "Make sure there's no mistakes in logging them," he shouted after Thrum. He turned to see her half smiling, half smirking. "What?"

She sat on the picnic table, feet on the bench seat, still grinning. "Just another one of your BGOs."

"We can't afford any mistakes. I trust Thrum, just reminding him, even if it's a blinding glimpse of the obvious. Besides – "

She patted the table top. "Come rest your weary bones. Been a helluva night."

"You can say that again."

"Been a helluva night,"

They laughed. It echoed through the trees before being swallowed up in the darkness. They sat side-by-side, holstered guns touching – he was right-handed, she left.

He said, "You know you disobeyed an order by going in?"

"What order?"

"What order? Does nothing I say matter anymore. It's as if – "

"I didn't mean it that way. I heard a noise and – "

"These days, I wonder what the hell I'm doing. Second guessing myself. I know one thing, I'm doing a lot wrong. Hell – "

"Michael stop it."

"Why do you sometimes call me Michael, instead of Mike?"

"I do?"

"You do. Sometimes."

"I dunno …?

"Yeah you do. You did that afternoon at my place."

Why the hell did he bring that up? "It's your imagination."

"Maybe so. But you do."

She should let it go. "Is it okay?"

"Is what okay?"

"The Michael thing – sometimes?"

"So you admit it."

"If you say so."

"I say so."

"Maybe it's another BGO – it *is* your name."

"Only my Mother called me Michael. To everyone else I'm Mike. Except with you – sometimes."

"Well, I'm in good company then." She felt his shoulders slump. Their guns butted together. Their legs leaned into each other. She saw the gray light of dawn filtering through the trees.

"Sometimes I miss her so much … I talk to her sometimes, you know. As if she were here. It helps."

"Is she here now?"

"We all need to talk to somebody."

"Absolutely." She put a hand on his knee.

"She's not here, like you are." He put his hand on hers. "She would've liked you. She respected strong women … she was the strongest. Man, how she put up with my ol'man, I'll never understand?"

"Love."

His head turned, eyes needing answers.

"She loved you. She did everything for you." She held his eyes, "Michael, you're as loved today as you've always been."

He leaned in and kissed her. He wasn't hungry, he was grateful. He wasn't out of control, he was deliberate. He held her mouth for the longest time. "Gritt, I am forever grateful to you. For you. For who you are. I can no longer lie to myself … I need you, want you. Somehow, we have to make this whole thing work, have to – "

She put a finger on his lips. "Shhhh. There's nothing we can't do. And this, between us, is already working. Just have to talk it through, work out the wrinkles. Figure out how – "

He took her mouth. This time it was desperate.

She was ready. This time it was unbridled.

She vaguely remembered placing their gun belts next to each other as the exhilaration raced from her mind to her heart to her core – fantasies being fulfilled beyond her imagination. The cool morning mist on her bare legs and the rough table on her naked butt heightened her arousal as he stepped into the heat between her legs. His thick thighs forced her further onto the table as he hooked his arms under her legs and lifted. Her elbows scrapped on the table as her head went back in a wave of excitement and expectation. She moaned, "Yes…."

He pulled her toward him. "I didn't hear you."

"Yes, Michael … yes." She wanted to shout his name. He pushed, hard, and the pulsating expansion deep in her heat ignited every nerve-ending of her being. She yelled into the morning light, "Yes Michael … yeees!" Her throbbing desire engulfed his rhythmic pounding and her inner heat released into a wet, stream of ecstasy as his climax possessed her.

This time it was the morning sunlight that shone on his new reality. And this time, reality was unconditionally beautiful – his very own Olympic champion. *Was she his angel in-waiting? Was it time to let go of fear? To trust?*

CHAPTER TWENTY-TWO

"Gimme a break Pops." Mike pushed back from the kitchen table and opened the refrigerator. "I know what I'm doing." He was hot, thirsty and annoyed. He'd come to talk with his father again, but the ol' man was doing all the talking, while grunting over a crossword puzzle.

Jack said. "Douglas was a hit. So if Goodall is too – what's a five-letter word for celebrity politician. Ends in d? – Then you got a mess on your hands. Ain't all politicians celebrities?" The pencil eraser worked feverishly on the crossword.

Mike thought how the nickname, *Jackhammer* suited his cantankerous father. He was the quintessential bull in a china shop. Or as Gritt said, "A bull in a glass house." Truth was, he could use his input, but he didn't need the attitude, spouting theories without even discussing how the murders are categorized, a basic first step in investigative work. If it isn't rape-murder, a burglary gone wrong, a drug killing, a murder-for-insurance or a domestic dispute, then what is it? He'd run through all of them with Gritt, but the ol'man was off and running at the mouth. Much of what he said was intended to challenge, not help, to reconfirm his father-knows-best image. He claimed a professional hit made the most sense, especially if Chrystine had been filing for divorce.

Mike didn't disagree. But the other possibility, the more frightening one, was that some deranged bastard killed Douglas and was after Goodall but surprised Chrystine by mistake. It could be a disgruntled ex-employee, one of more than fifteen thousand. He kept an open mind, but his number one theory was a professional hit, hired by Goodall or possibly the ex-husband. Number two, a deranged ex-employee. The mounting problem was that Gritt was holding on to the third alternative, a spurned lover. Even his father had mentioned it.

Should open up to Gritt. But no way to my ol'man.

Jack groaned. "Five letters … d, d, d…. Shit – "

"That's four. And it doesn't end with d," said Mike.

"What?"

"Shit doesn't end with d." Mike looked down at the puzzle, covered in eraser crumbs. "You need six letters. Try Arnold."

"Uh?"

Mike sat silent.

The pencil hovered over the blank boxes as Jack rattled on. "Ya' gotta get forensics to give ya' a break. Get on their ass. There's something in that bedroom crying out to be found. Turn the house inside out. Turn Goodall's life inside out. You'll find something."

It was another blinding glimpse of the obvious and Mike rebutted with his own. "We're all over it. Ballistics, blood, trace evidence, canvassed the neighborhood, twice, Ms. Goodall's victimology – "

"Uh?"

"Her background. Why she might be a target." He watched as Jack ignored him and penciled in A-R-N-O-L-D. He felt that flutter of expectation, a son's need for acknowledgment. Instead, he got the usual no thanks, no credit. *It's only a crossword.*

Jack said. "Follow the hit theory. Divorce filing in those social circles doesn't make for much of a motive. Even so, killing her is a stretch. And why would her Ex want to cut off his source of money?" He shrugged. "But you gotta do what you gotta do." The little, empty white boxes haunted him. "What's the name of that damn TV show, you know … same name as Goodall. Alex … Alex – "

"Trebek."

"The show!"

"Jeopardy."

He started to fill in the boxes. Stopped. Erased. Tried again. Erased.

Mike spelled it. "J-E-O-P-A-R-D-Y."

Jack said. "Know what I think? That shooting at Syntex speaks volumes. Somebody's out there taking serious aim at people. I'd get on it. Before he does it again. Maybe doesn't miss next time."

Mike ate two more chocolate chips and drained his coffee. He missed Billy, who always curled up in the corner waiting for his chocolate chip. He usually sat at Mike's feet, but not when Jack was around – always moved further away. A dog's sixth sense. Mike wished he had the same sense to stay away from Jackhammer. "We're all over it. Crime scene, interviews, records. We'd do surveillance if we had someone to surveil. But there are anomalies."

Fancy-ass words pissed Jack off. Just flaunting his college education.

"Both Douglas and Goodall scenes could be fixed. And who in their right mind would fire a rifle, trying to kill someone, then throw the shell casing in the nearest trash can?"

"Any sick, stupid, confused, idiot, crazy enough to do it in the first place. We're not talking balanced mind here. This guy is angry. Psycho. Schizo. Depressed, flatter than flat iron."

"Exactly," said Mike. "Schizophrenics usually don't do things like this. They're not capable of it. They – "

"What about that Ohio Freeway sniper. Said he was paranoid schizophrenic and he – "

"There's a lot of misunderstanding about paranoid schizophrenia. First of all, they're a very small percentage of the population, it's simply over diagnosed and blown out of proportion by the media."

"Media. Assholes blow everything out of portion."

"Proportion…. If this is a deliberate attempt to kill CEOs then it's highly unlikely the work of a schizophrenic, they're too disorganized. Psychopath? Maybe. But it's not like we have a series of killings here. Two murders do not a serial killer make."

Jack had tuned out and was nose-down in the crossword. He had no time for book psychology, what he knew was street psychology, reality, not theory.

"Depressed people, the kind laid off, usually aren't prone to violence. They're down and out, at times can't control their anger, but rarely do they go shooting people. They're not psychopaths, not schizophrenics. But if they do kill, they go on a rampage, go postal. They don't serial kill. That takes premeditation, planning, cunning."

"Where'd you learn that crap? Not in the real world. Look, the criminology book ain't gonna help ya' here. If they're linked, why wouldn't it be a wacko wanting revenge?"

"Who says they're linked. The only common denominator is that Douglas was CEO at Syntex and so was Goodall. But for Christsakes," he hammered the table, "it was *his wife* who was murdered."

"By mistake."

"No! Not a mistake. The burglary was staged. Not some psychotic idiot. And the Douglas one was no fool either. Point blank, clean, quick."

"That was robbery."

"Come on."

Jack pushed. "Maybe they're not linked. Coincidence. Or some idiot got the idea after Douglas was wacked. Figured it was a helluva way to get rid of these guys. So, he goes to try it on Goodall, surprises the wife, panics and shoots her." He gave his son a what-do-you-think-about-that look.

Mike said. "Whoever did it, had access, the alarm code. Goodall wouldn't be handing that out as part of employee severance packages. She could've been the target."

"Then track it down. But don't discount the village idiot theory." He jotted another word into a box and changed the subject. "By the way, I spoke to Captain Hyll. Give him a call. He'll get you some help on boppers."

Mike fumed. Again, he was ignoring procedure, freelancing, after he'd asked him not to contact Rochester. It was time to go.

He glanced at the pink, plastic clock on the wall, remembering the day his mother bought it at Sears, he was with her. Like most Saturdays, she'd taken him shopping with her. First Sears, then

Goodeve's market, then ice cream cones, then Linley's drugstore for her arthritis medicine – gold shots. He'd always thought gold was a funny name for medicine. She'd taken a lot.

"Gotta go."

Jack penciled in another word. "Keep me posted. Especially on Sentry Hill."

What's with this keep me posted bullshit? Who do you think you are, my shift commander? He let the slap of the screen door speak for him, but the echo of Sentry Hill poked his heart. When his mind wasn't immersed in work, it was on that wonderful night – morning – and her. *Must compartmentalize.* As he walked down the drive, the village idiot theory crystallized in his mind more than he wanted to admit. He'd better get Gritt on it or he'd end up being the idiot.

CHAPTER TWENTY-THREE

Mike was at his desk pondering the wall of the building next door. It was his view on the world from his isolated spot in the world – a cluttered office, stacked with files, plants and a sense of pride. No knickknacks, no frills. There was a collection of photos over a leather couch that looked more like parched mud than genuine leather. There was Mike with the mayor; Mike with the Governor; Mike with his sister, both in uniform; Mike and the Syracuse football team, he was number eighty-seven in the back row; and Mike with his grandfather, all dressed up in his 1930s police uniform, sitting in a wheelchair at the seniors' home. He also had a photo on his desk of his family of three – Billy, Mercedes and himself.

He didn't look at the photos much; he preferred to stare at the blank wall because the nothingness allowed his mind to search for answers among the chipped bricks. Today, they weren't very helpful. He half-smiled at his corny thought, *I'm up against a brick wall*. But he wasn't laughing. As Gritt had said, it would be good to laugh more and get back to chiding her about her bad clichés, which she butchered just for a laugh. *Speaking of the sexy devil.*

She came through the door like she was charging to a finish line. She never knocked. Didn't need to. She had open access, unlike the rest. At first, her appointment as Chief Deputy had ruffled Scott Waggs, a twenty-two-year veteran and top investigator, who'd expected the appointed. But everyone had settled in and there was a minimum of office politics.

If his desk hadn't stood between them, he was sure she would've run into his arms – which would have been wonderful, but inappropriate – in case someone was watching. She winked and gave him an I-know-something grin.

"Deputy Matsuta got something. Could be connected. We were discussing the case in the patrol room. I mentioned the geezer we interviewed on Sentry Road who said he'd seen a 2008, 2009, dark car about the time of the shooting. Didn't think it was much. But Matsuta heard me. Recalled seeing a similar year, dark gray, cruising past Goodall's place a few days ago. Coincidence? You know what they say about coincidences – "

Mike held up his hand as if to say please. "Get a plate?"

"Negative – "

He dropped his feet off the corner of the desk without taking his eyes off her. *Fuck, she's sexy when she's pumped.*

She continued. "Maybe his drive-by was a return to the scene of the crime. Nut cases do that. Can't help themselves. Berkowitz, 'Son of Sam' did it. That Williams guy, in Atlanta did it. It's slim. But I've asked for a list of all employees dismissed from Syntex in the last two years. Had trouble getting it. Some asshole Vice-President said it was 'quite improper.' I threatened. Got a call from his highness, Goodall – offered full cooperation. Should get the list in a few days."

"Few days? What do they think this is an invitation to a wedding? Get it. Today! Tomorrow latest! None of this few days' shit." He kept firing. "How are you going to comb through fifteen thousand names? Looking for what?"

She loved his intensity. It fired her up, in more ways than one. *Concentrate girl, concentrate.* "Maybe something will pop out. Most deputies know people who've been laid-off. I'll circulate the list. See if anybody knows anybody driving a 2008, 2009 gray vehicle – "

"Dark gray."

"No point going to DMV without a plate."

He flopped onto the couch. "Anything on the coins?"

Geez he looks sexy stretched out on that beat-up-bag-of-stuffing called a couch. "Can't match the partial. But guess what? That Liegerman guy hasn't been back to work. Whoever was trying to scare him, did. He's Goodall's hatchet man. The guy who rolls the numbers."

She grinned.

He rolled his eyes. "Tumbles the numbers."

"Yeah, that too." Her baby-blues were sparking. "Guess the big bucks they pay him covers up the stench of death he creates with his sharp pencil. Maybe that bullet in the wall dulled his pencil."

He chimed in. "And blew out his calculator." Her laughter was infectious.

She sat in the big chair next to the couch. *Like to sit next to him … on him.* She loved the stimulating conversation, and being close to him. "Maybe his bottom line needs a new set of Pampers. I'm telling you, this guy was shit-scared that night. Hiding under his desk. When I told him a high-powered rifle would go right through the desk, you should've seen him move. Except he didn't know where to go. Stood motionless, like a rabbit in the headlights – "

"Deer."

"Whatever … then ducked behind the sofa. Guess he thought it was an armored tank. But ain't gonna help if this nut really wants to get him." She bounced up and paced.

He said. "I'll bet he's out buying an armored SUV right now." What he wanted right now was her. All of her. She was animated and excited, and exciting. He absorbed every inch of her athletic perfection and his pulse quickened in rhythm with her steps. He was slipping into fantasy. *So fucking sexy.* "Maybe this guy is more desperate than crazy?"

"The employee?"

"The who?"

She stopped in front of him. "The guy doing the shooting. The village idiot. A disgruntled ex-employee. Desperate enough to resort to killing … with nothing left to lose."

"Maybe?" He wanted to keep going, but couldn't hold his train of thought – any thought. He just wanted her. Here. Now. On his desk.

She continued pacing. "Except the shootings are different. Very few similarities. Maybe no connection. One obviously a pro. One maybe a pro. Other not a pro." She paused. "One a jealous lover … just saying."

"Not unless the lover is a crazy. A wacko. So angry he goes ballistic with a .38, a .22 and a .30-30." His anger blocked his sexual fantasies. "Please! Use your head."

She winced. *That hurt.*

He watched her return to the chair, and that moment of silence separated his battling needs – her, the case. "Get that list. Start with those laid off the longest. Cross check hunting licenses. Make sure – "

"Yeah, yeah. I got it."

He watched her rise. Strong, committed, ready … graceful. "And find someone who owns a .30-30." His voice had cooled, but his insides still churned as she walked out, taking his undeniable, unrequited needs with her. "And find me a village idiot."

CHAPTER TWENTY-FOUR

After a week of nauseating hype, the media had moved on and categorized Chrystine Goodall as a follow up story. Today's headlines were about Alexander Goodall and his latest announcement. Mike heard part of the news on the radio.

Syntex has announced another round of restructuring that will target several departments and two plants. CEO Alexander Goodall said, Over the ensuing months we will be reducing staff by twenty-four hundred employees. Most will be through early retirement and natural attrition....

The announcement driveled on with empty platitudes and corporate jargon that every citizen in Westhaven despised. He wondered how brother Don rationalized this one. On one occasion, he had admitted it was a giant shell game and Goodall and Douglas were just sophisticated con-men, pocketing millions and then moving on to the next sick company as if they were doctors of mercy, when in reality they were doctors of destruction. Don was angry – had been most of his life – but he was seen as mister nice guy to almost everyone, except Mike. He had most everyone fooled, including their father and did an admirable job of presenting the *Walton Family* image. Twice Mike had been called by deputies to incidents involving Don's daughter Sissy. Once when drinking was suspected. They let the kids off. The second time she was caught at age seventeen having sex in an open convertible up on Sentry Hill. Again, they let her off. And Mike never told Don, not so much to protect Sissy but Don. Something stopped him from shattering his big brother's make-believe world. He'd always got along with the old man, or so he thought, because he presented a bullshit picture and his father had to lie to himself because Don was the only one who had any semblance of a relationship with him. Don had made a career of propped-up images while in constant fear of his tower of Babel crashing down.

It was after six and Mike was hungry. The phone rang before he could order the pizza. "Cougar."

"Fuckin' bastards. Psychopaths! They – "

"Pops! Stop. Who? What?"

"Fuckers fired Don."

CHAPTER TWENTY-FIVE

It was a good thing Irene wasn't home or Dick would have yelled at her. She kept throwing out his newspapers. She'd better not have thrown out the ones with Chrystine's pictures. He went to the basement where she stacked old papers and flung them around until he found his prized editions. He slumped into his chair and savored the images. He never used to look at Playboy or trashy magazines, but he did peak at the Victoria Secrets catalogue and his daughter's fashion magazines sometimes. Until he got so depressed, then he quit looking, except for Chrystine. Her pictures were the only thing that gave him any sense of pleasure. Outside of his family, she was the only decent person he knew – and she was dead.

The phone rang. *No fucking way I'm talking to anybody.*

The voice was an irritating squeak. "Mr. Ryder, this is Dr. Borachi's office. You haven't shown up for your appointment. Our policy is to charge you if you don't notify us in advance. Please call to make a new appointment." Click.

He shouted into the empty house. "Fuck you. And you, and you and you. Fuck your policy. I'll do what the fuck I want, when I want. Maybe I won't come and see that uptight bitch anymore. Lot of fuckin' good she's doing me. I'm crazier than when I first went there. Yeah, maybe that's it. As she makes me look inside myself I get sicker and sicker with what I see. A complete asshole. Useless. No fuckin' good to anyone. But I used to be. I did a lot for that fuckin' company. Had great ideas, opened new markets, set up new dealers. How about the new promotional material and the advertising campaigns? That was an industry first. I put your fuckin' company on the map for the first time in fifty years. And what thanks did I get? None!" He rose from his chair and charged at Dr. Phil on the TV. He kicked the screen. His ankle screamed, but Dr. Phil kept gabbing; going on about how we are where we are in life because of choices we made. "Bullshit. I'm in this sinkhole because of choices other assholes made. Trump murdering jobs with tariffs, Obama with Chinese labor, Goodall and Weiss cutting thousands, my old man, my twin brother…." He whirled around, eyes searching. There, on the mantle, a replica of Rodin's, *The Kiss* – a wedding gift twenty-eight years ago. His mind screamed, *it'll never be the same*. He grabbed the sculpture and split Dr. Phil's head with it. The explosion – actually he remembered it was called an implosion – was scary. He had no idea it would make such a mess. Shit, back in university when they dropped a TV set off the roof of the fraternity house it hadn't seemed so bad. Of course, he wasn't standing six feet from it. Broken glass everywhere, stinking smell. And his hand was bleeding. But he felt better. He'd shut Dr. Phil up. He crumpled onto the couch, into the quiet.

He wasn't sure how much later it was when the phone pierced his peace. The first thing he saw was the trashed television, *how the fuck did that happen?*

The answering machine did its routine. "Dick … Sid. Gotta talk. Dick, pick up." He waited. "Call me. Or meet me at Frankie's. Be there in an hour."

He stared at the dead phone, the dead television and the dead Chrystine in the newspaper. *Fuck, everything's dead…. I'll go see Sid.*

He left the deadness and cranked up the car, mumbling, "at least it ain't dead, yet."

Frankie's was overflowing, and the din was all Dick could take. People yakking, drinking and eating as if it was their last meal. *For some it might be.* Maybe if he stayed at Frankie's every day and just drank he'd die of liver disease. That would be a relief. And Irene would get three-hundred thousand in life insurance. That would be a win-lose. A win for Irene and the kids; a loss for him, a real loser.

Sid was animated. "Listen, listen. I was talking to the guys at the Argyle Street plant and we think the shooting at head office and

Goodall's wife's murder are connected." He ignored his companion's glazed stare. "Everybody's trying to figure out who it could be. You know, some guy, mad as hell and out to take care of business. Gotta tell ya', none of the guys were too upset if that's what's happening."

Dick's eyes narrowed as anger bubbled into tumbling thoughts. *No. Those degenerate assholes wouldn't care. What do they know about a woman like Chrystine. Nothing. She's just a name in the newspaper to them. They hate Goodall, who doesn't? But they don't care that she was an innocent victim of a righteous deed. Trying to kill Goodall is laudable but making a mistake with Chrystine is unacceptable. Besides, what do they know, they still have their jobs. Wait 'till they've been on the dole for two years and see how they feel. By then you can't even think straight. You stop thinking, you stop doing anything.* He sniped at Sid. "What do those assholes know? Nobody was out to kill her."

"Goodall was the target. Listen to this. The bunch of us: Jamie Morgan, Phil Madison, and Harlan what's-his-name, got a theory. Remember Buford Viles? He's been laid off, outta work for two years. Wife and kids left him, bank foreclosed on the house. Went to live with his brother down in lake country somewheres, in a two-room shack. Harlan was saying the brother does odd jobs and kinda lives off the land, hand to mouth. A hunter. And Buford's a crack shot. Harlan's gone huntin' with him. Get this. Says he owns a .30-30. That's what the newspapers said was used at head office." Sid's voice was ringing like a slot machine. "Jackpot. One plus one could add up to Buford Viles."

Dick really didn't give a shit. Either you know, or you don't. And Sid didn't know. He didn't even fucking understand. "Could be."

"Dicky boy, this is huge."

You keep calling me Dicky boy and I'll show you the pointy end of a .30-30.

"Everybody's talkin' about it … and you don't care? Man, you're really in the tank. Isn't that shrink helping you? Gotta pull yourself together. Find a job. You could – "

"Fuck you … find a job?" His eyes looked like there was a brush fire inside his head. "You don't fuckin' understand. There are no jobs. None. Never will be. For me, for you, for most of us. They're gone. Gone to robots and computers and to China and India. And McDonald's, flipping hamburgers. Or cleaning rich peoples' houses. Yeah, that's what the fuck I'll do, get a job as a maid. Work for Goodall, now that he doesn't have a woman around the house." His eyes went sad. "Don't you get it Sid? You and your stupid ass cronies, speculating yourselves into a myth. Goodall is the only winner. He and all the rich assholes running the show. Here, Rochester, Pittsburgh, New York, wherever they are, wherever they implement their waste management practices. Yeah, they waste good management like you and me. And they'll keep doing it until we're all out of work … or dead. So stop with the speculation. Just let this guy go about his business. If he's knocking off assholes like Goodall, Liegerman, Douglas, then more power to him. But I hope he doesn't make any more mistakes like Chrystine." He stopped, his venom dispensed.

Sid, never short on words, picked up the gauntlet. "Right on Dicky. These assholes deserve it. Who knows, maybe our messenger of death will get the message across – stop with the genocide or *you're* next. But you're right, too bad about Mrs. Goodall."

Sid continued to talk through lunch and three scotches then paid the bill, leaving a twenty percent tip for Helen. Dick thought, *fuck, must be nice to be able to leave that kinda tip. Maybe I should be a waiter?*

He drove aimlessly and with no air-conditioning the humidity and his depression made his brain feel like a blender processing mud. He cranked down the windows and headed out of town. He didn't see the flashing red and white lights until the siren made him jump. When he looked left the deputy was pointing at him to pull over. *Fuck you … no Richard, get hold of yourself.*

In the mirror he saw the deputy approaching. *I'm done.* But in a few minutes, he was on his way, feeling lucky that the deputy hadn't looked at the front of his car that was beaten to shit. But he had a fucking seventy-two-dollar ticket. Now he was pissed. Needed a drink. He stopped at an ATM, tried withdrawing a hundred dollars and got a *funds not available* notice. He tried fifty. Same response. On the third try the machine coughed up a twenty. He headed to the Home Plate.

• • •

Deputy Fred Trowell had handed out tickets to every weirdo you could imagine, but the guy in the Ford had acted stranger than usual. Initially, he hadn't said a word. Handed over his license in silence and when asked if everything was okay said, "Sure." Nothing came up on the plate check, so he wrote up the violation. When he gave him the ticket the guy looked like he was going to jump out the window. He was seething, the artery in his neck was twitching and his hands gripped the wheel with either fear or anger.

Later, he related the story to a couple of the guys back at the station and they laughed about it.

Deputy Eric Waters asked. "What make of vehicle?"

"Ford Taurus – rust bucket."

"What color?"

"Dark gray."

"Check the board. They posted a car like that."

After chatting for a while Trowell went to his patrol car and punched up his MDT (mobile data transfer computer). There was an alert: A hit-and-run. Two guys in a van had been injured. The description was similar to the car he'd ticketed. He'd check it out after coffee.

CHAPTER TWENTY-SIX

Gritt was ready to run out of Mike's office. "We got a positive ID. He's placed in the vicinity of both shootings. Let's pick him up."

Mike held up his hands. "Whoa, step at a time. Let's be sure we've got everything."

"Look at what we got." She counted on her fingers.

He couldn't divert his gaze from her fingers. She noticed.

Smiling, she asked, "Sheriff, do I have your attention? Ex-employee. Down and out. Family disintegrating. Seeing a shrink. Car placed at both scenes." She went back to her little finger. "In a hit-and-run. Beat the neighbor's fence silly. This guy fits the profile like a sock."

"All circumstantial. No witness. No prints."

"I called that consulting psychologist over at State – can never get his name right – Doc Panterescu. Said he fits a profile. Maybe manic depressive, borderline psychotic, probably in a deep depression and acting out anger at those he blames.

Part of Mike wanted it to be a village idiot; it would be easier to solve than a professional hit, a lot better than a serial killer, and would get rid of the scorned lover theory. "Yeah, but this type isn't prone to killing. Some violence, like beating fences to death but not people. Too many unanswered questions."

She said, "Yeah but there's a pattern in everybody's behavior."

"You'll figure it out – soon I hope."

He watched her leave, a little deflated, walking as if she'd just lost a race, feet dragging, shoulders sagging. He'd wanted to hug her. Kiss her. And …

· · ·

Dick didn't usually look out the window, especially in the

morning because when he felt shitty the sun hurt his eyes. But this morning, even with the sun blistering off everything, he was sitting in the back of the living room watching the bastards watch him. They'd been there since last night, two different unmarked cars. One a shit-brown Chev, which was there now, the other a white Ford. He didn't understand why they didn't just come and get him. *Good thing the Taurus is in the garage. Guess they're gonna wait 'til I come out? Assholes.* He wanted to run and never come back, but brooded for a while then checked the window again. The shit-brown Chev was gone. He ran to the bedroom, yanked a suitcase from under the bed, threw in some clothes and headed for the basement. In the far corner, beside the electrical box was a piece of plywood paneling fastened high up on the wall. It had a rusted handle in the middle of it. He stood on a box and pulled on the handle. The panel popped out. Gingerly, he extracted from the dark hole a long object rolled up in a blanket with several strips of duct-tape wrapped around it. He cradled it under his arm and went upstairs. Still no car in the street. He took a wooden yardstick from the broom closet and exited to the garage. The blanket and yardstick went in the trunk and he backed out.

He drove the speed limit with no idea where he was going, he was just going. Maybe a long way away. Buffalo? Syracuse? Albany? Then he saw him. A cop. The acid convulsed in his stomach and the speedometer crept up as he fought to push back the anger. *Should've had a drink before I left.* He said out loud. "Don't panic. Go slow. See if he follows you." He headed for the New York Thruway and entered the Rochester bound ramp. The cop dropped the tail at the tollbooth. Dick laughed, "Rochester, here I come, ready or not."

CHAPTER TWENTY-SEVEN

Gritt was on the phone with one of the deputies and Mike could tell she was upset. "Why'd ya' wait? Could've radio the troopers. Fuck.… Com' on in." She dropped the phone like a hammer.

He eased her frustration. "Rochester will spot him."

"Contacted them. Got a BOLO (Be on the lookout). They'll notify if they spot his car."

"Let's get inside Goodall's life." He called investigators Waggs and Gibson in. He was about to turn his prime suspect's life on its over-inflated head.

Scott Waggs was the best homicide detective in Western New York. After twelve years in Washington DC, he'd come to Westhaven after his wife insisted on getting him out of one of America's murder capitals. In DC he'd started in Narcotics, was on the Hostage Negotiation Unit, did undercover and as detective first-grade investigated over a hundred homicides. Ironically, after three years here, his wife left him and went back to Virginia. He liked Westhaven, so stayed. Mike was glad he had. Hodge Gibson was the antithesis of Waggs. That's why they were a good team. Gibson's reason for being a cop was primarily so he could legally tote a gun, actually two guns. His standard issue Glock .45 and a .32 in a Velcro ankle holster, and thirty extra rounds of ammo. His philosophy was, 'When it comes to me or them, I'm the one comin' home.' One night he'd responded to a burglary in a department store over in Jonsville. Not waiting for back up, he went in. It was dark as hell inside and when he saw the perp with a shotgun, he drew on him and told him to drop the piece. He got no response, so fired, once. The mandatory internal investigation was a total embarrassment for him because the perp had turned out to be a mannequin in hunting gear. Hodge's strength was his knowing the street, where he had a lot of respect and connections. He had more snoops and snitches than any ten cops. He too often freelanced, but usually got results. And right now, they needed results.

Mike started. "I know we've all been working ungodly hours, but it's gonna get worse. I want to reshuffle things a little." He looked at Gritt. "You focus *solely* on Ryder. I'll focus on Goodall. Scott and Hodge will back me up. We'll tear down every door in his life and either eliminate him as a suspect or arrest him. Solomon, Hoffman, Hinton are cooperating but they're being cautious in case they go after him in a wrongful death suit."

She whistled. "She haunts him even after death."

"Even after he has her killed," said Mike. "Maybe?"

All agreed, if Goodall did it, he would've paid big. Waggs and Gibson would review evidence from the scene, including a partial footprint from the garden. Forensics had a plaster cast of it. Gibson would talk to his street people and see what he could get on a hit man being in town recently. Gritt would stay on Ryder, and Mike would follow up with the law firm and interview Goodall again.

Mike wrapped up the meeting with some bad news. "Might have to set up a task force on this."

"Shit!" Gibson shook his head and chucked a chunk of chewing gum in his mouth, followed by a toothpick. When his temperature went up the gum and toothpick went in. Talking through the gum he said, "We don't need that crap. It's a fuckin' distraction."

He was right. It would turn into a feeding frenzy with everybody running all over, more intent on out-doing the other factions than doing what counted. Mike's guys were already working twenty-four/seven, grabbing scraps of sleep here and there. With a task force it would get worse. And frustrated, tired deputies were not the best investigators.

Mike shrugged. "Pressure from above. And the media will be relentless – unless we make progress, fast. I can probably hold off a week."

Gibson said. "I've got a druggie who's tapped into a dealer. They might know if a stranger was in town to do a contract. This snitch is a wanna-be G-man ... wants some credit against his next bust."

"Gritt, get hold of DMV," said Mike. "And get Ryder's birth certificate, blood type, prints. Let's get this thing going in some direction, any direction." *And not in the direction of a love triangle.*

CHAPTER TWENTY-EIGHT

The curtains hung like wet dishcloths in need of a good breeze, but it wasn't the heat and humidity that was smothering Mike, it was the anxiety, guilt, anger. He was flat out in his recliner, wearing only Joe Boxers, watching the ballgame on his big screen TV. He was about to go to bed, but the Mets had just hit a three-run homer to go up by two. Normally, he'd be up and cheering but he hadn't budged. He loved baseball and the Mets were his team. He hated the Yankees. And he was hating this job. It made a not-so-good life worse, although he knew that was a copout. He also blamed the job for perpetuating the acrimony with his father, but again, he knew it was another copout. *I'm a copout.* He'd always allowed his father to play big shot at his expense, and on this case the ol'man was the worst he'd ever been – *should kick his ass out of my life for good … and let Gritt in.* But none of that would solve the murders. He'd had over six months to get a solid lead on the Douglas case and he had squat. Now Chrystine's. She deserved more; life not death, love not abuse. If that bastard Goodall did this, he'd hang him by his balls in the middle of town and let Syntex ex-employees stone him.

The feisty Mike resurfaced a little and he grabbed at it, telling himself that problems were to be solved, not wallowed in. And he had Gritt's support, in more ways than one. Their relationship was a good thing, if he could sort out how to make it work. But for now, it had to be a secret. *Fuckin' secrets … be the death of me.*

This was not the first time he'd questioned his decisions. His hiring Gritt. His one-night stand with Chrystine. *I'm a sucker for beautiful, smart women. But still just a village idiot.* He never got to know Chrystine but Gritt he knew, instinctively, from day-one. She was special. Perhaps too special for him, the village idiot, all dressed up like a big, tough cop.

He'd made a lot of questionable career decisions, including the original sin of continuing the father-son legacy that stretched like the long arm of the law from his grandfather to him. But he no longer nursed the doubt that he might have gone into police work to get respect from his father; he'd picked sheriff because he liked the idea of being a public servant, and accountable through public election. Not a 'lifer' like his ol'man on the city force. And unlike father, he didn't need to be a hero. And Gritt had made it a whole lot better.

The phone rang. "Cougar."

"Rochester just called. A shooting. You at home?" Gritt's voice telegraphed alarm.

"Yeah."

"I'm coming buy. Ten minutes."

Why would Rochester call about a shooting?

"They've got a shooting. She's dead, at the scene. Several shots. Rifle. From a distance."

He knew.

"Guess who? A Heather Trott. Head of Scelltone."

Another CEO.

While waiting for her to arrive, he turned the Mets off and slipped on jeans and a T-shirt. He fidgeted with his Joe Boxers because he usually didn't wear them under jeans, they were just for hanging out around the house. But he'd hurried, and now they were creeping up on him. And that wasn't the only thing creeping up on him. This Rochester murder would open a floodgate of public outcry that his finger-in-the-dyke would not be able to stop. Two CEOs dead, another's wife dead – it went beyond coincidence. It was a nightmare. Maybe a serial killer?

She looked glum walking through the door and dropped onto the couch like she'd just lost a 1,500-meter race. "We got a problem, right here in River City."

"From the movie, Music Man." He sang, " ... trouble with a

capital 'T.' And it rhymes with 'P' – "

"What?"

"The song. " And it rhymes with 'P,' and that stands for pool ...'" Except for us, it's a pool of blood, too many pools."

"No shit."

"What do you know?"

"Was it really called Music Man? You sure?"

"I'm sure. My mom loved it. Watched it with her, more than once." He sat down next to her. What did they say?"

She laid her head on the back of the couch. "Like I said, not much. They'll keep us posted. Said they called just to give us a heads up. Because of similar MOs." She sighed. "That's it."

He put his hand on her leg.

That feels good. She swung her eyes from the ceiling to him. He looked like an oasis, a safe place for a thirsty, hungry woman to run to. The tension released from her body.

As his hand moved, her eyes turned vulnerable, looking for release, relinquishing control, asking for him. He took her breath away, then her mouth and tongue. She cursed her belt, her gun, her boots. The last thought she had was how a deputy's gear was a serious barrier to spontaneous sex. He solved it, carrying her to the bedroom and removing everything – slowly, deliberately. Except her underpants. He laid her on her back, stood next to the bed and swept his T-shirt over his head and stepped out of his jeans. *Joe Boxers, not Jockeys. Haven't seen those before ... so fucking sexy.* He laid beside her and rolled her on her side, facing him, inches apart.

He whispered, "No touching. I just want to absorb you. Look at you. Feel you without touching you. Marvel at you. Soak you up. Indulge in my wildest fantasies." He put a finger to her lips. "Shhh, not a word."

Outside she was still. Inside she was in turmoil. *How can I not touch him? This is crazy. The heat coming off his body is driving me nuts. I'll try for a minute. If I can?*

If she moves, touches me, I'll devour her. The pull is ... hang in there Cougar. This is unimaginable, unforgettable. Be strong ...

His eyes ... my god, he's in complete control. I can't move. Where are his hands? I can't look. His chest is moving. Oh god ... he moved, his lips moved ...

He whispered. "I'm going to touch you, gently. Don't move, just feel my fingers on your skin."

Her body was on fire. *Oh my god, his fingers ... on my thigh ... under my panties ... I just went wet ...*

Slowly Cougar, slowly ... don't rush.

I can't. "Michael ..." She slammed her body into his. He gasped. She clung to him. "Michael, Michael, Michael ..."

He turned onto his back, rolling her on top and pulling every inch, every ounce, of her to him. They were one. There was nothing else. Nothing.

CHAPTER TWENTY-NINE

As dawn broke so did the humidity and the downpour overwhelmed the windshield wipers, forcing Mike to slow down. On a good day it took ten minutes to get to his father's, he was already fifteen. He'd refrained from contacting him last night – wasn't going to spoil a great night with Gritt. She went home about two, after two more incredible sexual adventures. *Hated to let her go. But best.*

His ol'man knew people in Rochester so he decided any help was better than no help, and he'd put up with the spewing. He couldn't reach him on his mobile so assumed he'd done a nightshift and could catch him at home.

He was surprised to see the taxi parked in the street. Usually it was in the drive, but the drive was empty, and the garage closed. He pulled into the drive to shorten the dash through the rain. Three knocks didn't roust his father. He opened the screen and hammered on the door, then tried it. Locked. Usually it wasn't. He peered into the kitchen. No sign of life. Must be out. *So why was the taxi here?* He flipped up the collar of his orange slicker and dashed to the side door of the garage. His father's Chrysler was gone. He shrugged, dumping water down his neck, "Shit." He waited in his patrol car and as the windows misted over it was like a protective cocoon and he slipped into a conversation with his mother, looking for comfort, and maybe some answers. She wasn't responding.

He called Gritt. "Morning. Any more from Rochester?"

"Nothing."

"I'll call Captain Hyll. Gonna go over."

"Where?"

"Rochester."

Gritt was silent. She was lead on Ryder; she should go to

Rochester. *Love to go together … can't.* "What about interviewing Goodall?"

"I'll get to that. Put together everything on the village idiot theory. I want a warrant."

Getting a warrant pumped her. "Call me from Rochester … and be careful."

At police headquarters in Rochester, Captain Hyll pointed to a chair. "Welcome to Fifty-One Division Sheriff. I've had a briefing from our CSU (Crime Scene Unit) and detectives on the Trott shooting. We don't think it's the work of a pro. Too sloppy." He explained that five shots had come from a .30-30. "Five shots are not the mark of a pro. Two hit the victim, one in the lower back, one in the head. Three missed. CSU found one bullet in a tree, five feet to the left of the victim. Retrieved five casings on the hill above the jogging path. Figure the guy was lying in wait. Had to know her routine. This was no random or impulse killing."

Mike said. "Same firearm as one of ours, but just one shot fired – missed by ten feet. If it's the same guy, he's a lousy shot. Might fit the profile of an angry ex-employee. We like this guy Ryder who might be on the run. We're doing background and asking for FBI profiler." He paused. "Ryder only came to Rochester yesterday. That's not much planning time."

Hyll said, "Not much planning here. Just had to know Trott was a jogger and where she jogged. Rest could be luck. Good luck for him, bad for her."

They agreed to treat the murders as possibly linked and look for evidence supporting the theory. But publicly deny any link. Mike couldn't reconcile the Ryder theory – which had merit – with Chrystine's murder. If Ryder went to kill Goodall that night and Chrystine surprised him, it was possible that he could've killed her, but not likely. One shot, .22 to the head wasn't the work of a wacko. Or a poor shot. They needed a profile.

CHAPTER THIRTY

Alexander Goodall lived by the clock, ran by the clock and expected everything to work like a clock. So the fact that eleven of his direct reports had been sitting in the boardroom for fifty-five minutes waiting for him was an indication that things were not running as they should. Everybody accepted that life might be in turmoil after losing his wife but what had surprised everyone was the way he'd reacted. He'd withdrawn for a couple of days and then it was back to business as if nothing happened. A few marveled at it but most knew it fit his nature and his nickname, "Ax." He was tough, ruthless and insensitive. There was no room for emotions.

Beyond the double doors of the boardroom, Goodall's office was like an overheated boiler room, filled with agitation – his. Mel Ebe, Carmencita Lopez from the local, law firm of Raleigh & Shay and a Brandon Sharko, a private investigator, had been with him for two hours and they'd yet to resolve much. Ebe had contacted Solomon, Hoffman, Hinton only to discover that they were already representing the late Ms. Goodall. Alex had gone ballistic when he heard Chrystine had been filing for a divorce. Ebe had gone to his second choice, Raleigh & Shay and been assigned Ms. Lopez, whom he wasn't impressed with. She hadn't said much, just listened with an engaging, damn near seductive, smile that partially diffused Alex's frustration when he looked at her – often.

Goodall had spent an hour telling his audience how he felt, what he wanted and what he expected. Problem was, none of it meshed. He'd said he was torn apart by Chrystine's death and the revelation that she was unhappy – an apparent surprise to him. He was furious at the local sheriff's inability to turn up any leads and he said over and over, he was committed to finding the murderer. The discussion was dragging because he was confusing everyone. He wanted Carmencita to represent him and keep the sheriff off his back but wasn't clear on why he needed the sheriff kept at bay. When she asked, he was dismissive. He wanted Sharko to 'dig up anything and everything,' but when asked about the probability of a professional hit he avoided the question. He wanted Ebe to meet with Solomon and diffuse any action on the divorce, especially public exposure. When Mel suggested it might be out of their hands, he unloaded a tirade.

He paced. These people were getting on his nerves. And he wasn't sure about the Lopez woman, although he did appreciate how well she improved the scenery. *Maybe she's worth keeping around.* Chrystine's demise was not working out as expected because she'd been idiotic enough to start divorce proceedings. He never thought she'd do it until getting an agreement from him to continue support for her kid. That kid was everything to her but just a half-million-dollar expense to him – a small contribution on behalf of his career. His strategy was being threatened. His plan to wrestle Syntex into shape in a couple of years and put himself in a position to become the next CEO of a flagging *Fortune 500* corporation could be in jeopardy. There was no room for error.

"Carmencita, I want you to come to a meeting with our two-bit sheriff. Put him in check if he gets overzealous." He looked from her legs to Sharko. "Get back to me regularly. Don't be low profile. I want everyone to see you on this. You can reach me anytime." He turned to Ebe. "See Solomon today, I don't care if it's at midnight in his bedroom, I want this thing truncated." He rose, as if he was going to raise his arms and bless the multitudes. He took a last glance at Carmencita's legs. "I have people waiting."

• • •

Mike's secretary, Hong, as reserved and unflappable as a Buddhist monk, buzzed him. "Sheriff, there's a Ms. Lopez here to see you. She represents Mr. Goodall. He's not here yet."

"We'll wait for him." *So Goodall thinks he needs a lawyer.*

As they entered, Goodall launched into a speech about how he wanted to cooperate, prompting Mike to think, *bullshit might work in business, but it doesn't cut it here. This is homicide, not reengineering.* Although the case against Dick Ryder was mounting, he found himself believing that *this* dick in a ten-thousand-dollar suit smelled of complicity. "Sir, I'd like to review the list of items you said were missing from your home. You listed, 'Cash, undetermined amount.' Could you give us a better estimate?"

"Two, three thousand dollars."

"That's a lot to have lying around?"

"It's relative. Cash is handy, and we keep it handy."

"Did your wife keep a lot of money on hand too?"

"Of course. She is, was, an impulsive spender. That night she could've had a couple of thousand dollars on her. And there could've been another thousand or so in the house?"

"Do you not use the safe?"

"Only for good jewelry. Which was not taken. The only jewelry missing was what she was wearing and what was in her jewelry box. As I listed. Her diamond was worth fifty-thousand." Then, appearing to be helpful, added, "That and the cash would certainly be enough incentive for a burglar."

"Who might've had the access code to your system?"

"My investigator said pros can deactivate them, the right guy can get by any system." He made no effort to camouflage the condescension.

"You think the motive was theft?"

"You've eliminated sexual assault, right? Could be some psychopath after me? The same one who got Douglas. And that woman CEO … Trott?"

Mike wanted to keep the arrogant bastard calculating. "Why do you say that?"

"Christ sheriff! I'm not the cop here. I'm trying to help.

Anything's possible. But *if*, and I underline if, someone was interested in hiring a hit man to kill me – sounds like it's right out of a Mafia movie – then that kind of professional would never make the mistake of killing the wrong person. They don't do that."

Mike's eyes held him. "Maybe it wasn't a mistake?"

"She didn't have enemies. Not those kind … Preposterous."

"You said earlier you weren't your wife's – I believe your word was – keeper."

"I know the life she lived, knew her friends and – "

"All her friends?"

Ms. Lopez interjected. "Sheriff is this necessary?"

"Her male friends?"

"Yes."

"Could she have had friends you didn't know?"

"Where's this going?"

"Did you ever have her followed?"

"That's irrelevant. The only time I've hired a PI was yesterday." He shot a glare at his lawyer as if to say, do something.

She did. "Sheriff, my client is here of his own volition. Need I remind you, he's a busy man. Speculation and conjecture is all well and good, but I suggest we leave that to you and your colleagues and make the best use of Mr. Goodall's time."

"If Mr. Goodall knows anything about the people surrounding his wife, anything, it could be important. Far from conjecture."

Goodall said. "I want to help."

Mike was aware of the constant switching in Goodall's posturing, from superficial caring to defensive irritation, he was covering the waterfront with suggested motives from robbery to a psycho to a hit. Mike was convinced that despite the hired PI and all the harangue, Goodall had no intention of helping. And he was lying. The question was how much? He'd planted one fat lie when he said they probably had two or three thousand dollars in the house the night Chrystine was murdered. Chrystine had told him that she purposely didn't keep more than a few hundred dollars in the house or on her person.

Ms. Lopez continued. "We believe the brutal murder in Rochester of Ms. Trott may be relevant. Needless to say, it has Mr. Goodall concerned. Do you have reason to believe there's some connection?"

"We've been in contact with Rochester police." Then he embellished to get a reaction. "We think it's quite possible that your wife's death was a murder-for-hire, intended specifically for her." He held Goodall's eyes – nothing. But he saw the same twitch in his cheek that he had seen when they met on the day of the murder.

"I told you, she had no enemies."

"That you know of."

Before Goodall could convert his exasperation into invective, Lopez placed a hand on his arm. "Sheriff. You're not suggesting that my client is under suspicion?"

"We've closed no doors, it's our job to – "

Goodall turned to his lawyer. "If he's threatening my reputation – "

"The first step is to eliminate Mr. Goodall and family members."

Ms. Lopez tried to assist. "But Sheriff – "

Mike put up his index finger. "Are there any family members on your wife's side?"

Goodall didn't answer.

"Like Parents? Ex-boyfriend? Ex-husband?" He didn't go too far.

"Her parents are dead. I'm sure there are several ex-boyfriends." He was fidgeting with his cuff link. "She was married before."

"Do you know where her ex-husband lives?"

"Never met him."

"How long ago?"

"Geezus." He looked to his lawyer.

Lopez took the cue. "Sheriff. In court this is badgering the witness."

Mike was as placid as the brick wall outside his window. "Ms.

Goodall never mentioned where he lived?"

"That was her business. We kept it that way, intentionally."

"Do you know of any reason why her ex-husband might have been angry with her?"

Again, he turned to his lawyer.

"Were there financial dealings between them? Alimony? Assets?"

"It was her business, not mine."

Another lie.

Lopez came to the rescue. "I think it's best you follow up on these issues after you've made some progress in the case, rather than taking up my client's time fishing."

Goodall rebounded. "I'm willing to cooperate but you have to be judicious with my time. I've an enormous commitment to resurrect this town's most important asset, Syntex, and despite my personal tragedy and our mutual objective to bring my wife's killer to justice, I ask that you respect what I'm doing for your town. In the long-term, all of Westhaven will be better off."

Under his desk, Mike's feet pressed into the hardwood floor and he pulled his chair in close to prevent himself from going up and over the desk to grab this egocentric bastard by his two-hundred-dollar tie and squeeze the sanctimonious pus out of his head.

CHAPTER THIRTY-ONE

Dick watched the blood trickle. Usually, the sight of blood made him gag but nothing seemed to bother him anymore. He didn't even feel a need for Irene. The blood oozed from the slice in his finger, *how much blood do I have to lose before dying?* It was a little cut from his son's Swiss Army knife. He fumbled in the glove box for a tissue, wrapped the finger and returned to whittling the end of the yardstick. He was sitting in the passenger seat with the yardstick between his legs, one end on the floor, the other in his tissue-bound hand. He was cutting a deep V in the end of the yardstick. It was hardwood and tougher than expected, especially because he didn't have much light. The overhead interior light was as dull as a crawl space and outside was black as shit. He was in the woods above the old Cattaraugus quarry. Back about a hundred yards, he'd passed a lovers' lane area, lots of beer bottles and cigarette butts, but no lovers. It was mid-week, so any teenagers trying to get laid had gone home by now. When he was a teenager, he never got laid, only had a couple of chances and screwed them up. He half smiled at his pun. Lois Hancock, his second girlfriend, had probably been his best chance. He was nineteen at the time and a virgin – not that he let anyone know. His buddies assumed he'd scored with his prom date, the not-very-pretty Judi Mayer. Truth was, he'd always been afraid of rejection and she hadn't handed out gilded invitations that said, 'Come fuck me.' But she probably would've if he'd pushed a little. Of course, he hadn't, not Mister-nice-guy, mister please-like-me-first then fuck-me-later. The guys made fun of his lack of effort when it came to girls, but they'd assumed he got laid by Judi because she was, well, bordering on ugly. He hadn't bothered to correct their misperception. But with Lois it had been different. She practically attacked him one night when six of them were camping. He was in a tent with his buddy Robert

Mankel – who was fast asleep – when she crawled into the sleeping bag with him. Before he was fully awake she had his sweat pants down and rubbing herself all over him. The scratchy-tingling of her pubic hair pushed him to a quick explosion, all over her. He never got it in. Robert never woke up. And Lois never did it again. He considered it his first time and never told anyone otherwise. He never had real intercourse until he was twenty-three and that was with some girl he couldn't even remember her name – it was at a keg party down on Lake Canandaigua. And Irene said she was a virgin when they married, but he didn't believe her. So he led her to believe that he was a lady's man before they met, bullshitting about parties and girls in his past. His whole life was a lie.

He snapped the knife closed, admired his handy work, climbed out and opened the trunk. He cut the duct-tape off the blanket and gently lifted out the rifle, holding it like a piece of fine china. The night was so still he could hear his breathing. There was barely room for the rifle, the yardstick and him in the passenger seat. It was hot so he opened the window but there was no breeze and he was oblivious to the cricket concert or the dance of the fireflies. The overhead light now felt like a heat lamp, but he couldn't move enough to reach the switch on the other side of the steering column. Suddenly, he jammed the barrel of the rifle into the overhead cover. It shattered like a chunk of peanut brittle, but the light stayed on. The next thrust took out the tiny bulb and buried the encasement an inch deep in the roof liner. He waited for his anger to recede. He needed courage, not anger. But there was no hurry.

CHAPTER THIRTY-TWO

Gritt had spoken to Rochester several times and there'd been no sighting of Ryder. It was twenty-four hours since the Trott shooting and the trail would go cold quickly. A warrant for Richard Roger Ryder had been issued but it was in conjunction with the hit-and-run, not homicide. But she figured Ryder could be the guy. She'd interviewed his wife, kids, neighbors, employees at Syntex and a guy named Sid Leavens. One of the telling pieces of evidence – it wouldn't hold water in court – was that Ryder had collected newspapers about the Goodall murder. Mrs. Ryder had shown them to her, piles of them. Could be an obsession? The Leavens guy had been fired too and said Ryder was depressed. He offered his own version of a suspect, some guy called Buford Viles. She made a note of it. Dr. Panterescu had spoken with Ryder's psychiatrist but because of doctor-patient confidentiality they didn't get much. Panterescu pointed out that the doctor-patient privilege didn't apply if there was an imminent threat that the patient might act again, but the psychiatrist claimed he wasn't capable of doing it in the first place, let alone again. He was suffering from stress and a sense of inadequacy, but he wasn't psychotic.

An arrest at this time would quiet things down even if later it proved to be the wrong guy, and this guy was crazy enough, and they had enough, so she'd pursue this and not push the love triangle theory, for now.

On her way to a meeting with Mike, Waggs and Gibson, she swung through the kitchen because at 7:10 am, the coffee and doughnuts were always fresh. There was only one doughnut left. She grabbed a coffee and the last doughnut.

As she sat down, she saw the new home of the doughnuts. Waggs had two, Gibson none – he was a health nut – and Mike had two, and a

Danish. *He's eating a lot, must be pissed.* Waggs and Gibson had done a complete background on Goodall and were briefing Mike.

Waggs said, "ME has a semen sample from the victim. She'd had sex that night. Sent it to the State lab for DNA, be a couple of weeks. But only works if we have a suspect to match it to. Under duress, we got a blood sample from Goodall. But his alibi looks tight." Waggs referred to his notes. "Forensic guys did get some hair and fibers off the clothes Chrystine Goodall wore that night, but she was in touch with a bunch of people, so don't hold much hope. They took fibers from underwear found in her laundry hamper. Not sure they're the ones she was wearing that night. Might be able to match 'em. Probably showered after sex." He closed the notebook. "We've been in touch with her ex. Alibi has been corroborated. But we still consider him a suspect. Thought we might fly to New York, have a face-to-face chat, see if – "

"Wait on that," said Mike. "Keep the pressure on Goodall, don't let him think the ex is a suspect."

Waggs shrugged. "Whatever."

Mike asked. "Gritt what've you got?"

They waited while she licked her fingers. "Sorry, got side-saddled … side-tracked. This guy Ryder. Richard Roger Ryder – try saying that fast, three times."

Gibson did. "Richard Roger Ryder. Richard Roder Ryder. Richa, Roder, Ryda."

They all laughed.

She watched Mike, *god he looks great when he laughs. And when he's serious … anytime.* She continued. "This guy is headed for the loony box. If he did it, he'll probably get off on temporary insanity. Everyone said he was on the edge. I expect Rochester to find him soon – if he's in the area. Hell, he could be halfway to Florida by now. No nation-wide yet."

Mike said. "May want to get a UFTAP warrant (Unlawful flight to avoid prosecution). Want him in custody ASAP, ostensibly for the hit-and-run. Still holes in a murder charge." He flipped through his notebook. "Interviewed Goodall, with his lawyer. And Jones at Solomon, Hinton, again. The divorce was a bigger problem than he's letting on. Big money damages and reputation damages. Problem is, I can't get much from her lawyers because they're protecting her interests. Can't blame them. But Goodall's lying."

"Like what?" asked Gritt.

"Wyatt Jones confirmed there was some ongoing contact between her and the ex.

Gibson added. "The ex said he'd never met Goodall but confirmed there was a financial arrangement. He was cooperative to a point, especially in clearing himself. But he seemed to be protecting someone. Maybe Goodall?"

Waggs and Gibson hadn't mentioned the daughter, so Mike didn't. Or that Goodall's financial support was half-million-dollars. He'd follow up.

• • •

Gritt hung up from Rochester and called Mike. "Com' on, com' on … pick up."

"Cougar."

"We got a match. A partial. The coins from Cedar Point. Rochester lab did what our guys couldn't. Used that superglue method. Guess who? Richard Roger Ryder. That puts him in Cedar Point. And Rochester – "

"Not necessarily at the scene," said Mike.

"Maybe at Goodall's place. If we can match that shoe print."

"I'll see where Waggs and Gibson are. Come on up."

Waggs and Gibson? I got this.

Mike should have been elated. He wasn't. He turned to the brick wall. *Despite the Ryder evidence, Goodall had to have something to do with this?*

Gritt walked in.

He turned back. *Damn she looks good.*

"It's a break." She high-fived him, *love to hug him, just for a sec*. "Although Rochester still has no sign of him. But his wife confirmed he owns an old rifle and it's missing. She didn't know what make or model, but her son said it was … you got it, a .30-30. Cedar Point and Trott, both .30-30s." She reached into her pocket. "Got a hundred says this guy's a lousy shot."

"Get somebody over to his house and bring in every pair of shoes the guy owns; boots, rubbers, runners. And if we only get a partial match on the shoe print, send it to the RCMP in Canada. They have a method of matching people's footprints to shoes – the inner sole of the shoe. Tell them it's urgent. And find out if ballistics can compare the slug from Liegerman's office with the ones from Trott. Run our slug over there, let their lab do the check. Want as much as possible when we collar this guy. Get a new warrant. Murder two."

"On it."

He stood up, smiled, high-fived and winked, *wish you were on me.*

If he winks twice, I'll jump him. "See ya." She was gone, loving the chase. She sent a deputy for the shoes, signed the slug out of evidence and headed for Rochester.

CHAPTER THIRTY-THREE

In the blur of activity over the past twenty-four hours Mike hadn't been home to sleep. He'd spent four glorious hours at Gritt's – well, he did get a twenty-minute nap between the fulfillment of sexual fantasies – and was just dropping around to the house to change and check messages. There was a message from his sister Emily, "Call me."

He tried her at home in Syracuse, no answer. She only called when there was good reason, so he left a message. Her job and family were overwhelming, with the ridiculous police hours and two, running-wild kids, he only saw her at Christmas. He'd always admired her guts for disassociating with their father—one day she'd told him to shove it and walked away. He should do the same.

She called back before he'd showered and changed. "Grumpa's not doing well." As kids, they'd always called their grandfather, Grumpa, at first with affection and later with sarcasm. "Gone downhill in the last week. Thought you should know."

He heard hesitation, maybe sadness. What she meant was … *and tell dad.* She probably ached for something from her father but long ago cut off that part of her. She'd been hurt too many times. The old man was too stubborn, too egocentric and too pained. Since the death of their mother, he'd been like a drunken captain on the good-ship Cougar, lost at sea, abandoned. Their mother had been the glue, the calm in the center of hurricane Jack. When they lost her to a higher-place, they lost their place, especially him. It was his tipping point, and the harder he tried the worse it got. Don withdrew, went to college and grew up outside his father's immediate reach. Mike was younger and had tried to work through it, but Emily was too young and could only deflect the vacillating emotions with rebellion. From green hair and marijuana to shoplifting and teen sex, she'd defied the rules, and her father. At seventeen she ran away to Florida, lived with some loser twice her age, joined the army and then came home and went to the police academy – maybe a retroactive reflex to try and please her father. It must have touched him in some lukewarm corner of his heart, but he didn't have the capacity to show it, so the relationship remained an ever-widening gorge between them.

Mike knew the source of the evil, well maybe not evil, but certainly destructive dysfunctionality; Grandfather, James Orville Cougar – Jack Senior. A wisp of a man, whose monolithic, tyrannical shadow had blackened three generations. All because he was a poor orphan, of sorts. His father had committed suicide in the crash of 1929, leaving his wife with young Jack Orville and twenty thousand dollars. His mother promptly put him in a Catholic orphanage – she said she couldn't handle him – and then went through the money one bottle, and many men, at a time. Mike was sure Jack Senior gave his only son his name with the tag 'Junior' as psychological puppet strings, tied to the expectation of building a son in his own image. It had worked.

Jack Junior hadn't visited his father in two or three years and they didn't talk anymore. They used to – yell would be more accurate. Senior had driven his boy to make something of himself: Be an eagle scout, be a Marine, be a cop, be a captain – a hammering litany of never-ending assignments. When the good son didn't make it, he heard about it, and when he did, the only mention was the next goal. Senior had been a beat cop, as tough as the pavement he pounded for thirty-three years, and he expected more from his son. Nothing short of captain, except Junior had come up short. Senior's big accomplishment was becoming the first union rep for his precinct and it drove him to be a die-hard union man. He often talked about the day he'd met Jimmy Hoffa, saying, 'That Jimmy Hoffa, now there's a man, a leader among men.' He adamantly claimed Hoffa was not a crook. Mike figured it was more about a man of small stature who hadn't made it, admiring another man of small stature who had – in his eyes. With his local union, he thought he was cock-of-the-walk, but now he wasn't walking at all and lived in a nursing home.

Emily, still searching for some umbilical tie had moved her grandfather to Syracuse so she could be there if needed. Dementia had set in and some days he talked nonsense, rambling on about disconnected events and people. Emily said, "Mike, can you suggest he find some time, now that he's retired, to drive over and visit Grumpa? It might do them both good."

"Good luck. He's out every night in that damn cab. Sleeps during the day, in the streets by night. That, and butting into my work, is all he does."

"May not have much time left. Some reconciliation might be good."

"See what I can do."

After the call he felt the usual muddy mix of emotions. He remembered a day when he was twelve; it was as vivid as the pigeon-shit pattern on the kitchen floor. He'd been in the basement and his father was marching in pounding circles around the kitchen, ranting while his mother sat quietly at the table. When there was a pause in the spewing his mother's voice, like the quiet proclaiming of the gospel, spoke. "Jack, if you ever lay a hand on Emily again I'll have you arrested." Mike remembered how frightened he was that night when he saw Emily in the bathroom. He'd inadvertently rushed in to get a band-aide as she was getting out of the tub. The ugly, purple-blue bruise obliterated more than half her tiny, white bum. He stared, she cried, and he ran out. He was too afraid to ask questions, afraid of the answer.

• • •

Saturday traffic on the New York Thruway was light, except for the begeezin, big trucks that rumbled across the countryside like a herd of killer whales. Gritt singing and tapping the steering wheel, chuckled as they all slowed down, spying her patrol car. Her chuckling was also happiness, exhilaration. Last night with Michael was unforgettable.

She indulged the memory as it rushed through her body. *He's amazing.*

In Rochester, she'd be getting a forensic report, but she still wanted to take a look at the love affair angle. She'd do some digging on her own. Ryder could've done Trott and Douglas and someone else Chrystine Goodall. There was more to that night at the hotel. Inexplicably, forensics had not been done in her hotel room even though the ME said she'd had sex the night she was murdered. That was a major oversight. It amazed her how sloppy police work could be – shameful. When the DA hears about the screw up, there'll be hell to pay. She'd do some cover-our-ass work.

Rochester's ballistics technician, Tina somebody-or-other, went over her findings, pointing to photos of the bullets. "Both slugs were lead jacketed, copper-coated, so the rifling is pretty good. This ammo is usually the choice of serious shooters. The one from the wall at Syntex is in worse shape but your people were careful enough to take it out in the chunk of dry wall. That helped." She shuffled the photos. "As you can see the lands – the raised spaces between grooves – are the same as those from the bullet out of the ground under Trott's body. This one went through her right arm, damaged slightly, probably from shattering a bone, but it's good enough. Here, we have the casing you found, and one from the Trott scene. Identical .30-30s rim-fire markings. Same rifle."

She asked, "Can testify to that?"

"Anytime, anywhere."

She stuck out a hand. "Thanks."

They were getting closer. Same rifle at two scenes. Ryder owned a .30-30. His prints matched the partial on the coin from Cedar Point. He was a depressed ex-employee. And he was on the run. She called Deputy Thurm Kier about Ryder's shoes.

"You get the shoes?"

"Yep. Seventeen pairs."

"Lab says?"

"Nothin' yet."

"Get me the lab." She didn't get the answer she wanted.

The technician said. "We've compared every shoe and there's no match. The plaster cast is larger, size eleven; these shoes are tens. Pattern's different."

"Get me Thurm." She waited. "Did you collect every shoe in the house?"

"Yeah."

"Son's too?"

"Son's?"

"Get 'em. Could've worn them. He might be psycho but he ain't stupid."

"The kid's bigger," said Thurm.

"Maybe size eleven … you think?" She hung up and said to the empty room. "You can lead a horse to water, but you can't teach him to drain the swamp."

CHAPTER THIRTY-FOUR

It was 4:15 a.m. and Alexander Goodall was alone in the back of his limousine gazing at runway lights that looked like tiny soldiers guarding his private jet. Next to him on the seat was his silent iPhone. He was still waiting for a four o'clock call. He didn't tolerate tardiness. But overall, he was pleased with developments. The board had given its blessing to phase two of his restructuring, not that he expected otherwise. He'd inundated them with facts, figures and strategy – information overload deterred a lot of questions. The reality was that he made the critical decisions and did whatever he thought best. The board, other than Carl Schodenhauer, was a rubber stamp. The goal was clear: cut costs, jettison unprofitable operations, sell assets to build cash and expand revenue by acquisition. It was the quickest way to turn this crippled company around. Sure, they could take a long-term view but that would not make the analysts happy or the shareholders rich, in the short-term. The stock had languished between twenty and twenty-four dollars for over a year and the analysts were not buying the new strategy. Today it closed down more than a buck. A signal that they didn't believe he could improve productivity. So, he'd solve that by cutting more; the stock would jump, and he'd convert his options. Publicly, he'd laid out a five-year plan but had no intentions of staying that long. Within two years he could clear as much as eighty million in stock options and then land a slot as CEO of a Fortune 500 company. That's why tonight's non-contact was so annoying. He didn't know this guy, but he'd made it abundantly clear what was expected – a call *exactly* at four. It never came. He tapped on the privacy screen and the limousine moved onto the runway. *Nobody circumvents me, this guy included.*

Before stretching out on the sleeper seat, he had a double-

Chivas and contemplated life since Chrystine. Not bad, but there were still hurdles. The divorce filing was a pain in the ass and Ebe hadn't come up with a way of blocking further action. He wondered if her ex-husband was behind it. He better not be, or he'd be on the short end of an empty bank account. He called Ebe and discussed negotiating the ex's silence. "I don't want this asshole coming back at me or saying the wrong thing when the cops get to him." He downed the scotch and slipped on a sleep mask as the jet whisked him away from his compartmentalized reality.

CHAPTER THIRTY-FIVE

New York, New York ... Mike silently hummed the Sinatra classic as he gazed at the magnificent island stretched out below. The plane was over the Hudson River, banking left and moving up the east side of Manhattan towards La Guardia. He could see it all, gleaming like an architect's model in the morning sun: Statue of Liberty, One World Trade Center, Chrysler Building, Empire State, and street after street, crisscrossing avenue after avenue like an elaborate lattice holding it all together. He'd love to bring Gritt to New York – almost did, then thought better of it. This had to be all business, and the two of them together, here, in the city that never sleeps, would be too much, too wonderful and too distracting. In two hours, he was meeting Grant Hawkins, Chrystine's ex-husband, for lunch at *Twenty-One* – Hawkin's suggestion.

The taxi let him out next to the Plaza Hotel. He wanted to walk down Fifth Avenue, window-shopping – not that he'd ever been a shopper. He caught his reflection in Bergdorf Goodman's window. He looked lonely, then he saw the mannequin in a black evening dress, tall, slender; suddenly, it was Gritt. He gawked. Then abruptly broke away, bumping into someone.

"Watch it buddy."

"Sorry." He shook the image but couldn't stop the racing of his pulse. *Get a grip.* He walked to Rockefeller Center, sat on a bench and went over the approach he planned with Hawkins. He'd keep it non-adversarial and tap into their common interest, Chrystine. His primary mission was to get Hawkins to implicate or exonerate Goodall. Waggs and Gibson had pretty much established Hawkins wasn't a suspect.

Hawkins was sitting at the table when the maître d' ushered

Mike across the room filled with overstuffed business suits clucking and preening like a bunch of roosters and hens. After introductions, he ordered a Bloody Mary and Hawkins got another "very dry Beefeater, straight up, two olives." His host appeared uneasy despite an inflated poise and a cloned Brooks Brothers image. He was cordial, but his eyes flitted, like a water bug on troubled waters. He spoke, almost whispered, "Mike, you know I've had a long conversation with your detectives. Told them everything I know. I'm surprised you'd bother coming all this way to go over the same ground."

"Have you been able to think of anything else?"

"Nothing." He sucked an olive off the swizzle stick like a fish swallowing a bug.

"What can you tell us about the Goodall's relationship."

"I'm not under suspicion, am I?"

"Did your wife – "

"Ex-wife."

"Ex-wife … confide in you?"

Hawkins pressed. "Is Mr. Goodall under suspicion?"

"Everyone's a suspect until eliminated. I understand you have an alibi." He saw relief in Hawkin's eyes. "Although we'd like additional corroboration." It turned to anxiety. He wanted to get at the Goodall angle first; before he pissed him off. "But we still have some details to tie up regarding Mr. Goodall."

They worked their way through appetizers with Hawkins talking about his time with Chrystine and how well their daughter was handling the tragic loss. "I suppose it was good that she didn't see her that often, you know, made it easier."

"How often did she see her?"

"She was very busy ... Chrystine. And Justine was wrapped up in her school, ballet and jujitsu. It wasn't easy to get together, but we made the best of it. Even when she was a baby her mother worked on Wall Street and traveled a lot. After the divorce, the adjustment wasn't so bad."

"How often did she see her mother?"

"Like I said … maybe, three, four times a year."

He was lying. Chrystine's statement filed with Wyatt Jones said she had been limited by Goodall to one visit a year. "When did they last visit?"

"Not sure…. Couple of months ago. Chrystine flew in for a weekend. They went to a friend's farm in Connecticut."

"Didn't they have a place on Fire Island?"

Hawkins looked surprised that he knew about Goodall's place on Fire Island. "Maybe she wanted to go someplace different?"

"Where in Connecticut?"

"No idea."

Mike let it go even though it was highly unlikely a father wouldn't know the whereabouts of his daughter, in case of an emergency. And Fire Island in May would be just the place for a young girl, not a farm in Connecticut. Hawkins wasn't as forthcoming as he tried to appear.

"Did you pay support payments to your ex-wife?"

The surprise was too obvious to cover-up, so he laughed uneasily. "Please. Do I look like I could keep her in the lifestyle she'd become accustomed to? They're filthy rich. She made a lot more than me."

"You're in advertising, right?"

"DDP, Shawe, Plett."

"They big?"

"There not BBDO. We have three hundred employees."

"You make a good salary?"

"Six figures."

"Low? Mid? High?"

His testiness began to show. "Is this necessary?"

"I can find out."

"Three-hundred and seventy thousand."

"What about bonuses, stock options?"

"I get a bonus if the agency has a good year."

"How much?"

He sucked down the second olive. "Seventeen."

"Stocks?"

"Forty-eight hundred shares."

"What are they worth?"

His patience was fraying. "Maybe ninety-thousand." He waived for the waiter, or some relief. "I thought this was about Chrystine, not me?"

Mike leaned in. "There's an old adage in my line of work that says, 'Follow the money.'" He held Hawkin's blue eyes. "We think money might have had a hand in Chrystine's murder."

Hawkins patted his lips with the linen napkin, glanced past Mike's shoulder and asked. "What's that got to do with me?" He waived at the waiter again.

"You told Detective Waggs you hadn't spoken to Chrystine during the weeks prior to her death?"

"So."

"Did you speak to her at all in the last year – other than during her visit to pick up Justine?"

"Of course. We weren't friends, but we did discuss our daughter from time to time."

"When did she tell you that she was filing for divorce?"

"From me?"

"From Goodall?"

"She didn't." He started poking at the Scampi on his plate.

"This is important." He didn't know what Chrystine had done, but she'd told Jones she was filing for custody of Justine. It would be unusual if she hadn't discussed it with the girl's father.

Hawkins was agitated. "I covered this with your detectives. What could that have to do with her death?"

Mike resented the adversarial tone. They were talking about this guy's dead ex-wife, the mother of his daughter, and this smug dandy was less than cooperative. There was a reason. "*If* she did speak with you, she could have said something that might give us insight into problems she was having. Or anyone new in her life."

"A lover?"

It was Mike's turn to poke at the food. "A business associate, someone in a charity, someone interested in her money." He was putting forth a string of options, moving away from Hawkin's first guess.

"What about a lover?" he asked. "She traveled a lot. If she was getting another divorce, who knows? Between you and me, she might have been unfaithful to me; there were occasions when her whereabouts were questionable. But we had a little girl and you know, you tend to look the other way in those situations."

"Did she tell you about any problems with Goodall?"

He blinked. "Never. He wanted it that way. Was fine by me."

"Did you ever speak to him?"

The eyes dropped. "No."

"We can check phone records."

"What?"

"Our interest is in Goodall. He hasn't been open."

"Look, I agreed to see you, buy you lunch. Cooperate. But all I'm getting is innuendo and aggravation. Whatever you want from him, get from him. I've told you all I know. I have a daughter to protect; she's gone through hell and I'm not about to let you rip apart her only surviving parent's life."

"How much support did Chrystine pay you?"

He dropped his napkin on the table, waved at the waiter and made a scribbling motion with his hand. "Check please." Then he tried to eyeball Mike. "I should say, none of your fucking business. But then you'd dig into my life and find out anyway. So, for the sake of my daughter's peace of mind, and what I hope will be your last attempt to disrupt my privacy, I'll answer what is, as far as I'm concerned, the last question. Half a million dollars." He signed the check, rose and walked past.

"Thanks for lunch." Mike was sure Hawkins had spoken to Goodall. Now, he would put Goodall through another interview and see how he felt sitting on a straight-back chair in a ten by ten room with coffee served in their finest Styrofoam.

His flight wasn't until six, so he contemplated taking in a bit of New York and maybe buying a little something for Gritt. But had second thoughts and went to the airport and caught an earlier flight.

As he walked into the concourse of the Rochester airport, Gritt was waiting for him. From a hundred-feet away his Chief Deputy's posture said more than he probably wanted to hear. She was upset. *She needs a big hug … can't.*

Through a genuine smile she said, "Bad news…. Tell ya' outside."

He had to pick up his pace as her long strides didn't stop until they got to her car. She slumped against it.

"What?"

She put a hand on his arm and it came out in quick bursts. "Been another shooting. Not here. Pittsburgh. Same MO."

"Think it's connected?"

"Happened middle of the night. Got a call an hour ago. Pittsburgh saw the Ryder BOLO, made a connection."

"What've they got?"

"Dead CEO. Head of a GE business unit. At a hotel near Penguin's arena. Some sort of conference. Shot in his room."

"What's the link? Other than he's a CEO."

".30 -30 slug. Three of them. Through and through. Dug'em outta the bed and floor."

"Forced entry?"

"Don't have much yet. Pittsburgh to keep us posted. If I'm betting, our Mr. Ryder is probably somewhere on a road outta Pittsburgh. What are the odds? Another CEO. A .30 -30. We gotta get this wacko."

"Let's talk to Captain Hyll."

She added. "I guess the Fibbies 'll be riding into town now. That's

151

all we need. Gotta keep 'em at a distance. Don't want them screwing with our investigation – I know them. And Rochester isn't gonna like them on Trott."

"I'll do what I can." It would be a turf battle, hopefully not a war.

CHAPTER THIRTY-SIX

Mike stepped into the darkness, hesitating to turn on the light. The black was soothing, easier on the screeching behind his eyes. But the emptiness was worse. He'd never realized how empty a house could be without some else in it. He flipped the switch. It didn't help. There was no Billy.

There was some relief in that Gritt was interviewing Mrs. Ryder again and Waggs was getting Goodall and Hawkins' phone records and Gibson had feedback from the street – a rumor someone had been looking for a hit man a few weeks back.

He put a package of frozen lasagna in the microwave and popped a Genesee. The cold didn't ease the eyeballs or his knotted neck, but it soothed the throat. The lasagna was bland and congealed around the hole in his stomach and the second Gennie didn't help. Exhausted, but knowing sleep had abandoned him, he surfed looking for the Mets game on the West Coast. All he got was the damn Yankees and Cleveland, so he watched CNN. He was about to switch when the announcer said:

In Pittsburgh a prominent General Electric executive has been murdered. Last night Dunne W. Riggins was found shot in his room at the Marriott. What makes this alarming is the fact that it is the third Chief Executive Officer of an American corporation murdered in the last six months. Previously, two CEO's were shot, one in Rochester, New York, the other in Westhaven, near Rochester. The FBI aren't saying whether there's any connection. Our Kyla Hewitson is at the scene.

Yes Lexi. There's little information at this time. We know Dunne W. Riggins was shot six times according to a source close to the investigation –

Mike yelled. "Three shots, stupid."

We don't have anything more right now. However, speculation is that this murder could be related to the two in Western New York State. Rochester is just a four-hour drive from here. But so far, the police aren't saying.

This is Kyla Hewitson, KDKA, Pittsburgh.

Mike hit the remote and the television went black. "Media. Hype, hype, hype. Screw up the facts, blow it outta proportion. Anything for ratings." He went for another beer, talking to the empty kitchen. "They'll have the public panicking for no good reason." He slammed the refrigerator door.

At one-twenty a.m. he went back to the office, for no good reason. An hour later, the knot in his neck snapped him from a miserable sleep on the couch. It was after three, so he decided to go see his father on the off-chance he'd be home. *Don't. Avoid him.* But the mounting reality about a serial killer made him willing to take his father's bullshit for any kernel of a clue.

The light in the kitchen was on and the silver-blue flicker of the television danced across the living room. His father was happier to see the three coffees his son was carrying than he was the carrier. Other than growling, "What're you doin' here?" He said nothing until he'd consumed the first cup. The television moaned on incessantly until Mike turned it off and tried to make conversation. It didn't happen, so he went to the kitchen. He remembered how his mother used to let the ol'man brood while she quietly went about her work. He yelled into the living room. "Wanted to talk to you about an angle I'm working on." He got no response. "Want some toast?"

Jack appeared in the doorway. "Why d'ya' turn off my fuckin' TV? *Apocalypse Now* was the best war movie ever. Why Martin Sheen ever did that stupid *West Wing* shit, I'll never know. Politicians are useless assholes. We need commanders; a few more Eisenhowers. Or that Mattis guy. World's goin' to shit."

"Want some toast?"

"Maybe we should just napalm the whole damn thing and start again."

Mike got out some bread. "Goodall bothers me." White bread was all there was in this house, nothing healthy. But there was always corn syrup, the one thing they had in common. His father liked it as much as he did. He toasted two slices, *he can make his own damn toast if he wants some.*

"Why's Goodall bug ya'?"

"I think he's been in touch with Chrystine's ex-husband. I met with him in New York … yesterday. He's covering … think for Goodall."

Jack talked through a slurp of coffee. "Goodall don't need him?"

"Reverse blackmail. Goodall pays Hawkins half a million a year. That's almost double his income. Lot of reasons to cooperate. Something to do with the divorce. Maybe Hawkins knows something. Something that could connect Goodall to Chrystine's murder."

"For fuck sake. Stop runnin' down blind alleys. Ya' got nothin' says he hired a hit…. Just theory."

Mike counted on his fingers. "The scene is fixed. Shooting is pro. She was filing for a divorce. And Hawkins? If there was a divorce, the half million would stop."

Jack added. "And if she's dead it would stop."

"Maybe not."

"Ya' saying they're working together?" Jack was more irritated than curious. "Goodall's too smart to involve anyone else. And half a million ain't gonna blackmail him."

Mike spread the thick syrup on the toast. "Not Goodall being blackmailed, him doing it."

"Ridiculous. Him blackmail a nothing ex-husband?"

"To shut him up"

"What are ya' doing on that loony Ryder?"

"If Goddall had her killed and Hawkins knew something, he'd have to quiet him. Money shuts people up."

"Ya' gotta find Ryder."

"We issued a BOLO."

"Get inside his life. His wife, relatives. Somebody knows where he is."

"We're doing that."

"Not fast enough."

His father reached over and took a slice of toast.

Mike's anger broke. "You want some toast? ... Here!" He flung the second piece of toast at his father – an instinctive fear made him aim for the cupboard door next to where he was standing. It slapped onto the door, face in, and stuck there as the anger stared across no-man's land. He saw his father's clenched fists rise up in front of him, as steady as two sledgehammers, then he saw the piece of toast begin a slow, slide down the door. When it flopped onto the counter Jack turned and walked into the living room. *Apocalypse Now* started up at the same time Mike began to shake. He knew he had to be the adult. It was typical of the old man not to listen to the request for toast, then seeing it, simply take it as if he had every right because it belonged to his son. For Mike, it wasn't the toast, it was the selfishness. It was always about him. He made four more pieces of toast, lathered them in corn syrup, sucked it up and entered the living room with his peace offering. Any shit and he'd be gone. "Remember when you went on special assignment to Rochester, when they had that serial killer, did ten prostitutes – "

"Eleven."

"And the press stirred up a frenzy?"

"They wanted my experience from the streets. Twenty years."

"You remember how it was handled with the press?"

"Fuckin' awful. Not because of the department but because of the press. They were relentless. Like vultures. You'd think we was the bad guys the way they criticized us. Course, we shut'em up when we caught the scum. That's what you gotta do. Nothin' else will stop those blood-sucking bastards. Turn up the heat and get a collar before the Feds get their nose so deep in, ya' won't be able to blow your own nose without their blessing. I'm tellin' ya' – "

"I know, I know." He held up his hands. "I'm asking if there are any tricks in fighting off the press? Maybe I should talk to Captain Hyll."

"Won't get shit from him. Lotta public relations mumble-jumble, but that don't stop the press. Only way to beat 'em is tell' em nothin'. Keep 'em in the dark. And while they're running 'round like chickens with their heads up their ass, you gotta be pushing every button you got. Informants, druggies, pigeons, witnesses. Lean on Ryder's family too. Ignore the press. Arrest somebody."

"I can't stall any longer. Have to hold a press conference tomorrow."

"Give 'em the Ryder story. Ya' got more than enough. If it's a bust, later you'll know more and be able to cover y'er ass. Remember way back, that Moose guy, the sheriff who handled the Washington sniper case. He was out every hour on the hour talking to the press. Told 'em too much. Shoulda kept his mouth shut. Christ, he had millions of people lookin' for a white truck. But it ended up being a blue Chevy car. Course, it wasn't all him, it was the politics of it." He took a piece of toast and the last coffee. "Another shooting and you'll be in the same box as Moose was."

"Please – "

"Lot of these guys want ya' to find them. Could be holed up somewhere waiting for the posse to arrive. These psychos are like that ya' know."

"He's not psycho. Sick, yes."

"You're splittin' hairs. He's crazy. That's all ya' need to know. Ya' need an arrest, today, tomorrow. Soon. Where's the DA on this?"

"We got a warrant. Problem is, I smell Goodall. And he stinks. Good chance they're unrelated. Ryder may have done Trott, but Goodall had his wife murdered."

"Who did Douglas?"

"Maybe you didn't hear me? They're probably unrelated."

"That might be the smartest thing you've said tonight." He shrugged. "Either way you win. Get Ryder and stay after Goodall. If Douglas is related, Goodall will lead ya' there. Put 'em both away and you're a shoo-in for mayor." He threw up his hands. "But what does an old beat cop know?"

"I can't say much on Goodall yet. Press would run like rabid dogs with it. But if I don't say something the implication is obvious – Ryder for all of them."

"All?"

"Including the guy in Pittsburgh."

"You're crazy if ya' think there's any – "

"You're not listening." Mike stood up. "What else is new?"

"What the fuck's that supposed to mean?"

"Nothing."

"My ass. Ya' don't want my advice, don't ask. If ya' disagree, say so. But don't give me your attitude. I listen. And I know a lot more than you think … sixty years 'round this town, twenty-seven on the force." He was yelling, "I know more than you'll ever forget" and his mouth was moving so fast he was talking backwards.

Mike couldn't resist. "You mean, 'forget more than I'll ever know.'"

"Up yours and your know-it-all college degree. If you know so much how come we're still talking about Douglas, six months down the road?"

Mike upped the volume. "I came here for insight, not ridicule."

"Ridicule? That's what ya' call it? Can't admit y'er old man knows more than you. Why else would ya' keep coming over here? I'll tell ya' what ya' gotta do. If you want to learn something, check your ego at the door young man. If ya' don't wanna hear what I got to say, don't ask."

Mike had to shut things down before they exploded. "Hear me out. I got different angles and I want to fill you in *before* you start with your answers."

"Hear ya'? I hear ya' loud and clear. Hearing is y'er problem, not mine. Y'er not listening to me. I been telling you for a week, get Ryder. Sure, if you want to poke around the Goodall angle do it, but the priority is Ryder, until you can either eliminate him or arrest him; neither of which you've done. Y'er problem is chasing too many leads with too few facts. Let me tell ya' about an investigation we did."

The old man was bouncing from one theory to the next as if he was playing a game of dodge-ball. Mike decided the best way to cool things down was to let him run himself out. Besides, he still had to bring up Emily's idea about going to Syracuse. Or maybe not? Jack told his story and the caustic odor drifted out of the room.

"I was talking to Em the other day. She was saying Grumpa isn't doing so well. Dementia. Memory going. Some days he's lucid, some not." He got no reaction. "I might have to go to Syracuse. Wondering if you'd want to come along, you know, drop in on him?"

"What happened to the idea of focusing on the job? When the hell are we gonna have time to go to Syracuse?"

Mike knew he was right. He didn't have much of a reason to go to Syracuse, except to get the family's two Attila-the-Huns together. However, he had thought of getting hold of his old criminology professor who was a forensic expert. "I'm planning on seeing an old prof of mine. Have him look at Goodall's finances. Professor Allen, he specializes in forensic accounting."

Jack grunted. "What about this dementia?"

"It's a mental processing disorder. The synapse connections are in constant decline and can sometimes be the forerunner of Alzheimer's."

"I know what it is. What's it doin' to him?"

"Memory loss, especially short term. Not long-term. Can also slip in and out of fantasies that make no sense. The other day he told Em, President Eisenhower had visited him." He offered a smile but got none in return.

Jack said. "He's crazy, right? If I ever get like that do me in." He put an index finger to his temple. "A .38, right here."

"Other days he's about as crazy as a fox." He tried the smile again.

"That's the real James Cougar Senior." Jack said it with an undecipherable mix of admiration and disdain.

"Em said he asks how you're doing."

"He just wants to make sure I'm doin' what he thinks I should. Shit, he'll probably leave a list of rules for me to follow in his will. You too."

"We should try and go Pops. He'd appreciate it and – "

"Bullshit." It was out like snake venom. "He don't know the word. But he'd like a chance to tell us what we're doing wrong and what he'd do if he was me. He may be crazy enough to think he's working for Eisenhower, but ya' can be sure he still thinks we're all working for him."

"If I can find a half day we could drive over and back. Quick trip."

"Find Ryder."

"If you think of anything, call me." It was an empty invitation, but it was an effort to rise above the animus. It might make the ex-cop feel better. And maybe he'd be able to get the three cops – two cops and a sheriff – together one last time. He wasn't sure why, but it sat well in a corner of his heart. When Jack picked up an unfinished crossword puzzle, he knew it was time to go. He needed to see Gritt – and hold her.

CHAPTER THIRTY-SEVEN

Gritt was in a hurry. She was heading to the station with lights flashing. She believed Mrs. Ryder, who said she didn't know where her husband was and had no reason to lie. But they'd caught a break. Ryder had called her Friday night, collect. That was four days ago. The day after Heather Trott was shot. He hadn't said anything other than he was okay and she mustn't worry.

It was 5 am when she called the telephone company and another forty minutes before she found the woman with the authority to release Ryder's records. She waited at the printer as the paper rolled out. There, a collect call, Friday, 10:47 pm, area code 716. *That's this area code.* The local number was in Oleans, New York, a couple hours south. And near the Pennsylvania border. That meant that on Friday night Ryder was two hours south of where Trott was shot. And maybe a couple of hours from Pittsburgh. She called Mike.

They met at the office and by eight had spoken to the Cattaraugus County sheriff, where Oleans was located. He would keep an eye out for the Ford Taurus. Now, there was nothing to do but wait. She hated waiting.

She swung by the kitchen and grabbed a coffee and a Danish. She should skip the Danish but didn't, *after all, I am Danish.* She spent the morning on the phone talking to Rochester, the lab and State police, who had an iffy report from a tollbooth attendant at the Batavia exit. Guy thought he'd seen a Ford Taurus, Friday around six. The banged-up front end caught his attention. If accurate, that puts Ryder west of Rochester and possibly heading south, maybe to Oleans, maybe Pittsburgh. They needed a sighting. What she didn't need was the next call.

"Hansen here."

"Deputy. Special Agent Edwards, FBI. They wouldn't put me through to the Sheriff. They gave me you."

"What can I do for you?"

"It's more, what can *I* do for you. We're heading up the Riggin's homicide investigation in Pittsburgh. Has possible links to a homicide in Rochester and your jurisdiction."

She knew this day would come and the Fibbies would roll in. Despite their forensic expertise, profiling and vast fingerprint files, their Achilles' heel was a cumbersome, bureaucratic machine that spewed out armies of agents running around playing arrogant cops. It often hobbled more than helped local authorities and had produced disasters from Ruby Ridge to Parkland Florida, not to mention the pre-9/11 vacuum. They needed them, but she swore if they got in her way she'd roll right over them.

Edwards continued. "I'd like to get a briefing on your investigation. I'll be in Rochester later today. Want the sheriff there." He wasn't asking.

Her teeth started chewing her sentences into chunks. "We're up to our ass. Heavy duty pressure. Not sure he can make Rochester." She was lying. Mike was taking a much-needed nap on his couch.

"Deputy, I'm leaving Washington in fifteen minutes for Pittsburgh. Then a flight to Rochester. I need confirmation now."

"No can do."

"I want someone there. Even if it's you."

She was aware that it was in their best interest to be there. If not, these cowboys would be running like a herd of buffalo over the case. "Someone will be there." If the FBI could link even Douglas and Trott then they could put some substance behind the theory that Ryder was out to knock off CEOs. The DA had called the motive 'preposterous.'

• • •

Gritt was driving, talking, laughing and slapping the steering wheel and Mike was riding shotgun. She'd had him laughing since they left the meeting with Edwards and pulled off the expressway, heading for Westhaven.

She said. "At one point I thought I might have to put you in shackles. Thought you were going over the table at Edwards. Loved it when you said he should hold back the troops, this wasn't Waco. I think he considered apologizing but then remembered apology wasn't in the Fibbie manual.

"Touchy."

She was having fun. "Hey, know the difference between Bigfoot and an intelligent FBI agent?

"I'll bite."

"Bigfoot's been spotted a few times." She slapped the wheel. "How do you know when an FBI agent is gonna say something stupid? When he begins a sentence with, 'At the FBI we always....'" They both laughed.

Mike said. "Did you count how many times Edwards mentioned he was recently with the FBI's JCTC – spewing acronyms out like we're supposed to be impressed."

"JCTC is the Joint Counterterrorism Center, right?

"Yeah. And TTIC is Terrorist Threat something."

She rolled on. "What do you call a lawyer who's lost half his intelligence? … A FBI agent."

The laughter was infectious and needed. The meeting with Agent William – 'you can call me Bill' – Edwards and Captain Hyll was worthwhile. Except they could've done without Edward's condescending attitude. All agreed there was a chance that the Douglas, Trott, Riggins' cases were connected. That was the FBI's focus. Ryder was the prime suspect. Edwards hadn't been convinced when Mike said his prime suspect for Chrystine's murder was still Goodall. What they did know was that Edwards was going to be a prime pain in the ass.

She said. "You know he said we could call him Bill instead

of William, but I think it's an insult to Billy's memory because Billy was smarter than this asshole." She paused. "You still think Goodall did it?"

"Had it done."

"Not Ryder?"

"I didn't say that. Just that Goodall is a prime suspect."

"Your prime. Not mine."

"You're sounding more like my ol'man. Been talking to him lately?"

She didn't respond.

He said. "I have. He's incorrigible. I think he's going to help and all he does is criticize. You'd think I'd have learned by now?"

"You're doing it for him. That's commendable."

"And stupid."

"You said it, not me."

"I think psychology says the father son bond is fundamental to a son's sense of self. Does my self-confidence look like it needs my father's blessing?"

"You're doing it to hold onto whatever might be between you. You're the strength, he's the weakness. Your tolerance and compassion keeps you going back. He's damn lucky to have you. And losing your mother – "

"Gritt, not you. I dropped that poor-me, victim crap years ago. Truth is, my old man's a bastard. If ever there was a father-son problem, it's between him and *his* father. And it isn't genetic. I don't ever want to be lumped in with them. They're King Kong and Godzilla in a battle to the death. I just have to make sure it isn't my death." He stared into the distance. "So why am I taking him to Syracuse?"

She smiled and touched his arm. "Armageddon?"

He didn't acknowledge her touch, just contemplated the passing fields, then shrugged. "What are you gonna do? He is who he is ... and his father ... who knows?"

She didn't know his grandfather, other than he was also a Jack, also a retired cop and in a home in Syracuse.

"Pops is a victim too," he said. "His old man is worse."

To her it was a rationalization for an irrational father.

He put his hand on top of hers.

She kept her eyes on the road.

"Want to pull over?"

"Is that a question or an order? You're a cop, you telling me to pull over?"

"What do you think?"

"Here … now?"

"You're a cop too so you don't have to … unless you want to?" He looked at her. *She's so fucking beautiful.*

She glanced. Caught his eyes. They were gleaming. And demanding. "Is that an order, sir?"

"It is."

"I see a side road up ahead. That what you had in mind?"

"No, what I have in mind you'll have to wait and see. But that road will do."

She turned onto the country road and slid her hand onto his thigh.

He pointed ahead. "Nice day for a walk in the woods. Let's check them out." He ran his fingers up her neck and through her hair.

They pulled the car next to a path into the woods and walked in. At first, he didn't take her hand. He seemed to purposely keep a little space between them. She asked, "What if someone spots the cruiser?"

"Not likely. And if they do, they'll figure we're chasing bad guys in the woods."

"Like cops and robbers?"

"Yeah. Like Bonnie and Clyde." He was smiling.

She couldn't stand it any longer and took his hand.

He pulled her to him.

His powerful arm wrapped around her shoulder and she pressed into him as they walked, arm-in-arm, hip-to-hip. The crunch of their footsteps was the only sound.

He stopped next to a towering maple. Released his arm and with two demanding hands backed her up against the tree. "Deputy Chief, I order you to remove your gun belt and place it carefully on the ground … and keep your hands where I can see them, at all times."

His grip was strong. Forceful. Her buttocks pressed against the bark. "Only if you remove yours too. I am not your prisoner, I am only guilty of wanting you and if – "

"And you will remove your handcuffs before you place your belt on the ground." He relaxed his hold on her waist.

She unbuckled and drop her belt to the ground. "If you want handcuffs, use your own. I will not be party to a criminal offense against an innocent woman. If you – "

"Innocent? *You* are the criminal. Criminally beautiful. Murderously sexy. Undeniably guilty."

"What happened to innocent until proven guilty? Where's my trial?"

"Trial? I'm the judge and the jury. The trial is over. You're about to be sentenced." He stepped back, unbuckled his gun belt and turned to place it on a log next to them. When he turned back, she was stepping out of her boots and black uniform pants. Her long athletic legs were spread in a defiant stance. "Maybe, instead, I will sentence you." She started to unbutton her shirt.

"To what?"

"To rape. Not *for* rape, to rape." She tossed her shirt away. "You are hereby sentenced to lawfully and rightfully rape your criminally insane Deputy Chief … insane about the most brilliant, wonderful, strong, handsome sheriff in America."

He struggled to get his boots and pants off quickly.

Her eyes filled with raw desire and she dangled her handcuffs in front of him. "Cuff me."

He took the cuffs and threw them aside, then grabbed her waist and turned her around. "Put your hands on the tree, keep them where I can see them. You have the right to remain silent. Anything you say – "

"Silent? Are you crazy? There's nobody for miles. I'm gonna scream. Make me scream …"

"Can and will be used against you … in a court of sexual fantasy. And you have the right to scream – "

She screamed – when he entered, when he came, and throughout the glorious flood in between.

CHAPTER THIRTY-EIGHT

Mike was amazed at Goodall's self-control. He and Ms. Lopez were squeezed into one of their interview rooms, face to face with him. It was smaller than most of the closets in Goodall's home, a nine-by-ten box with a three-by-three table, two chairs and two Styrofoam cups. Goodall looked like he was going to throw up when he first saw the room. Gritt was next door watching on a monitor.

Mike had been questioning them for almost an hour and he'd remained calm, damn near emotionless. Ms. Lopez parroted the requisite lines to protect her client but several times he dismissed her answers, only hiding behind her when asked about the divorce.

Mike asked. "Again sir, at no time, did you know your wife was filing for divorce. She never mentioned – "

"Enough! If I say something once, that's it. I'm not in the habit of repeating myself."

"Would you agree to a voice stress analysis?"

Lopez jumped in. "Don't insult us. Mr. Goodall is cooperating. Unless you intend to charge him with something, this interview is over." She placed her hand on Goodall's arm, and left it there. "Let's go Alex."

Right after they left, Waggs, Gibson and Maya Lee, an assistant DA, gathered with Mike and Gritt in the office area Waggs and Gibson called home.

"Some show that was," said Gritt. "They're more like Jack and Jill than client-lawyer."

"She's a whole lot more at ease with him then she was last time," said Mike.

Waggs turned a chair around and sat. "Usually a place like this unnerves our guests but he didn't get ruffled until the lie detector idea."

"Might have been premature suggesting it," said Mike. "Couldn't help it. Bastard's lying. Pissed me off."

"Wouldn't' have got nothin' anyways." said Gibson. "Was too prepared."

"He's lying about the divorce stuff. And Hawkins," said Mike. He'd tried to catch him in contradicting stories, questioning him about a fixed burglary scene, the handing out of the alarm code, and if he'd ever heard of a Carlo Santini, a small time hit man – who was actually in prison. He didn't get a reaction. What they did have were his and Hawkins' phone records indicating Hawkins had called the law firm of Turnbull and Ebe. But Mike didn't mention it. Didn't want to, yet.

Gibson said. "Might have somethin' from an informant. Word is there was this here guy, Sal Ignagni, big time bopper, outta North Philly. Was in town about a month ago. One night."

"A month?" Mike's voice was flat. Chrystine's murder was only sixteen days ago.

"I'm diggin'. But these guys are hard to track. Got a call into a buddy of mine at Philly OCU (Organized Crime Unit). See what they know."

Mike said, "Month doesn't fit. Unless … here for a meet. Set things up, case the place. Check where Goodall was a month ago. In town, out of town? Pin down this Ignagni's whereabouts." He turned to Maya Lee. "Can we get a warrant?"

"For what?"

"Goodall's calendar, travel schedule, personal notes, iPhone. Anything to do with his coming and going?"

"I'll try. Don't go after the business files."

"Can we get his secretary's stuff? Guys like this live through their secretaries."

Waggs asked, "Bring her in for questioning?"

"Do it there, see how cooperative she is."

Gibson said. "Know what we didn't do? Check that shoe print with Goodall's shoes. Did ya' see how many pairs of shoes the guy had?

More than a friggin' outlet store."

"Check'em all. Turn up the heat. We'll either get more cooperation or more lawyers."

Gritt grinned. "I got a hundred on the legal beagles."

• • •

"Sue the assholes. Twenty, thirty million. I'm going to – "

Mel Ebe hit the button to cut off the speakerphone as Goodall's words ricocheted off the walls. The junior partners didn't need to hear a murder suspect's undisciplined utterances.

Ebe asked. "What is it?"

He listened to his client's outrage at sheriff's deputies who were removing files and papers from his office. Goodall was in Nashville and had his secretary on another line, but she was unable to do anything about it. So he did what he always did, called his lawyer. Ebe told Goodall what he didn't want to hear. "If they've got a warrant we're better to cooperate. Get Lopez over there."

"She's not there."

"Not where?"

"In Westhaven."

"Where is she?"

He didn't respond.

"Get someone else over there."

He responded. "They're on their way. She said it was highly unlikely it would do any good that – "

"Who?"

"Who, what?"

"Who said it was unlikely."

"Lopez…. Spoke to her earlier. Bastards have no right to my files. Tell me how to stop them."

"Depends on the warrant."

"Depends my ass. Talk to Brook. Tell her what to do. When

the lawyer gets there, tell him what to do. Brook will call you." He bellowed into another phone. "Brook, call Mel on the other line. Yes, for Christsakes, he's in his office." He was back. "Talk to her, them, anyone you have to. Then call me back. I'm here at ICP, with the CEO."

Mel waited for Goodall's secretary. *How did Alex talk to Lopez earlier if the police had just arrived at his office?* Knowing Alex, he knew where she was, and it was exactly where she shouldn't be. Mel understood the temptation of nubile young women – he had his own addictions – but unlike Alex, he never fished from the company dock. Carmencita Lopez was a new player in Alex's game, eager and sexy, a vulnerable combination for a guy who could never steer clear of an alluring skirt. She was in Nashville.

CHAPTER THIRTY-NINE

Gritt went to the Hilton to follow up on loose ends. The manager set her up in a meeting room and she got her essential request in first. "What're the chances of gettin' some coffee?"

"No problem?"

"Any Danish?"

"No problem."

"Couple … lemon maybe?"

Room service delivered coffee and a platter of sugar-coated calories. Croissants, muffins, Danish. No lemon. Before she'd finished the first Danish, a waddley, squat woman came through the door. She looked like a Russian shot-putter. And her accent sounded Russian.

"Meez? Mr. Frank say I see you. My name Mrs. Krazov. I speak before to poh-leece." She stood in the doorway like a granite head stone.

"Come in. We're just following up. Please … sit." She was so short she just slid her backend onto the seat. Gritt continued. "You're the head housekeeper?"

"No, no. Assistant head. Meez Suzanna is head."

"You were on duty night of the July 6th. Right?"

She was nervous. "I tol Sheer-if. I know not 'bout lady keeled. Who stay here. Room seven-one-seven. Phong clean room. Five-and-ten before eight that morning."

"Who's Phong?"

"She work 'till four. Off … 'till Sunday."

"I'd like to talk to her."

The woman waited, as if expecting more questions.

Gritt found herself talking like her. "Ya' send her. To me. Now?"

"Ya', ya'. Sorry, sorry. I not know you mean." She trundled out as fast as her thick legs would carry her.

In a few minutes a demure, slight girl walked into the room, her expectant brown eyes taking in the deputy as if she was facing a dangerous animal. "You wanted to see me Miss?"

"Come in, come in." Gritt assessed her. Couldn't be more than twenty-five. Pretty as a picture. Asian. This might be harder than she thought. "It's Phong, right?"

"Yes, Phong Li." Her English was perfect, not a trace of accent.

"Where are you from?"

"Buffalo."

"Do you live in Westhaven?"

"Yes ma'am."

"How long have you been here?"

"Four months."

"How long in Buffalo?"

"All my life. My father is Chinese, my mother Vietnamese."

"I'd like to ask you about room seven-seventeen, on the morning after Mrs. Goodall stayed there. You know who she is?"

"Yes ma'am."

"Have you spoken to anyone else from the sheriff's department?"

"No."

"No one questioned you!" It was a statement of dismay, not a question.

"No ma'am. I just told Olga, Mrs. Krazov, when I did the room. Same as always. Nothing unusual, you know."

Gritt started slowly. "I have to ask a few difficult questions. Need you to think carefully. Don't be embarrassed."

Her eyes widened.

"It's possible that Mrs. Goodall had someone else in her room that night, a man. She may have slept with him. Was there anything you noticed? Any little thing? Something left behind maybe?"

She replied as if answering a spelling bee in high school. "Like sex?"

"Like sex."

She didn't hesitate. "I see this often you know, so I didn't think anything of it." She shrugged her tiny shoulders. "All the towels were used – eight. Bed covers were on the floor and the bed linens were stained with semen marks, you know. Not unusual. And the waste basket next the bed had tissue in it, you know, like afterwards."

Gritt nodded. "Anything else?"

She shifted in the chair. "You know, a few hairs." She paused and her eyes brightened. "Something else. There was a scratch on the bureau that wasn't there before. I did that room the morning before too. I would've noticed. Could've happened during the day, maintenance fixing something."

"Is the bureau still there?"

"So is the scratch. I reported it to Mrs. Krazov. But maintenance hasn't done anything about it. It's not bad."

Gritt stood. "Can you let me in the room?"

"Maybe Mrs. Krazov should. I'll get her."

Krazov stood like a sentry at the door while Gritt looked around the room. The scratch was noticeable. A small round indentation, maybe a quarter of an inch across with a slight tail. As if something heavy had been dropped. She told Mrs. Krasov that the room would be off-limits and went to get her camera. She didn't want to call the forensic guys in yet. Half an hour later, she'd taken photos and placed yellow tape inside the door. She returned to the second floor and completed several more interviews, but they bore no new information. She polished off another Danish and called a lab technician to come and take a look at the bureau. It might be nothing, but you never know.

Back in room 717, she poked around waiting for forensics but found nothing. After the photographer had finished she asked, "How come you guys didn't do this earlier?"

"Did what?"

"Take photographs."

He nonchalantly replied. "No one booked us. I checked the log before coming over just now, nothing. I'm the only photographer in forensics, so beats me?"

"No forensics done?"

"Rest of team could've come. But no one asked me."

No point pressing him. "Send those to my mobile. And blow up the best close ups, print them, and put on my desk. "And thanks." *Mike will be pissed when he finds out forensics didn't order photos.*

CHAPTER FORTY

That evening they caught another break. Olean's sheriff called. A local service station operator remembered the beat-up Ford – on the Friday night. The driver had gotten five bucks worth of gas around 11 pm. Gritt's first question was, "Sure it was five bucks?"

"That's what he said. Remembered 'cause he paid with three ones and eight quarters."

Five bucks wouldn't get him to Pittsburgh. "Any description?"

"Matches what you gave us."

"Any idea which way he headed?"

"Guy said he went west on Highway 17."

"Where's it go?"

"Jamestown. Or south on two-nineteen to Bradford."

"That's in Pennsylvania?"

"Just over the line."

"Keep your eyes peeled. He's still out there."

It wasn't much. Four days is a long time for a guy and his car to disappear. Has probably abandoned the Ford and picked up another vehicle. But how? He's not a car thief, probably wouldn't have the slightest idea how to get one, and according to his wife he's too broke to buy anything – except five bucks of gas. That suggests he could still be in the Olean area. Or could have taken a bus … That's it. He had two days to get there because Riggins wasn't shot until Sunday night or Monday morning. She would notify local authorities to show Ryder's ID at bus stations and the Marriott in Pittsburgh.

She contemplated booking off for a couple hours, maybe see if Michael wanted to, then she got a call from the lab.

The technician was monotone. "Blew up the photos and checked samples."

"Samples?"

"I took dust samples."

"And …"

"Scratch is recent. Some residual dirt – lazy maids. Maybe a week's worth." He continued with an inordinate amount of technical explanation then finally got to the good part. "I'd say it was caused by a relatively blunt object, either dropped or set down quickly. Or a lighter object thrown down. But I lean to the former. Because the tail of the scratch is too short to have resulted from a thrown object. It's a guess, but based on the depth of the indentation, I'd say maybe a couple of pounds."

"The something weighed a couple of pounds?"

"Maybe little more."

"Any guesses?"

"None. Nadda."

"Gimme a maybe. A range of things."

"Can't."

"What about," and she rattled off a list. "A briefcase? Ice bucket? Bottle of booze? Shoe? Electric razor? Some kinda sex toy? Vibrator? She got a quick no for each item. "Chains?" she got a pause. "Chains?"

"Maybe. If heavy enough. But not likely."

She couldn't imagine Mrs. Goodall into kinky stuff, but you never know a person's dark secrets. "Handcuffs?"

"Not heavy enough. Have to be thrown down. No. Scratch doesn't go in the right direction for that. Something like cuffs would slide all the way across. Mark would be longer."

The list was getting desperate. "Lighter? Cellphone? Gun? – "

"Maybe?"

"What maybe?"

"A gun. Guessing – that's what you wanted. 'Bout the right weight. Corner of the grip could have done it. Or – "

"Or what?"

"Speculating … understood?"

"Yeah, yeah."

"Let me do couple measurements and run a couple of tests. Maybe–"

"What?"

"I'm looking at my own Glock in its holster, pancake model, sitting here on the counter. The snap on the holster is just about the right size but … it's a stretch. You'd never get me to testify to it."

She said. "But it could have been a gun. Right?"

He didn't respond.

"Do the tests and call me back." She hung up. *A gun*? Could the person who killed Chrystine Goodall have met her in the hotel and later in her home been carrying a gun – the one that killed her? And she knew it, but wasn't afraid of it, or him. Someone she trusted. Her husband? A friend? Hotel security? A bodyguard? Or maybe the gun was hers, carried for protection? Most people who carry a weapon to protect themselves are shot by it. A lover could have gone home with her and the love turned to anger and murder. But one shot to the head? That's someone who has shot a gun before. Once again, she felt the rush of the hunt.

CHAPTER FORTY-ONE

It was quiet inside the Blazer, too quiet, and neither the blather of the radio or the whirr of the road could fill the void. There was nothing new on the case so Mike had tried to talk about Jack Senior. That's when the silence set in and his father drifted away to wherever guys like him go in their head. Usually he argued like hell with talk-radio callers but today he'd tuned them out. Mike focused on the monotony of the New York Thruway. *Thank god it's a short trip. Besides, what mattered is that he came.* Although Jack had said he was coming because he wanted to hear what the fancy-ass forensic professor had to say, Mike suspected that it was more about the same bond, the curse, that threw fathers and sons into the lion's den. Emily had made it clear, she didn't want to see her father so the plan was to visit Jack Senior first and use the meeting with professor Allen as a reason to leave, especially if things got tense.

The retirement home was moderately pleasant compared to most that he'd been in during the course of his duties – everything from death by heart attack to disarming crazy people brandishing knives, hammers, crutches and nail files. One time they'd investigated a homicide, where a guy ninety-nine killed another guy ninety-three. Hit him twenty times with a bedpan – full. Then the man who did it died a week later, of natural causes.

Jack Senior was on the first floor in a pale, pathetic little room. It was as cold and plain as the urinal on his nightstand. And it was as if someone acknowledged this insipid state of affairs by planting a small garden of roses outside the window. Their aroma almost overcame the musty smell that seems to collect in areas where old people collect. Mike recognized one piece of furniture, an old dresser from his grandparent's house. It was the only touch of warmth. Senior was sitting in a wheel chair, blanket over his knees, gazing at the roses. He didn't look up.

"Hi Grumpa. How you feeling?"

He turned. No recognition, no acknowledgement. Then barked in a croaky voice. "Where the hell's George? Thought George was comin'?"

"George who?" asked Mike.

"Get him on the phone."

Jack Junior stood back like a non-participant.

"There's no phone Grumpa. George couldn't come."

"Said he'd be here. I'm countin' on him. Never let me down. Get him on the blower." His eyes were no longer vacant, gradually filling with moisture, more like a life-feeding lubricant than tears. He looked at Mike as if his son wasn't in the room.

He asked again. "Who's George?"

From behind him his father said, "His old partner."

Senior repeated. "We got work to do."

Mike tried another approach. "Look who's here." He took a half step back so his father was front and center.

"That ain't George."

Jack said, "He's on his way."

"Damn well soon enough. Always late. But there when I need him. Good man, George. Ike's gonna want to meet with us, you know."

Mike kept the dialogue going. "Meet with who?"

"George and me. When's he coming?"

Jack replied. "This afternoon."

"This afternoon? That's no good. Meetin' this morning."

"It's already afternoon Grumpa. It's three-thirty."

"Then where's Ike? We met at the White House. He said first thing this morning. He's never late. Not like George."

Jack poked. "Who's Ike?"

"Don't be a smart ass young man. I'm talking about the President of the United States. Won't stand for disrespect."

"No disrespect intended." Jack was playing along with the dementia, which was, if nothing else, more relaxing than the reality.

"See to it. Go on, get to it," said Senior.

Jack disappeared down the hall leaving Mike unsure whether to go after his father or stay with his grandfather. "Dad's gone to look for George."

"Dad who?"

"My dad. Your son."

"Jack? Good man Jack. Don't tell him I said so." He winked, as if he knew exactly what he was doing.

"He came to see you today, to have a chat."

"Where is he? Hell, I can't talk to him if he ain't here."

"He'll be right back."

"Always late. Like George. Where the hell's George?"

"Jack 'll be right back."

"Jack who?"

Mike strained to keep his eyes from rolling in frustration. "Your son. He's looking for George." He put a hand on the blanket – the old man's leg felt like a wooden stick. "He'll be right back."

"Good. 'Bout time he did something. Can't just keep restin' on his laurels you know. Police work demands complete commitment, night and day. Sacrifice, sacrifice. That's the way we did it in the forty-third. Jack's gotta do more if he expects to make captain. Hell, he ain't even a lieutenant yet. Don't know what he's thinkin'? Needs to make more of himself. There's no higher callin' then working for the public good, protecting people from the scourge of the earth. The world needs more heros."

"How you doing Grumpa?"

"Never better." He yanked a blue-veined, age-spotted hand from under the blanket and half-waved it in the air. "This place is a pain in the ass." Then, unexpectedly, he reached for Mike's hand and dropped his voice. The adamancy was gone. "You know, Jack's really a good kid. Means well. Does okay. I don't tell him because gotta keep the pressure on, keep pushin' him. Time is against us. … Lot to do."

Mike felt the change from blathering to lucidity. He hoped to keep it going until his father got back. It would be good for him to hear this.

"Retirement was his problem. Should never have retired. Could have been so much more, climbed to the top. Time on idle hands is bad you know. He's clever you know. Shrewd boy. But needs discipline, a harness, to rein in that drive. Yeah, he's got drive. Kid took on anything. Good boy, even if a little misguided at times. But …" His alert blue eyes flicked up, then drooped. "So, when Ike gets here, I want my partner in the room. Nobody else. Ya' hear. Nobody."

Suddenly, Jack was standing in the doorway. During the rest of the visit Jack stood back and Senior was oblivious to his son. The plan had been for Jack to stay and visit with his father while Mike went to meet with professor Allen, but Jack left with Mike and never said another word about the visit.

Professor Allen's office should have been called a closet. A closet jammed with everything you would expect in a professor's office and a few things you wouldn't expect. Books of course, hundreds of them. Files piled like a house of cards, teetering on disaster, a computer with the keyboard buried under a stack of papers and more pens and pencils than a Bic factory. What was incongruous was the wall behind the professor. As small as it was, it must have had more than fifty photos on it. All framed in the same cheap, five by seven, frames. Each was a picture of Allen with a dignitary, of sorts. Mike recognized Leona Hemsley, F. Lee Bailey, Michael Milken, Bernie Ebbers, Martha Stewart, Michael Cohen, Paul Manafort. The burly professor and his tattered chair occupied the only remaining space.

"Quite the collection," said Mike.

"My rogues gallery. I have more, but these are my favorites. A pictorial resume. I call it the good, the bad and the ugly. The good is that it was good for me. The bad is that most of them were bad. And the ugly is that most of the consequences were ugly."

Mike noticed a computer-printed motto taped to the wall under the photos. It read, *Follow the money*.

Jack stood in the doorway. Probably wondering where he was going to sit in the closet. Mike was a little awkward, so simply said, "This is my father, a retired police officer." He didn't explain why he was there, so Jack did.

"I'm giving my son a hand. Thirty-years experience goes a long way in a case like this. I'll listen. You two carry on."

 Mike said he wanted the professor's assistance in the Goodall end of the case. "To quote your motto, we want to follow the money."

Jack said, "Yeah. We're big on this guy. With his money ya' should have no problem coming up with the money for a hit. But cash is hard to trace ain't it professor?"

Allen said. "Depends. Like any case, you construct the circumstantial evidence to a point that any blue-blooded hound dog or assistant DA can paint a trail for the jury. If you're lucky, the guy'll confess before you get to court."

Jack wouldn't shut up. "Not this guy. Wouldn't fold in a junkyard compressor."

Mike asked. "Professor, what do you need to get you involved?"

"Let me come over to Westhaven. This has the makings of a high-profile case and I have a penchant for high profile." He smiled immodestly.

Jack said. "It's high profile, but Mike's no Sheriff Moose – although he's good with the politics."

Mike smiled a fake smile. His father was pulling his typical crap. First a criticism, then a compliment – of sorts. *I should've dropped him off at the local precinct so he could trade his bullshit with some old-time cops. Or dumped him at a mall – that would've killed him.*

They agreed with the professor to meet later in the week.

Driving back, Jack was enthusiastic about Allen's involvement and offered up suggestions. "My guess is forty, fifty grand. That's what it would take for a big time hit like this. We're talkin' no trail, no evidence, not a trace. But you can't hide that amount of money easily. This ain't no two-bit hood or biker. Goodall would go big. Somebody outta New York." He looked over. "Ya' got a tail on him?" He knew the answer. "Shit! He could've already made the payment." He shrugged. "Maybe the professor can track the first payment?" His silence was obvious disapproval of what he considered a slip up by his son.

He was right.

CHAPTER FORTY-TWO

Mike knew when they came through the door it was good news, bad news. Good from Waggs and Gibson, bad from Gritt. The two detectives had an almost indiscernible smile on their face even though it was out of character for these two to smile. Gritt looked like she'd just run a four-minute mile and lost.

Gibson said. "Got something. Not definite, but something. Talked to my guy in Philly OCU. They had a tail on Ignagnai and last month he left town for one night, got a plane, to … yep, Rochester." Then he frowned. "Couldn't keep the surveillance and didn't notify Rochester police. Stupid! You'd think it would be the first call they'd make. Guy could've been in Rochester to whack someone."

"Probably did," added Waggs.

"Rochester isn't Westhaven," said Mike.

"You musta got an A in geography," chided Gibson as he enjoyed stretching out his story. "If you can't bring the mountain to Mohammed, bring Mohammed to the mountain."

Gritt rebutted. "Yeah. And you can bring a horse to the water, but you can't make him swim."

"Drink…" said Gibson.

"Says who."

Waggs said. "Guess what Goodall's calendar showed on that day?... Rochester. Actually, it wasn't in his calendar, it – "

"What?" said Mike.

"It was in his secretary's. She's an efficient, woman. Notes on everything. I'm sure Goodall appreciates it. Until now. She'd written in, as clear as day, To Rochester."

"No time on it though," said Gritt.

"She'd written it at the bottom of the page. And she had a 5 pm meeting marked above it."

Gibson picked up the story. "Two things. We combed through Goodall's phone records for the last three months, including mobiles – has three. Numerous calls to Philadelphia; checked them all. Legit business, except for one." He paused. "He called an ex-employee, a Vincenzo Pomante. Was a VP of finance at Microhe Systems when Goodall was CEO. Nothing wrong with calling an ex-employee – for old-time sake, catch up – except this employee left Microhe for suspected fraud, financial embezzlement, tampering with evidence – shredding it. Nothing proved. Goodall, in fact, fired him and made a public announcement condemning him. Now he's calling him? We thought it odd. Checked Pomante's background. Nothing in the past but guess where he's working now. River Creek Casino. According to records, River Creek is legitimately owned. But according to OCU, the mob have their hand in it. Now, what if you were Goodall and you wanted to get in touch with a hit man. Maybe an inquiry to an old employee, he's certainly not a friend, who just might be hanging out with people who know people, who know Ignagni?" Gibson cracked a smile.

Mike asked. "Any record of him contacting Ignagni?"

"Nada."

"What about his phone?" asked Gritt. "They can encrypt messages. But FBI could crack it."

Gibson said, "Could contact a buddy at FBI."

"Let's call him," said Waggs.

"Not sure it'll work," said Mike. "Some phones use military encryption. If Goodall called Ignagni, it may be his secret."

Gritt added, "Each unit has a private key and there is only one per person. If Goodall encrypted a message it's as good as gone. Out over the airwaves and into his company server behind a firewall. Can't be decrypted unless you have the private key. And we ain't gonna get it from Mr. fancy-cufflinks. Only guy who could open it is him, or the guy he sent it to. And I don't think we'll be getting' any cooperation from a mobster."

"Where the hell did ya' learn that shit? asked Waggs.

"FBI. They are good for something."

Mike said. "I've got a forensic accountant coming in. He'll be all over Goodall's records."

She looked at Gibson. "Tell him the rest."

"Get this. OCU hasn't seen Ignagni since then. They're puzzled. It's not like him. He's always around Vito Busillio, the boss."

"They looking for him?"

"Not really. If he's fled their jurisdiction they figure good riddance."

Mike dropped his feet off the desk. "It's something. Might connect Pomante to Ignagni." He acknowledged Gritt with a smile. "Sounds like the phone is a dead-end." See what Philly can do for us. Keep the FBI out of it this part, for now."

Gritt jumped in. "A guy like Ignagni can – "

"Work on your Italian Gritt," said Gibson. "It's pronounced, In-ya-nee."

Gritt ignored him. "Could disappear for months. Years. This might be one time those assholes could help."

"Gritt has a point," said Waggs.

"Everybody deaf? I said keep the FBI out of it ... for now."

Gritt saw Mike's frustration. Something was chafing just below the surface, something he wasn't talking about. *I thought we were now sharing everything.*

Mike said. "Goodall drives a Mercedes. Silver. Not the most inconspicuous vehicle. Maybe somebody in Rochester saw something."

"I'm on it," said Waggs. He and Gibson we're up and gone.

"Gritt, got a minute?"

She eased into a chair in front of his desk.

"I think both Ryder and Goodall theories are valid. We each have our inclinations, but I don't want turf battles. There are too many angles and not enough of us. And not enough time. So ..."

He's beating around the bush.

"I want us to stick to two tracks. Goodall and Ryder. You on Ryder, Waggs and Gibson on Goodall. Anything Waggs and Gibson get, they bring to me. You too."

"You're the boss." She meant it but she also intended to dig further. *Going to follow my hunch.*

CHAPTER FORTY-THREE

Gritt entered the lounge at the Hilton and stopped to let her eyes adjust. At the bar was Jackhammer in conversation with the young bartender. She retreated and went outside and moved her patrol car around the corner. She waited ten minutes before returning. Jack was gone. She took a stool.

The bartender – the same Mister enthusiasm – approached. "Chief Deputy Sheriff, right? You just missed the sheriff's father. Good guy."

Gritt nodded, her gut tightened.

"Tough questioner. No wonder you guys use him from time to time. Lot less conspicuous."

She took out her notebook. "How's that?"

"Like he said. You guys are in uniform. Stand out. He's less conspicuous. Makes sense."

"Did you help him?"

"Hope so. Told him what I told you before. Was able to recall the people in and outta here that night. Busy night. Had to go to the cashier twice."

"Anybody in particular he was interested in?"

"Nope. Other than Mrs. Goodall. More who was with her. Couldn't tell him anything more than I told you. Told him to see Raul, food and beverage manager. He would've been in the ballroom and seen more."

"Where'd he go?"

"Told him where Raul's office was…. Get ya' a drink?"

Gritt left, pissed at the bartender, and Jack. The kid was a jerk. Talking to anyone who said he was the sheriff's father. Idiot. And who the hell did he think he was, poking around? Mike will be pissed.

She found Raul Sanchez in Conference Room B, down at the front setting up a bar and talking to Jack. She waited until Jack left. She asked Raul about the night in question and what Jack had been asking.

"Just general questions," said Raul. "About what I remembered 'bout the lady. He also asked about the sheriff – said he was his son – and needed to confirm he'd been here. Told him I didn't see him. He pressed me, but I told him no." Raul dropped his voice. "He told me there was speculation the lady was with the sheriff that night. Wanted me to confirm. Couldn't. He also asked if I saw some suspicious looking guy in a trench coat. I hadn't … then he left."

Gritt went to her car, needing a moment to clear her head. In the solitude, the words rolled through her mind in neon, *the lady was with the sheriff. Couldn't be. What the fuck was Jackhammer doing?* Her emotions sunk. She trusted Mike. There had to be an explanation. Whatever … she'd standby him through wind, rain, sleet, snow, sex – even murder.

CHAPTER FORTY-FOUR

Bill Edwards was irritation personified. He was irritated that Mike wasn't at the meeting, he was irritated at the selection of doughnuts and he was irritated at the coffee. And Gritt thought he walked and talked as if he had a permanent irritation up where the sun doesn't shine. But tact was departmental policy, so she would do her damnedest. Edwards was here to review the status on Ryder, and as much as she didn't like to admit it, they needed the FBI. Ryder had vanished. Hadn't been seen since last Friday and they had no calls from the Cattarugus County sheriff, whose involvement Edwards had dismissed with a shrug.

"We got it covered in Rochester, Pittsburgh and everything in between. Just want to be sure we're on the same page. We're bringing in a profiler. Here tomorrow. So let's go over what we got."

This guy is about as bright as his dull blue tie. We've been asking for a profiler for weeks and now he's the big shot bringing one in. Asshole. She filled him in despite stupid questions aimed at showing how smart he was. She was mad at herself for having procrastinated on getting the Cattarugus sheriff's department and Pennsylvania State troopers to check bus stations with a photo of Ryder – she'd gotten side tracked with the Hilton stuff.

She said in the most tactful voice. "William, I have a suggestion. Let's get Ryder's photo shown along the routes heading south and west out of Oleans."

Edwards had already closed his briefcase and for a moment looked embarrassed. But as quick as a G-man, he recovered. "You haven't done that yet? I just assumed."

"Figured you guys best suited to do it."

"Yeah." He popped open his expensive, aluminum, look-how-important-I am, briefcase and made a note. "We'll take it from here. It's a little late but – "

"Better late than not."

"I want you and the sheriff at a meeting tomorrow morning with the profiler. Say seven." Then he tried something that he was incapable of, levity. "And maybe the coffee will be better early in the morning."

She smiled and showed – instead of threw – him out. *I hate tact.*

· · ·

The next morning Edwards introduced them to the agent from the Criminal Investigative Unit. "This is Andrea Tuckwell – you can call her Andy – one of our top profilers. She'll develop a criminal investigative analysis."

It's a profile asshole. Call it what it is.

Tuckwell was the antithesis of Edwards. Everything about her was clarity. A deliberate voice, an unassuming attitude and eyes that actually engaged you. They spent two hours going over the case and, surprisingly, Edwards had little to say. Tuckwell wanted everything on Goodall as well as Sid Leavens, who they had little on, and Buford Viles, who they had nothing on. She was also interested in Grant Hawkins. "I'll visit each crime scene, meet with the ME, then get back to you. Late tomorrow afternoon? I can tell you this, it has characteristics that fit Ryder, but not completely. I'll need more on him. And the Douglas, Trott, Riggins crimes have a common print. But not Mrs. Goodall. Doesn't mean it's not the work of the same person. Usually, we can quickly divide crimes into general categories; like psychopathic or schizophrenic or organized, disorganized. This one is a mixed bag."

Great, thought Mike. "Like what?"

"Chrystine Goodall sounds planned. Staged burglary. Clean. An organized killer. Psychopathic type assassin. The Syntex scene was sloppy, a disorganized killer. More schizophrenic. Same for Trott scene;

except schizophrenics usually aren't capable of doing these things. Yet, Douglas, that's well organized, weapon left without fear. Taunting by the killer. That's psychopathic. But all premature right now."

Edwards stood up and snapped his fancy briefcase shut. "Let's leave it until tomorrow."

Gritt stood up. *Don't know why he opened it; never made a note. Just drank coffee – and never commented on the special Colombian coffee I bought. Probably couldn't tell good coffee from bad manners.* She smiled, and Edwards took it as a nicety that prompted the use of a new word in his vocabulary.

"Thanks." He ushered Tuckwell out as if she was a show dog under his tutelage.

The next day Andy Tuckwell came alone. She told them she would be preparing a report, but for now she'd give them a verbal. She started with the most frightening point. "It *could* be the same killer for all four murders." She emphasized, "That's only a maybe at this stage. Because there's plenty of evidence to the contrary."

Mike had heard lots of profiles and too often, in the end, there were too many qualifiers to base much on them. But right now, he was open to anything.

Tuckwell continued. "Ryder doesn't fit the Goodall murder. He could Trott, maybe Riggins, not likely Douglas. I spoke with Mrs. Ryder as well as his psychiatrist who has diagnosed his mental state in the schizophrenic, disorganized category." Tuckwell scanned her notes. "She said he's depressed and impulsive, manifesting in psychotic behavior and the fact that he doesn't have a history of schizophrenia doesn't mean he isn't. I don't agree with her. I don't think he's schizophrenic. I think he's deeply depressed and no longer able to cope. Events have overwhelmed him, driven him to irrationality." She flipped through her notes. "The little I got from his wife about his background suggests a lack of self-esteem, and latent anger. All of which are exploding as he loses coping mechanisms. His reasoning is distorted, he thinks everybody is against him. Blames everybody else." She underlined something in her book. "There are telling characteristics: avoidance of responsibility, increased drinking, bursts of uncontrollable anger and retreating from the reality instead of dealing with it. And refusing to take his medication because he even blames his psychiatrist." She leaned forward. "If he sinks low enough he could turn to suicide or homicide. He may never have done anything violent before because he was able to cope, nothing had come along that he couldn't handle. Being fired wasn't enough but after more than a year could change that. His underlying instability and sense of inadequacy could've driven him to erratic behavior. Could be beyond reason, beyond coping."

Gritt made a mental note. *Maybe yes, maybe no. Who knows?*

"I can't, yet, rule him out of the Goodall case. The staged burglary is too obvious to be a pro. And the untouched nude body of Mrs. Goodall is an anomaly. Definitely not the work of a psychopath nor a schizophrenic – they usually touch, play, disfigure the body. The presence of semen has to be considered although post death – necrophilia – was not evident. Someone like Ryder would be too overwhelmed to do anything but run." She looked at them as if to say, that's about it. "You need to DNA him. His collection of newspapers and driving by the scene could be post-event regret. Or nothing more than a depressed unemployed man with nothing better to do than get immersed in the most sensational murder in the town's history."

Gritt made another note: *Get DNA sample from Ryder's hairbrush.* For her there were too many ifs, ands, ors and maybes. The summary sounded like, maybe it's Ryder, and maybe it isn't. She went more with is, than isn't.

Tuckwell went on to outline her preliminary thoughts on how Goodall may or may not fit. She was certain that he had nothing to do with anything other than his wife's death. And if he was involved in that it was only by hiring a killer. This was not a killing of passion. The staged burglary was not the work of a pro but could have been someone hired for a small amount of money, a few thousand bucks. Which opened the door to other possibilities, other enemies of the victim.

Gritt made another note: *Small time hit man?*

This brought Mike back to Grant Hawkins while Gritt was stuck on – sick about – a possible love triangle.

Tuckwell was going back over the Douglas case, off to Rochester again, and would be back in a few days. After she left, Mike and Gritt sat glumly, staring across the table at each other.

Gritt sighed.

"Good stuff," said Mike.

"I feel like I just played a game of whack-a-mole."

"Nothing definitive but she's added meat to the bones. I want more on Hawkin's relationship with Goodall. And Chrystine … Goodall."

Gritt ventured in. "You think he had something going with his ex-wife? Like a renewed interest … an affair?"

"No, for Christsake! A dispute over money. About their daughter. Something? Anything?"

She wanted to push, but not too much. "Maybe Hawkins had something on her. Threatened blackmail. She threatened to cut off his funds. He hired a small time hit man for a few thousand bucks." She watched his eyes. "Or she was having an affair, and Goodall knew."

He turned to the brick wall. "Leave Goodall to me. You've got your plate full with Ryder – and cowboy Edwards."

"Michael."

He didn't turn.

"There's something we should talk about."

"You handle it."

"Can't."

"Get help."

"Can't."

"Will you get off the 'can't' for Christsake." He turned. "Are you paralyzed or something?"

"Kinda."

He was angry, but his heart wasn't in it. He was yelling at Gritt without the volume. He wanted her gone but wanted to hug her. *Shit … go do something. That's what a chief deputy does. Takes care of things when the boss can't.* "Gritt, I'm counting on you. This is a mess. We need focus. And make sure the Fibbies don't get us off track. Keep Edwards on Ryder, you keep onhim. And Ryder. I'll turn up the heat on Goodall and Hawkins. Their ass is mine."

"What about other angles?"

"Forget it"

"Sid Leavens? Buford whoever? Follow up at the Hilton – "

"Back off. You know as well as I do, we only have so many resources. We've got two murders in our jurisdiction, maybe linked to two more in other jurisdictions, and you want us chasing flimsy leads. Do I have to make every sensible decision around here?" His voice had an edge but his eyes were measured. "Okay. I will. You stick to Ryder. That's it. No, wait. You want more? More than Ryder and Edwards? Okay. Follow up on Leavens and Buford Viles." His eyes dropped. "Update tomorrow."

The diversion was obvious. Her stubbornness was more obvious. "I found some interesting things at the Hilton."

"I don't give a shit what you found." He stood up, bouncing his chair into the wall. He was spitting words he seldom used. "Gritt, what the fuck don't you understand about no? No Hilton. No follow up."

"FBI are looking for Ryder. Don't need me."

"And I don't need your hunches getting in the way." His voice trailed off and he turned back to the window. "Not right now."

"You're the boss." She couldn't bring herself to say any more. When she left, her feet were dragging, and her heart weighed a ton. She didn't give a shit about the case, all she cared about was him. She hoped she wouldn't regret her hesitancy, opting to protect their relationship rather than the case.

CHAPTER FORTY-FIVE

Dick Ryder was slouched in the seat, barely seeing over the steering wheel. He'd been driving on the expressway for the last half-hour because he was tired of all the back roads, school bus stops and hick towns. He'd been driving around Pennsylvania and New York for days, actually mostly nights, and lying low during the day. He'd stayed in flea-bag motels for almost a week but was now sleeping in the car to conserve money for gas. He had thirty-seven dollars and fifty-two cents left. Now, he had to get off before the tolls started on the Thruway. He would head for Jamestown then back toward Oleans. He really liked that park and quarry where he'd spent the first night. It was serene and quiet there. Peaceful. And the water in the quarry reminded him of the Caribbean, almost turquoise. But cold as a witch's tit. Yeah, he'd go for a swim and get the grime off. Better still, he'd hide and watch those crazy teenagers skinny dipping at night. He pushed the Ford up a notch to get there before dark.

He stopped outside Jamestown at a gas station, filled up and bought two Cokes, a jumbo bag of chips – Ruffles, he loved Ruffles – and three Mars bars. Walking out, he noticed the pay phone. He stopped. He could hear Irene's voice, soft, understanding, forgiving. A horn blared, and he jumped back onto the curb. Some asshole in a pickup gave him the finger and roared away. *You fuckin' lucky asshole, I got a .30-30 in my trunk.* Irene's voice was gone. Just like his life was gone. Taken from him by corporate raiders – that's what they called them. They should be called rapists, mass murderers, psychopathic killers. Like Sid had said, they're no better than Bin Laden or ISIS. They had a cause and the loss of innocent lives meant nothing to them. But they'd be sorry.

He started the car, looked in the rearview mirror and froze.

Pulling into the station was a state trooper. Too late to run. He'd wait until he parked and came toward him, then he'd take off. That way he'd have a bit of a jump. The trooper stopped right behind him, climbed out and closed his door. He would wait until he was alongside the car. Sweat soaked his underarms. He pressed on the brake pedal and eased the shift into drive. He saw the trooper's belt buckle and gun in the side mirror. Then it was gone. He checked the rearview mirror. Nothing. Slowly he turned his head, just in time to see the trooper entering the gas station. He lifted his foot and the car slipped onto the highway. A mile away he veered onto a country road heading east. He laughed out loud. "Stupid cops. Can't catch me."

There were more cars than expected at the park. This could be risky because he needed to drive over the grass to the quarry, but it wasn't allowed. He'd done it before but that was late at night. He'd wait until all the yahoos went home. He parked at the far end of the lot and pointed the car toward the boat ramp so he could watch the idiots taking their boats in and out. Most of them were those stupid seadoos that screamed around the lake annoying the shit out of everybody. He smiled at the thought of taking out his rifle and picking off a few of the yahoos.

He wasn't sure how long he'd been dozing before he heard the tap on the window. It scared the hell out of him. He was staring at some fat, bulbous gut in a shit-brown T-shirt, worn by an oversized hillbilly who was grinning at him like Nannu the whale. Dick's fear subsided into puzzlement then resurfaced as anger. He glared at the guy then noticed the second guy. Another loser. Nobody wore shorts and black socks, except this asshole. And he had one of those Australian outback hats, a fake cowboy hat with a string. He looked goofier than Nannu. Dick rolled the window down an inch.

Nannu spoke. "Hey good buddy. Jus' wonderin' if ya' might do us a favor? We gotta park us our RV and boat. And only spot is here at the end of the lot. Can't squeeze 'er in with you here. She's a bit bigger than yer Ford." He laughed as if he'd actually said something funny.

Dick pulled his cramped body upright and, for a second, almost did what was right, start the car. Instead, he got out. Both Nannu and Black Socks stepped back. Dick tried to control his rage as he opened the trunk.

"What da' ya' say goody buddy?" He watched Dick reach into the trunk and asked, "What's that for?"

Black Socks moved back against the boat and trailer. A cheap, blue, fiberglass thing with a Mercury engine hanging off the end of it. He mumbled. "Just askin.'"

Dick walked around behind the boat. Nannu tried to keep a friendly tone in his voice. "Hey! Not lookin' for trouble good buddy. If you don't want to we'll figure – "

Dick raised his arms and took aim.

Nannu's eyes screamed louder than his mouth. "Noooo."

The first swing of the tire iron smashed into the outboard motor. A few paint chips flew off. Dick was mad there was so little damage. Three more swings and the engine casing split. The next one knocked the propeller off. The commotion had brought two unsightly women out of the RV, but they quickly retreated when they saw their stalwart men as immobile as plastic G.I. Joe figures.

Dick climbed into his car and sped away. *That'll teach you to fuck with Dick Ryder.* The last he saw, Nannu and Socks were standing in front of their dinky blue boat with the worthless motor. As his anger subsided, he collected his thoughts: *That was stupid. Now the police will be all over your ass. And your access to the quarry is cut off.* He drove south, took a couple of side roads and pulled into an overgrown lane that disappeared into the woods. He swung his arm and fist against the passenger seat again and again and made a guttural sound. Then he cried, not sobs, just tears, and whispered, "Irene, Irene." He sat for hours, only moving to swat at the pesky mosquitoes. It was after ten when he opened the trunk and brought the .30-30 into the front seat. He held it for a while, stroking the stock then placed it on the passenger side and covered it with the blanket.

Just after midnight the Ford eased back into the park with headlights off. There were only a few cars in the lot and at the far end Nannu's RV and boat. Dick forced the wheels up over the curbstones and drove across the dew-laden grass. He had to go around the far side of the RV to get to the quarry. Fortunately, there were no lights on. The tires squished in the wet grass like a kid's rubber boots and the engine rattled like a can of stones. He was crawling past the RV when a light came on, illuminating the hood of his car. Then the light was partially blocked. In the rear window of the box-on-wheels was Nannu, backlit in all his naked glory, peering into the blackness. The light from the RV moved across the car. Dick held his breath then heard a bellow from inside.

"Hey. Somebody's outside. Get the gun."

Dick tramped the accelerator and the car fish-tailed across the open space and into the woods. He could see the hiking trail that he had gone down before; it was just wide enough for a car. The Ford careened down the trail, lights bouncing off the trees as he fought for control. Speed was critical because that asshole whale in the RV would have the cops back real soon. Time was running out.

• • •

"I'm tellin' you deputy. It was the same guy. Went like a bat outta hell right down there into them there trees. Me and Bruce here heard shots. Right Bruce?" He didn't wait for Socks to reply. "I was in the Canadian Army, I know shots. Like firecrackers. Pop! Pop! Pop! Right Bruce? Three, maybe four."

The deputy said. "He ain't there now. Nobody. Kids go down there all the time to neck and get pregnant. Wouldn't surprise me if they was firing a gun. Or firecrackers. They're all gone by 'bout three a.m. Just checked. No cars. No shell casings. Beer bottles, used condoms and burned out camp fires. The usual."

"Was him. Same car. I'd know it anywheres. Same bastard who

beat the crap outta our motor."

"We'll file a report. Without no plate number."

"Told ya' I was shocked. No chance to get a license. Nor Bruce."

"We'll let you know if we locate him." They were trying to convince the deputy that an unidentifiable car in the middle of the night was the same one they had no license plate number for from earlier in the day. The disinterested deputy left, then pulled up to the refreshment stand for a burger and coffee. It wasn't exactly breakfast, but he'd been out here twice, once to answer a call at 12:20 a.m. and again at daybreak to check the quarry. He knew it was teens fooling around. There were tire marks across the grass and down the trail to the flat rocks above the quarry where they end. The whole thing was a waste of time and he was reluctant to write it up. But he had to because it was an official complaint filed by Mr. King of the RVs, a Dave Pollock from Mississauga, Canada. *What's that? Someplace outta the movie Dances With Wolves?*

CHAPTER FORTY-SIX

Gritt held the phone away from her ear while doodling on her calendar. Special Agent Edwards was rambling on with a litany of the obvious, the gist of which was that the infallible FBI had covered every inch of northern Pennsylvania and southwest New York. "If Ryder is moving around, he isn't doing it in these parts. Certainly not by car, bus, train or plane. Or foot."

She asked. "Any news from Agent Tuckwell?'

"It's only been twenty-four hours. We're good but not that good."

Tuckwell's that good, not you. She kept doodling.

"We're playing phone tag," said Edwards. "I'll reach her later."

She looked at a yellow phone message on her desk. Tuckwell had called her ten minutes ago. "William, I've got a call. Get back to you."

"Sure, if you need anything just – "

She hung up and dialed Tuckwell – got right through.

Tuckwell said, "Chief. Thanks for returning my call. I left a message for Bill Edwards too. In your interviews with Mrs. Ryder did you determine when her husband began to change?"

"Don't think so."

"What about co-workers? Secretary?"

"Hadn't worked for almost two years."

"What about this Sid Leavens? Did he have anything to say?"

"I'll check my notes."

Tuckwell said, "I'll talk with Mrs. Ryder."

"See you tomorrow."

• • •

Tuckwell came alone. "Bill had to fly back to Washington."

Without the tight-ass, tin-cased Edwards showcasing his stupidity everyone was more relaxed and even the Colombian coffee tasted better. Tuckwell's update contained a few key points. Her discussions with Ryder's psychiatrist, revealed a troubled man. They'd been able to get the doctor-patient confidentiality waived because there was a strong likelihood that he was a danger to himself, and others. He'd been in therapy for a year but had made little progress. The doctor was stuck on a particular diagnosis and not open to the simpler but possibly more dangerous assessment that he was no longer able to cope with reality. Tuckwell didn't hide her criticism. "Psychology is still far from being an exact science and yet so many practitioners are too intent on being exact. She thinks his psychosis stems from an impulse disorder. I checked his childhood and even though people had good things to say about him, he had signs of trouble." She counted on her fingers. "Ostracized by peers, nerdish, overly protective mother. Could be impediments in developing coping skills. And a sense of inadequacy now that he can't cope. Fearful that he has lost control." Tuckwell emphasized. "It's urgent you find him – ASAP."

CHAPTER FORTY-SEVEN

Mike kicked the wall. "Shit." He'd spilt water over the bookcase trying to water his philodendron. *You're losing it Cougar. If you can't water plants without screwing up, how the hell you gonna solve two murders?* He was angry at himself for being so irresponsible. First Chrystine. Now Gritt. *Women.* But he knew it wasn't the women, it was him. He'd tripped over his loneliness and succumbed to his carnal needs with Chrystine – no excuse. And Gritt. But she was more. It was more powerful. More conflicting. More troubling. More wonderful. His anger at himself and his hunger for her constantly clashed. Just being near her was tough. Her closeness … voice, laughter, smell, all too distracting. He mopped up the mess, then stared at the brick wall.

Two hours later he was cracking his knuckles and dipping chocolate chip cookies as his father slurped coffee. The tiny kitchen with the pigeon shit floor felt like shit. It hung in the air and the air had to be cleared. They'd been kicking the case around for an hour, but nothing was new.

Jack said. "Saw Gritt at the Hilton the other day."

"What?'

"You heard me."

"Gritt?"

"I was at the cab stand. Good spot."

"Thursday? Friday?"

Jack saw the anxiety. "Ya' havin' a problem with Gritt?"

"Insubordination. Told her to leave the Hilton alone."

"Why?"

"Her job is Ryder."

"Why stay away from the Hilton?"

"Ryder is between here and Florida or Mexico. Not at the Hilton."

"Maybe she's got a sniff of somethin'. Gotta let her get at it."

"This whole thing is a big enough mess without her wasting time."

"Maybe it's not a waste of time?"

He stopped cookie dipping. "You on her side now? Wasn't it the all-knowing, cop who said we should stay focused on Ryder and Goodall? Narrow the investigation?"

"I don't know what Gritt knows. But I do know if she's at the Hilton there's good reason." He saw fear in his son's eyes. "Do ya' know what Gritt knows?"

"Pops! Please. This is tough. I need your advice. Non-judgmental. Objective. Think you can do that? This is about a whole lot more than the case. My career. My life. Just listen." He looked for some redeeming quality. "Let me get it out before you jump all over me."

Jack didn't reply.

He stared into his coffee. "It's hard to know where to start."

"How about the end?"

"I don't know what the end is. That's the problem. I'm stuck in the middle, up to my ass. Can't think straight. Can't function. Can't concentrate. Can't even water plants without screwing up."

"Mike."

He mumbled into his mug. "I had an affair with Chrystine Goodall."

"I know."

He met his father's eyes.

"I know," repeated Jack.

"What?" He looked like an eight-year-old, caught in the cookie jar.

"Doesn't matter."

"Doesn't matter? Here I am thinking – "

Jack shrugged. "Shit happens."

"Not in the middle of the biggest murder case in Westhaven history."

"I've done bigger. Nobody needs to know."

"You know."

"Who else?" asked Jack.

"Soon everybody." Mike's emotions tumbled.

"Who else?"

"I don't know…. Maybe Gritt – suspects."

"Maybe?"

"She'd tell me." He looked up. "How'd you know?"

"I'm a cop. Streets are still mine."

"You followed me. Had someone follow me?"

"Point is, I can help. That's why ya' came isn't it? To figure a way out?"

They talked for a while. It was a release for Mike. And Jack was pretty good, considering. He listened and gave some simple advice that he repeated six different ways. "Like I said, nail Goodall's ass and no one will be interested in looking into his wife's past. Put the pressure on him. Get evidence, arrest him. He had her killed. You don't need the assassin to make the connection. Get that professor on the money trail."

After leaving, Mike thought about how even-keeled Jackhammer was and how unconcerned he seemed about his one-night stand with Chrystine. Maybe he knew more than he was saying? And if Goodall ever found out … there'd be no saving his career. He slowed the car to collect himself. He punched the dashboard. *I'll get this bastard. Or kill him myself.*

CHAPTER FORTY-EIGHT

Mike had forgotten how long-winded Perk Allen could be. Many times in his class, he'd fallen asleep and right about now he was ready to go face down on his desk. It was probably a mistake to have let his father attend the meeting, but he'd done it as a *quid pro quo* for his silence. But Jack's attention had checked out twenty minutes ago. The kindly old professor had stacks and stacks of computer print outs and was determined to go through every one of them. Fortunately, Waggs and Gibson weren't there because Gibson would have walked out after five minutes. Waggs was in Philly and Mike hadn't invited Gibson because he wanted to avoid the inevitable friction between he and Jack.

Allen droned on. "So, you can see there is nothing un-toward in all of these transactions. Large sums moving around, all seemingly legit."

"What do you mean 'seemingly'?" Mike asked, partially on instinct and partially to stay attentive.

"Haven't been able to trace all the transactions to off-shore accounts and I've ignored the obvious ones."

"Obvious ones?"

"I have to categorize the transactions in order to get them down to a manageable size for my first pass. You see ..." Allen went on explaining the process and Mike waited as long as his patience would allow.

"Professor Allen ... perhaps the short version."

"Sorry, sorry ... I do go on, don't I? Of course, the short answer." He turned a stack of computer printouts around and pointed to many highlighted lines. Mike couldn't see the figures from where he was and Jack didn't appear interested, but the professor pressed on. "Here's an obvious transaction. Three-hundred-thousand dollars to his margin account. Another? Ten-thousand to his checking account. I followed that one. No unusual disbursements from his personal account after that. A twenty-five-thousand transfer to his daughter's college tuition account. And there were several others to the same account over the course of the last year. Smaller amounts. And here's another hundred thousand to a bank in Nassau. I tracked that to a withdrawal in Nassau and a night of heavy gambling. Gambling isn't breaking the law, although it's a crime that anyone can throw away that much money on gambling." He looked for a reaction but got none.

They concluded the meeting with the conclusion that they had nothing yet. But Professor Allen left under a head of enthusiastic steam, unlike Mike who didn't have much enthusiasm for anything.

Jack was optimistic. "He's as boring as bat shit but that's what gets these bastards. Goodall has made a mistake somewhere and your ol'prof will find it." As Jack got up to leave Gibson came through the door. It was like two bull elephants meeting at a narrow river crossing. Their greeting consisted of a couple of grunts. Neither moved. Then Gibson shuffled back the minimum required to let Jack through the door.

"What's he doin' here?" asked Gibson.

"Seeing me."

Gibson wasn't buying it, but let it go. "Waggs called. Apparently, the mob is lookin' all over for their prize hit man, Ignagni. They're as mystified as anybody. He never came back from Rochester. They're worried he's gone to the Feds and in a witness protection program."

"Has he?"

"Don't know. Edwards is checking. Feds are closed mouthed about that stuff. Might never know. Not soon enough to help us. But we got something in Rochester. A silver Mercedes, 500. In a McDonald's drive-thru on the same night Goodall's secretary marked his calendar. A kid noticed it. Said he loved the car, made him drool. It was after 1:00 a.m. Pretty conspicuous."

"Kid give you a description?"

"Older guy."

"That's it?"

"He's a kid, drooling over the car, not the driver."

"Anybody else in the car?"

"Kid didn't know. But … he saw the vehicle pull over in the lot. Nothing unusual 'cause lots of people drive-thru then eat in the lot. Thank god for the kid's addiction 'cause he saw another guy come over and get in the Benz."

"Don't tell me. Couldn't ID him?"

"Didn't see where he came from. Or leave. Didn't see the Benz leave either." Gibson tried optimism. "We can put Goodall in Rochester. Meeting with a stranger on the same night Ignagni arrived in Rochester."

Mike said, "I can hear the DA's first question. And how many silver Mercedes, owned by older men are there in Rochester or New York State or any state?"

"Kid got a partial plate."

"Now you tell me. Fuck, enough with charades. No time for this shit."

"New York. Got two letters and three numbers … Sam, David, blank - 7,3,2. Goodall's is Sam, David, King, 7362."

"Close, but no cigar. But Goodall doesn't have to know that. And he doesn't have to know Ignagni is missing. What about that Pomante character, the ex-employee?"

"I'm flying down this afternoon. They're bringing him in for questioning. Waggs and I'll put him on the rack."

"Call me as soon as you have anything. Make the connection and we'll get an indictment. Need to nail this bastard."

Gibson left. *He's wound up tighter than a cheap yo-yo?*

Mike called Gritt, who was halfway to Oleans. "Why you going there?"

"Following up on Ryder," was the quick retort. And she couldn't resist. "Like you told me to."

"Yeah, yeah. When are you back?"

"Tonight."

"See me as soon as you get in. It's important. Very."

"Ten-four."

. . .

Mike was beat. And trapped. And sick of coffee. He sat alone at the counter in Frankie's and between refills, Helen gave him space. At this time of night there weren't many customers and except for one, a Sid Leavens, they left him alone. Leavens had stopped and given him his two cents worth – worth less than a penny – then sat down with some other guy over by the window. Apparently, no one had been to interview him since Mike had told Gritt to grill the guy, as well as a Buford Viles. Again, it was Gritt he was waiting on. They'd agreed to meet at Frankie's at eleven because she hadn't eaten since noon. Apparently, she had some good stuff. But Deputy Thurm had said he saw her at the Hilton, again.

Mike's nose was in the coffee cup when the flat-iron hand clumped down on his shoulder. He knew.

"Don't go face down in that coffee son."

"Hey Pops." He didn't want to say it. "Have a seat."

"For a minute. Gotta get some fares."

Mike knew it was bullshit. His old man didn't give a damn if he made a dime driving cab. "Trade you jobs. I'll take the cab, you take the case."

"Anything from your prof?" He eased onto a stool as Helen approached. "Two black, no sugar doll. To go."

"Nothing."

"Gibson?"

"May have something on a hit man out of Philly."

"Get it! And arrest the bastard. He may not be as tough as ya' think. Big man in the corporate world; just another fish in our tank.

Put some pressure on him."

Mike was relieved when Helen brought the coffee. "Let you know when I hear from Allen."

"What about the other stuff?"

"I'm waiting for Gritt. She's thirty minutes late."

"Do Goodall and you won't have to worry about the other."

Mike stirred his coffee that didn't need stirring.

"Here comes that ass Leavens. See ya." Jack left.

The black coffee went blacker as the shadow of Leavens spread across the counter. *Not again. If you sit down, I'll have Gritt turn your life inside out.* He looked up. "What can I do for you Sid?"

"It's what can I do for you. I've followed this case closely Sheriff, know Dick Ryder well. I know you can't find him. Your deputy spoke to me briefly on the phone … haven't heard since."

"She's been out of town. Back tonight. She'll be in touch."

"This Buford Viles. Interesting character," said Leavens. He had a theory that Viles fit the profile for shooting CEOs and the window of Liegerman's office. He didn't mention Chrystine.

Mike feigned interest and cracked his knuckles. The amateur detective rattled on. *Stubborn bastard, I should team him up with Gritt and send them both after these phantom suspects.*

"The Goodall woman. That's different. That's a sex crime."

Mike damn near threw the coffee at him.

"I see you agree." He lowered his load onto a stool. "Was talking with your ol'man the other day. He wasn't buying it but didn't put up much of an argument." He went on to explain how he figured it was a lover who went home with Ms. Goodall that night and after their dalliance an argument got out of hand out and he shot her, then made it look like a break in.

Mike boiled. He wasn't about to encourage this Perry Mason wannabe and he would've left if it wasn't for his tardy deputy and his instinct to be politically correct with the public. He asked, "You seem to know quite a bit. Where do you get all your information?"

"Here and there. It's mainly inductive."

"Inductive? That means you have to have the right details to work with. To draw your inferences and build a theory."

Leavens grinned as if he was now on the homicide team.

Mike continued. "So, to conclude that Ms. Goodall went home with someone and had an argument that ended in her death would mean you had to know something we don't know. The kind of detail we're searching for." Leavens was somewhere between pleased and puzzled. "What is it that you know Mr. Leavens?"

Leavens realized he wasn't on the team.

"And how could you know it if you weren't there? Tell you what. Be at my office tomorrow morning, 8 a.m., sharp. We'll have a few questions for you."

"I didn't mean … it's in my head, you know – "

"Helen…." He held up his empty cup. "Mr. Leavens, we'll take this up in the morning."

Leavens skulked away like a scolded dog.

Gritt came through the door spitting out an apology. "Sorry. Had a lead. Took longer than expected."

"Yeah?"

"Saw Mrs. Ryder." She wasn't about to add ... *and Jackhammer at the Hilton*. Or that she'd collected a DNA sample from Ryder's hairbrush. She'd learned in Olean that Ryder was seen at a Western Union office and they'd traced a money wire from Westhaven. She'd come back and gone straight to Ryder's home and after a few minutes of questioning, Mrs. Ryder admitted she'd had her son wire the money. She'd sent only two hundred dollars because she wanted him to come home soon. But it meant he had enough to buy gas and travel – to Pittsburgh or wherever?

Helen approached. "Coffee Gritt?"

"Thanks."

Mike quizzed. "Thought you were starving?"

"First things first." Mrs. Ryder had invited her in and offered her some leftover Rigatoni and hot sausage so she wasn't hungry now. She talked about the money and filled him in with the usual standard good news, bad news scenario. The bad was that the FBI had turned up nothing on Ryder's whereabouts. The good was the Cattarugus Sheriff had. A week after the last sighting and a ton of nothing from the FBI, the sheriff had had a sighting of Ryder. "One of his deputies had put in a report of a disturbance in Cattarugas Park and a description of some nut-bar beating the crap out of a family's outboard motor. It fit Ryder. Get this, later that night his car was spotted again in the same park."

"And?"

"Nothing."

"The car?"

"Nothing. Yet."

Mike surmised. "If it's him, he's not wandering far. Hiding, but not running. Afraid, disturbed, depressed … maybe plotting. Sounds more like a lost soul than a psycho killer. Call Tuckwell."

"Now?"

"No. Day after tomorrow when Ryder arrives in Oklahoma."

"She's at the Hilton."

"They have phones there don't they?"

Gritt called, then reported. "Tuckwell says it fits. Probably slipping deeper. Can't cope with anything anymore. The anger at a motorboat could turn into another killing. Or he'll hide in depression. Could return to the scene of one of the crimes." She took out her roll of bills. "I got a hundred says he goes to Rochester. Looks like he likes parks and Heather Trott was shot in a park."

"I want you on nothing but this loony. We know where he was a day ago and he's not likely running. Find him – before Edwards and his band of not-so-merry men do."

"I'll start with Leavens. He knew Ryder."

"I've got Leavens in the morning. I'll deal with him. Hasn't got shit but want to close his flapping mouth. Get what you can from Oleans."

Gritt felt the weight of her gun belt as she prepared to mention seeing Jackhammer at the Hilton. Before she did, he got onto something else.

"I'm getting a warrant for Goodall tomorrow."

"Really?"

"Gotta problem with that?"

"Got enough on him?"

"If Waggs and Gibson come back with what I think they will."

"What about the DA and a grand jury?"

"Not going to wait. Want this bastard in my jail. Sweat him."

Gritt wanted to do what she always did, play devil's advocate, with the two of them going at it. Analyzing, breaking it down, reconstructing it, flipping the angles, weighing the evidence. It was what they were best at. When his mind was in a groove, he was amazing, a modern Socrates articulating the rule of law, logic and justice. But for days, he'd been distant, no discreet winks, glances, touches. Not even hugs, let alone sex. He was like a depressed Hamlet. She couldn't find the guts to bring up the Hilton. She should, but couldn't. *Maybe tomorrow.*

Mike added a new piece to the Goodall case. "We've got two interesting phone calls by Hawkins to Ebe. He called a week before Chrystine … Ms. Goodall's murder, and again three days after. The only two calls in the last year."

Gritt noticed the hesitation whenever Mike mentioned Mrs. Goodall.

"He either knew something or was in on something. If Goodall doesn't give us what we want, I'll go at him again."

"And the chances of that are?"

"We can sweat Hawkins too."

"More than Goodall's bags of money or fear tactics? Hit men are a dime a dozen to a guy like this. He's probably got Hawkins scared shitless."

"Obstruction of justice is jail time and Hawkins is no Stonewall Jackson."

"Fear built the Berlin Wall."

"Freedom brought it down. We'll give the dapper Mr. Hawkins a choice. Freedom to keep buying his clothes on Fifth Avenue or weekly visiting rights for his daughter to come see him. I figure he learned something from his ex-wife around about the time of that first call to Ebe. According to Jones, she hadn't yet filed divorce papers when Hawkins called Ebe. So Goodall didn't know that a divorce was imminent. Did Hawkins? Did he call to tell Goodall, through Ebe? Unintentionally triggering a murderous process. He may have been contemplating blackmail or just getting into Goodall's good graces, afraid of losing his half million. No way Chrystine … Ms. Goodall could afford the same level of support. We'll get it out of him. But we don't have to wait before arresting the town's favorite CEO, Mr. pin-stripes and cuff links." He drained his coffee. "Let's get out of here."

She so wanted to go with him but right now separation was best. "Let me grab some food. I'll catch you at the office. Twenty minutes." As Mike left, Gritt ordered another coffee – she hated deceiving him. Made her want to throw up.

CHAPTER FORTY-NINE

At ten the next morning Mike's day was brightening. At eight he had shaken Leavens up enough that he wouldn't be spewing his ridiculous theories around and now he was about to shake a bigger tree and see what falls out. He loved this part of the job, especially when he was arresting a son-of-a-bitch like Goodall. It was one thing to walk into a broken-down tenement building or a stale-beer smelling bar, but strolling into the self-indulgent, executive offices of an arrogant asshole, now that was a high.

"Excuse me sir, you can't go in there." The pleading secretary didn't even get a sideways glance.

He was like the lead dog in a pack of five. Right behind him were Waggs and Gibson and behind them two deputies. He hadn't needed the phalanx, could have done it with either Waggs or Gibson, or let them do it. But this was a watershed event, although he wasn't too sure how deep the water was or whether he was about to sink or swim. He'd gone over and over what they had on this bastard and still, something gnawed at him. Maybe it was because Gritt wasn't completely onside. Or without confirmation of Ignagni's involvement, the connection was weak. In the end, it was his father's premise – arrest the bastard and all the other stuff will go away – that had him striding down the carpeted hall at Syntex. He'd prepared his PR woman for the media barrage, anticipating headlines: *Syntex CEO arrested, accused of murder.*

When the door to Alexander Goodall's inner sanctum swung open the CEO didn't even turn around. He was looking out his wrap-around windows and rambling on, his back to an oval table where three people were supposedly listening to him. They turned and had trouble closing their collective mouths. The five officers' presence didn't come close to filling the pretentious room, but suddenly it felt much smaller.

In mid-sentence, Goodall realized that attention had been distracted. He swiveled around. "What the – "

"Alexander Goodall. You are under arrest for the murder of Chrystine Gallagher-Goodall." Mike liked using Chrystine's maiden name. *She wasn't really a Goodall.* "You have a right to remain silent; anything you say – "

"Get the fuck outta my office – "

" – may be used against you. You have the right to the advice of an attorney before and during questioning. If you – "

"Get out!" He yelled over the approaching detectives. "Brook, Call Mel. And Carmen."

Hey asshole. It's Carmencita. Have a little respect for your women.

The three executives were frozen like ice carvings affixed to the table, as they saw, perhaps for the first time, their boss sweating. The armpits of his crisp, blue shirt suddenly looked like a dog had visited a fire hydrant. Even from across the room, Mike could see the purple vein twitching beneath his eye, like it did the first day he'd interviewed him. It was a small confirmation. But could mean nothing.

They gave Goodall no executive privilege. Drove him in through the wire, remote control fence and processed him – fingerprints and photo – like any other criminal. Mike's adrenaline high was complete when he left the handcuffed Goodall in the county jail. He would've liked to slam the cell door but let Gibson do that. Twenty minutes later Carmencita Lopez was in his office.

She looked impressive in her trendy legal threads and best defensive stance, hands on hips, Bosco bag tossed on the chair. "The audacity. The temerity. The disrespect you have shown my client. You didn't have to cuff him in the middle of your circus act, in front of his people – "

"He's charged with murder. That's what we do with felons."

"On what evidence?"

"He'll be arraigned tomorrow morning. Until then you can visit him here in county jail."

"You'll have my motion to dismiss before the end of the day."

"See the DA about that. Your client is being processed, you can see him in a couple of hour."

"A couple of hours?"

"We'll let you know. You can wait in the visitor's area if you like." *She's just another of Goodall's trophies and what she doesn't realize is I'm doing her, and a lot of women, and Chrystine, a big favor.* His anger would not recede.

CHAPTER FIFTY

Gritt parked her car in the parking lot behind the Hilton. As far as Mike knew she was halfway to Oleans. She would go, but first some clarification. She found Raul and asked him what she should have asked the first time – did Jack ask to speak to anyone else? He had – kitchen staff. She found a bus boy, Eli Sanders who told her he'd spoken to Jack and told him he'd seen a cop come through the kitchen about eleven.

She asked, "What exactly did you tell him?"

Eli said, "He got pissed 'cause I di'nt remember much. I told him, when I sees the po-leece I looks the other way and goes 'bout my business."

She asked. "Was the man going through the kitchen wearing a uniform?"

"No ma'am."

"How did ya' know he was a cop?"

"I knows po-leece when I sees one. I knows the sheriff."

"Did you tell the other man that?"

"His ol'man?"

"Yes."

"No. He di'nt ask."

She was on the road before turning the radio back on, in case Mike was looking for her. She considered stopping for coffee and doughnuts but her stomach was cramping, and so was her mind. And her heart. She couldn't make sense of this. Mike at the Hilton after eleven, Jack looking for a man in a disguise? Could it have been a PI, someone hired to follow Mike? Or Chrystine Goodall?

The trip to Oleans was unproductive, and her stomach was still unsettled, despite the Tums. She and the deputy had revisited the park and quarry and turned up nothing and the FBI couldn't find the Canadian and his RV. More importantly, she had to figure out how she could get ahead of this unresolved mess at the Hilton before it ruined Michael's career. It would be the race of her career.

CHAPTER FIFTY-ONE

Jackhammer was half-hammered and hammering on Mike. The problem was sitting on the kitchen table – Jack Daniels.

"Fuckin' courts. That flaming, liberal-ass Judge Newman would let every criminal out on bail if he could. Shit! Goodall murdered his wife. Bail – million bucks – pocket change to that asshole. Tell me they took his passport?"

"No."

"Shit…. Even the law is on the side of scum. Corporate America – all scum. And they write the laws. Supreme Court is there because of the President's appointments. President is there because of big money. Big money is there so crooked companies can get what they want. It's all about money." Jack knocked back another burn of bourbon. "How's yer prof doing? What are yer big city investigators coming up with? Let's nail his ass."

"Assistant DA made a good case for flight risk. Judge didn't buy it. Carmencita made a strong argument – all that good, corporate citizen crap. Said we were desperate for an arrest and made up this cockamamie theory about her client."

"Made up my ass. Gibson got anything?"

"Tomorrow." Mike wasn't going to tell his father what Waggs and Gibson had because too much resentment on top of too much bourbon was a bad idea. But they'd squeezed Pomante and there was a connection to Ignagni. He had made the introduction. Waggs had the FBI going after Ignagni's phone records. That plus something from Professor Allen, and Hawkins, and they'd have Goodall's ass back in jail.

• • •

Alexander Goodall's jet picked Mel Ebe up in New York and they were in Bermuda for lunch, and on their way back by mid-afternoon. At twenty-seven thousand feet there was no risk of surveillance. Goodall had told Ebe everything and they had a defense strategy. Goodall was upbeat but Ebe wasn't sure if it was habitual optimism or innate arrogance from a career of seeing life through a different lens. But that was good because a client convinced of his own innocence was better in front of a jury. Ebe wasn't completely skeptical but some of the evidence would be pretty damaging if it came out. However, if they prevented it from surfacing, then the whole thing might get thrown out. And he had another piece of information – only speculation – that could be leverage to stop the investigation in its tracks. He hadn't told Goodall. PI Sharko had heard a rumor at the local, cop hangout that the sheriff had been seen in the company of Chrystine Goodall. Sharko was now looking for a small-time PI, a Willy Neef, who supposedly had something on the sheriff, on the night of the murder. Ebe wanted to get to him before the sheriff did.

CHAPTER FIFTY-TWO

Mike was in early because he had a meeting with Perk Allen. Jack was sleeping it off. Last night things had deteriorated quickly and as much as he'd tried, he wasn't able to get away before a final blow up. He'd floated the possibility that all the murders might have been committed by the same psychopath, who rigged the crime scenes so the police wouldn't connect them. Jack's eyes had bulged in their sockets as if he'd been shot in the ass with a stun gun. He exploded. Knocked over the Jack Daniels and pounded the kitchen counter. It had frightened Mike. He knew how violent Jack could get. He railed for five minutes calling his son every denigrating thing his bourbon-choked head could come up with, and unloaded about his tough life, deprived childhood and miserable father. His parting shot was, "String up Goodall. Then ya'll get the rest." Mike left and made a long overdue decision. No more waiting, he had to completely detach himself from his father. When the old man was sober, he'd sever all ties.

As he entered Allen's hotel room he was struck by a touch of irony. When he was at university he, and all Perk's students, entered his classroom with trepidation, wondering if today would be the day for one of Perk's infamous pop quizzes. They were legendary, or more accurately, Perk was legendary in how he played with students' heads in his twisted game of quizzes. They were worth eighty percent of your mark and you never knew when they were coming. He'd even do two quizzes in back to back classes. Once, he did three in a row. It bordered on mental cruelty, but it worked. Whether you liked or hated accounting, you were always prepared. Now, the student was testing the professor. He hoped he wouldn't flunk.

Allen was still in his pajamas – *flannel in the middle of summer?* And as good as he was at accounting, he was as bad at environmental cleanup. Underwear, socks, shirt, slacks, hairbrush, toothbrush, wet towels and unfinished breakfast, had no order or place to be, except away from the table buried under paper. He cleared his briefcase from a chair and scanned the room for an open spot to put it … the bed. "Have a seat Mike."

He recognized the tone in the know-it-all professor's voice. Mischief. In his inimitable way, Perk started with a droning explanation of what he'd been doing but as he proceeded his voice quickened, like a kid telling a story of how he'd found all the little Easter eggs before uncovering the mother of all eggs.

"Remember how I said Goodall had a college tuition account for his daughter. Standard income tax shelter. Nothing untoward. I saw the deposits and transfers in and out. Never gave it another thought. My oversight. Broke a cardinal rule. Always check the obvious and never assume anything." He smiled but never stopped his patter. "Of course, that's why he used it, a cover. There'd been a debit to the account of twenty-five thousand this summer. That's about the time tuition might be due at school. However, on my second pass I noted that there were three other previous debits, each for nineteen thousand and evenly spaced between a-year-ago June, January and this past June. A couple of calls confirmed it was the semester-by-semester tuition fee. So what was the twenty-five?" His voice was now skipping along. "Checked the date again. Same day he met with the guy in Rochester. So …" The professor stopped as if he was about to say, pop quiz. Instead, he stood up, hands over his head, looking for high-fives. Mike did him one better, he high-fived and then hugged him. This was the best pop quiz ever.

"Professor Allen, how can I thank you?"

"After you arrest this guy just make sure I get a photo for my little gallery."

"You got it."

Twenty-five thousand. That was enough to buy a hit man. Immediately, he'd subpoena Goodall's bank records. It still wasn't a closed loop but all he needed was enough to break Goodall down. He could threaten to involve the IRS if Goodall couldn't show that the withdrawal went to tuition. Guy like that was probably hiding a lot more than twenty-five thousand.

Waggs and Gibson had gotten in late the night before and they were probably sleeping, but this was too good. He called. "Know you must be beat, but gotta see you. We've got something. One hour. My office. It'll make your day."

Waggs groaned. "I'll see your something and raise you one. Make that two. I'll make your day." He hung up before Mike could ask what he had.

CHAPTER FIFTY-THREE

Gritt needed Hodge's help on this phantom, trench coat guy that was apparently around the Hilton on the night in question. She caught Hodge rushing to a meeting with Mike and only got a couple of names off the top of his head as he shouted back, "The guy Willy Neef is a real sleaze-bag." She decided to start with him.

Westhaven wasn't a rotting-from-the-core town but if it had a festering pocket this was it, between 32nd and 46th Street, between Foster and Woodward Avenues, where street numbers were missing and plywood substituted for most store windows. She stopped to inquire at the Palm Hotel, an infamous flophouse. Things were looking up when she was told Neef operated out of the place next door, what might have passed for a three-story office building, thirty years ago. On the ground level was Alichi's Fish Shop and W.K. Neef, Private Investigations was on the top floor. There were a handful of what could hardly be called businesses in between. Steve's Trophies & Sports Memorabilia that looked like it had been forgotten a decade ago. Wong's Imports had three padlocks on the door, Olivia's Psychic Readings didn't have much of a future or past and Yolla's Novelties had obviously redefined prostitutes as novelties. *At least it's creative.* She skipped up three flights of stairs with the smell of Alichi's carp, Wong's incense, Yolla's cheap perfume and too many years of dust, dirt and rot right behind her. As she knocked on Neef's door, she unsnapped the catch on her holster.

"Enter."

Two men – slugs with teeth – seated in front of a dirt-gray, metal desk, turned and involuntarily let their eyes speak, *Fuck, it's the law*. It was surprise, not fear. A third man, dressed in a ninety-nine dollar suit, looked more pissed-off than surprised. She let her hand graze the comfort of her Glock. The cheap-suit had just passed an envelope across the desk to one of the slugs. He straightened up and with no attempt to hide his defiance said, "Sheriff."

"Chief Deputy."

"I'm William Neef, PI. What kin I do for ya'?" He looked at his clients. "Was jus' finishin' up here."

Scruff and Scum still hadn't turned on their brain lights and just stared, not able to calm their fight or flight instincts. Her left hand and arm were on full alert and she hoped her open-holstered gun would push the two dullards to logic and inaction.

Neef said. "Right. Butch was jus' finished. Right Butch?"

The one with a stubby ponytail that was shorter than his cobweb beard made an effort to think. "Yep … yeah. Done. All done. Yep. Just leavin'." He whacked his IQ-twin on the arm. "Bob. We're outta here."

Bob, who obviously couldn't afford a rubber band to ponytail his matted hair, looked like a pit bull that didn't understand the command. Or did but couldn't override thirty years of attack training. The two stood in unison and every one of their mangy body parts worked overtime to give off a marking scent – hands in pockets, puffed out chest, mutinous face – all said, *Fuck you, fuck the law, fuck everybody*. They stepped around her, uncertain as to whether they should maintain their defiance or be relieved they were being handed a get-out-of-jail card because the deputy just wanted to talk to their partner-in-sleaze, Willy.

She closed the door behind them, not so much for privacy but in hopes of keeping Alichi's carp stench from mixing with Butch and Bob's body odor. "Couple of questions Mr. Neef."

"Call me William. Most knows me by Willy, but I prefers William. More professional, ya' know. Am a licensed PI."

She saw him wrestling to change character from his natural, animal hostility to some superficial con. He was nervous. That might make for easier answers. As Willy gradually wet his armpits, she asked to see his license, gun and permit. "Figured in your line of work you'd be packing something bigger than a .38?"

"I like the .38. Easy handle. Easy conceal. Used to have a – "

"Ever own a .22?"

"While back, yeah. Had a .357 too."

"Where's the .22?"

"Real canon…. What? … Sold it." His voice was balky. Implied intimidation.

She knew the M.O. Typical low-life. "To who?"

Neef grunted. "What? The .22?" What's this about Sheriff?"

"Chief Deputy. If the Sheriff was here, you'd be in handcuffs. Sold to who?"

"Some dealer."

"Willy? Where were you the night of the sixth – this month." She locked onto glazed eyeballs that looked like they'd spent most days staring into a beer bottle.

"Beats me. Terrible memory for dates." He opened a drawer in the desk. She put her hand on the grip of her gun. "Slow …"

He pulled out a tattered notebook and rummaged through it. "The sixth, sixth … sixth. Yeah. Had an assignment. Sorry, confidential."

"Guess the work you're doing for your upscale clientele, Butch and Bob, is confidential too?" She got the blank-can't-think-fast-enough look. "Wouldn't take us long to run the Bobsie twins' rap sheet. Bring 'em in for questioning." She risked a guess about the envelope. "PIs don't usually pay-off clients, with cash. Partners are they? I'm sure that PI license is worth a lot to you?"

Neef's eyes said fuck you, and every muscle in his scrawny frame pulled at his dysfunctional brain and screamed, hit her. She knew Willy was ten times angrier and wilder than he seemed, and could be over the desk before she could get her gun out. Fortunately, she'd taken the bullets out of Willy's .38 and dumped them on the desk. So it was holster speed versus hurdling speed. "Willy. Just looking for a little cooperation."

Willy's brain worked. Eyes receded, and his voice filtered the anger. "Look! It's just that … well, I don't have a lot of good payin' clients. And … well, this here client, he's important. And if I was to – "

"Divulge too much?"

"Ya' see my point. Exactly."

"You need to see my point." She had to ratchet up her side, not to appear weaker, like two, trumpeting walruses. "I'm working on a murder investigation, you're working petty crime. You either answer a few questions here, or here soon won't be here. Get a warrant and turn this little den of rat shit into its former trashcan self."

"The sixth uh?" He sat down for the first time and faked thinking. "I was on assignment downtown. For a client. Was about – "

"You said 'he.'"

"I did?"

She sighed impatience.

"Right, right. He had me doggin' someone." He tried a plea. "Deputy, ya' know I can't divulge who. Fuck, it's private … good money."

"Okay – for now." She went fishing. "I understand. Instead of my asking questions, let me do the talking. You don't have to answer anything. That way you protect confidentiality. Except, if I make a wrong statement. Then you need to shake your head. That way I'll know I'm on the wrong track. No confidentiality broken, right?"

Willy was working hard at running the words through whatever was up there. It probably sounded like a trick question to him, but he might see it as an easy way to get rid of the cop, knowing if she got a warrant he was done.

"Yeah … okay."

She hooked a thumb into her gun belt, next to the Glock, and started letting out the fishing line. "You were retained by your client for surveillance. To follow someone, a male, because he suspected the target might be having an affair? At the time, he didn't know, only suspected?" She got silent confirmation. "On the evening in question, the target went to the Hilton at around eleven, eleven-thirty and you followed, wearing a trench coat and hat? The target entered by a rear entrance? Went through the kitchen? You took the same route?" No negative response so far. She added the next item, watching for a reaction. "Saw a black bus boy in the kitchen?" Willy's eyes retracted, probably realizing he could be placed at the scene. "Followed the target upstairs in the hotel?" She got her first negative nod. "Target didn't go up?" Another negative. "Did go up?" No reaction. "You didn't follow?" No response. "So you remained in the lobby and waited until he came back down?" Gritt went to work on a timeline. "He was back down in less than thirty minutes?" Got a negative nod. "Less than an hour?" Another negative. "Less than an hour-and-a-half?" No nod. "You picked up on the surveillance?" An unexpected negative response caught her off guard, but she realized it might be Willy who was off guard. *Why would he not pick up the target*? She asked, "You stayed at the hotel?" No response. "For less than half hour?" A negative. "For less than an hour?" Confirmation. "Then you left?" And now she set the hook. "Your surveillance was done?" She got a partial negative nod, twisted into a second-thought confirmation non-nod. It was as good as a lie, although not much good in court. The surveillance wasn't over at one-thirty a.m., but he hadn't followed the first target. But he waited for some reason – maybe to follow Chrystine Goodall? She asked in rapid succession, watching for nods, twitches, flinches, or nothing. She hoped for nothing. "You knew your client before he hired you?" Confirmation. "Your target was Sheriff Cougar?" Maybe a twitch. "You didn't follow him because you needed to identify who he was seeing?" Confirmation. "You waited and when Mrs. Goodall came down you assumed it was her?" Confirmation. "You followed her home and – "

"No fuckin' way. Ya' ain't pinin' no fuckin' murder rap on me. I … I.D. her and that was that. Come back here right after."

She had an unexpected opportunity. Scumball's reaction had come from animal instinct, not reason, some mixture of anger and fear had him spitting denial. She figured he'd followed Ms. Goodall home. But she didn't want to open that can of worms here, alone, with this half weasel, half mongoose, even if the .38 was empty. Now that he was talking, she fired off a couple of final rounds. "Trust you have an alibi for your whereabouts between one-thirty and five?"

"Yeah … yeah. Butch and Bob, they'll vouch for me. Was with them. 'Til mornin."

"Last thing. *I'll just pick a number.* "Your client paid you ten-thousand dollars?"

The non-confirmation was not silent. "What? Deputy, yer fuckin' insane. This interview is over." He stood, muscles straining like steel cables.

She took a step back to ease the confrontation.

"I ain't ever seen that kinda money. If I had, I wouldn't be here fuckin' wastin' my time with you."

She saw a morsel of thought flit behind his eyes.

"He hired me for surveillance, no fuckin' murder."

She left it there, hanging in the air with Scumball's bad breath, Yolla's perfume and Alichi's carp. She'd gotten more than expected – not enough, but lots to work with. In her mind, Neef had cleared Mike. Except she had to establish Mike's whereabouts between one-thirty and four. She'd ask him … soon, when the time was right. She'd confirmed it was just surveillance-for-hire. She hadn't cleared Neef. Because this guy was capable of being a two-bit, two thousand dollar hit man, and he fit the profile of a small-time hood trying to become a big time hood. But Willy's defensive reaction to the suggestion of murder, and to the ten thousand dollars, felt real. As she walked into the grime of 39th Street, she wondered who, other than cops and johns, would ever come down to this subterranean wallow of existence.

CHAPTER FIFTY-FOUR

The upbeat was so up in Mike's office that the always serious Hong was smiling. Waggs was chiding Gibson about how he'd caused such a commotion at Philly airport security last night because he'd forgotten to declare his second weapon, the .38 on his ankle.

Waggs turned to Mike. "I think Hodge was auditioning to be an air marshal. He got introduced to a couple of 'em. Then they talked to some mucky-mucks at Homeland Security. Damn near missed the flight."

"Bullshit. They held the flight for us," said Hodge. "And it was worth it."

Mike said, "Enough. What've you got?"

Waggs said. "You first. You said you had something."

"Sorry, I'm pulling rank. I say who goes first. And you guys go first."

Gibson explained how they'd gotten Vincenzo Pomante to crack. "Like a rotten egg. But the best part is Hawkins. But before I get to that, let me tell you about Rochester." He seldom smiled but his eyes were jumping. "I went back to the McDonald's in Rochester – was hungry. Just kiddin'. Wasn't happy with how little we had on the night Goodall was there in his Benz. Saw the kid again and lo' and behold he had something new. A new friend. This other kid, Tyson, had been working that night too. We didn't know it, but he was out back putting garbage in the dumpster when Goodall pulled over. He gawked at the Benz too. Saw the other guy get in the car. Gave us a pretty good description, even – "

"Hodge, come on, you're killing me," groaned Mike.

It was Ignagni. Kid had two good ID markers. Short. Bald." Gibson unrolled a piece of paper and placed it on the table. "Did this

232

sketch with the artist." Then he put photo of Ignagni next to it. "A match in any court. And the kid picked him out of a photo composite."

As Waggs went back to the Hawkin's interview, Mike was visualizing the nails going into Goodall's feet, then his hands, as he spread them out on that thick, mahogany table in his office. For good measure, he even put a nail through each of his French cuffs, replacing his gold cuff links. Then he saw him in prison garb, cuffed and shackled and shuffling into a cell that was slightly smaller than his executive office. *Soon you bastard.*

Waggs was saying how they'd dropped into Hawkin's office. "Nothing like a couple of investigators to brighten up an egocentric, image-conscious guy's day. He went from pissed-off to pissin' his pants before we were through with him. Phone records showed he'd put a call into Goodall through messenger boy Ebe, and according to Hawkins, he did it in the interests of his ex-wife and their daughter. He told Goodall she was going to ask for a divorce so she could spend more time with her daughter. We weren't buyin' it, and when we told him there'd be a subpoena for his testimony, he came clean. Adding that Mr. Goodall had offered to make sure he would not be financially challenged by the loss of annual support. When I asked why Goodall would give him one damn dime, he rather proudly said he was able to provide ongoing information that was of value to Goodall.

Mike asked. "Did he say what?"

"His second call was an up-date about her plans and he passed on what must have been a real gut-wrencher for Goodall. Maybe the straw that broke the camel's back. More motive. He said his ex was having an affair with someone."

Mike was silent.

"That's about it."

Mike asked. "No more details? Did he say who the affair was?"

Waggs looked at Gibson, Gibson at Waggs. "Didn't ask."

"Leave it with me. We'll get the indictment. Good work."

As Waggs and Gibson walked down the hall Gibson said. "Shit, I thought he'd be jumpin' up and down, callin' the SWAT team to go get public enemy number one. Something's bugging him."

Hong announced the call like any other. "Senator Harriet Rodder, line two."

Mike had already received a harangue from the Mayor, and the DA was doing his best to shield him and the case, but the heat was on. And about to get a whole lot hotter. A call from Senator Rodder meant Goodall was calling in big chips, although Mike considered her a light weight – way too political, and a woman who'd never understood the difference between 'principle' and 'principal.' She wasn't on his Christmas card list, he wasn't on her fundraising list, and she wouldn't know or care about some smalltown sheriff who lived hundreds of miles from Manhattan. There were no votes for her in this phone call but there was a bag full of campaign money from Goodall, Ebe and friends.

"Good morning Senator."

"Senator Harriet Rodder. How are you Sheriff … Cougar."

He guessed the pause was while she looked down to read his name off notes. She probably had very little information on anything other than the fact that Goodall was a big contributor. She paraded out a few pleasantries and then got to the point. How important Mr. Goodall was, how important Syntex's survival was, how important jobs were – she never explained if she meant the ones he'd downsized or the ones he hadn't canned yet – how important the founding principle of innocent until proven guilty was, how important she was, blah, blah, blah. The only thing she forgot was how important it was to catch Chrystine's murderer – of course, as a junior Senator she didn't have to deal with reality, only money and bullshit. In the end, she delivered her best punch, a body blow, not intended to knock him out, just to straighten him up. She spoke of all the funding she'd raised in her last campaign and the election machine she had in Haven County, speaking as if it was a patented, life-saving technology, "… especially important to a sheriff facing an election next year." Mike wanted to gag, but instead gave her feigned acknowledgement. No point pissing her off because he needed as much time as possible to bring down Goodall. He said he understood and that he'd take her comments 'under advisement.' Which meant he'd file them where they belonged, in the toilet.

He could dismiss the Senator all he wanted but he couldn't ignore the reality. The pressure was going to rip the investigation open and expose everything. Goodall's lawyers had served a 'motion to dismiss' and someone had gotten to Pomante, he'd disappeared. The next step was to secure Hawkins as a witness, but before he could make the call he got a call from him.

Hawkins sounded nervous. "Sheriff. I wanted to talk to you directly. Is this line secure?"

"It's the sheriff's office, we don't tap our own phones."

"I have some valuable information."

"That's good."

Hawkins went on to say how the information would be of great interest to Goodall and his defense team. The not too veiled threat irritated Mike. This guy was a key witness and here he is negotiating information for assurances that he would not be called as a witness.

"Mr. Hawkins, whatever it is you have will come out on the witness stand, there's nothing to negotiate."

Hawkins was agitated "You'd better make this worth my while Sheriff. Mr. Goodall would." He hesitated. "Chrystine, in trying to candy coat for Justine the pending divorce and explain that there would no longer be summers on Fire Island and winters in St. Lucia, told her that she had recently fallen in love with another man."

Although Mike had just heard this from Waggs, it was like being hit twice with a baseball bat. Hawkins was talking but it was as if he was shouting from the far end of a tunnel, every word echoing in his head.

"Chrystine could be so child-like when it came to romance. She told Justine things would be different that there'd be less money, but more happiness. Then she dropped the bombshell, the bombshell for your case. She told Justine she was seeing a policeman."

Mike's heart was the only organ in his body that kept working. His brain stopped. Stomach stopped. Nervous system stopped. There was no semblance of thought. Slowly he strung fragments together. *Getting a divorce. Another man. Romance ... maybe it wasn't him?* He was only aware of the fear.

Hawkins talked, Mike didn't hear. "Thought you might like to look into that little tidbit sheriff. He blathered for another minute, repeated his demand not to be called as a witness and said good-bye.

Mike repeated to himself something he often said about criminals he caught, *nine times out of ten, reality catches up with everyone.* He poked around the office watering plants and trying to find reason amid the chaos in his head. The best the emptiness could summon was, *Chrystine is dead. I might as well be dead. Regardless of what happens, I have to get Goodall. Where's Gritt when I need her?*

CHAPTER FIFTY-FIVE

The Mets were losing, Mike was empty, Gritt was dragging. She asked. "Think another cold beer might make us feel better?"

"First one didn't work."

She headed for the kitchen.

"Another beer, then we gotta get at this thing."

They'd come to Mike's house to work on the case. He'd wanted to get away from the office and she wanted to get closer to him. He'd changed into his old reliable jeans and white T-shirt and she'd left her gun belt, cuffs and body cam in the hall. When she came back with two cold ones, he sank into his recliner and turned up the game, "Bases loaded, nobody out. First time in something like forty-two innings." Then he gave her a kiss on the cheek – buying a few minutes before the inevitable.

That kiss is a like a single, I need a homerun. But it loaded my bases. Time for a grand slam. She liked baseball but not now. She grabbed the remote and hit mute.

"What?"

"They're not going score. And I need to."

He didn't protest.

She stood in the middle of the room, as if uncertain where to cross a deep river. "Before I ravage you, there's something we need to discuss … and then you're mine. All mine!"

She sat on the couch and plunged in. "I met with a sleazy PI, a Willy Neef. Ever heard of him?"

"What?" He didn't look up, just kept watching the muted Mets.

"He was following you."

He turned. His eyes were exhausted. "When?"

"Night of the Goodall murder."

"Who is he?" He was back looking at the TV, but not watching it – bases were still loaded, two out.

She sat on the arm of the chair. "I dropped in on the scum. He might even be implicated in the Goodall murder. He was – "

"You think? Like me?" He glanced at the game. The batter struck out. "Figures."

She ran a hand through his hair. "Tell me."

"What's to tell?"

"Whatever you want. And only what you want." His depression filled her heart as she stroked his hair.

He was silent.

"You know your ol'man is involved somehow?"

"Surprise!"

"Seriously, I think he knows more than he's telling us – you."

"No shit." He put his hand on her leg. "He knows … about Chrystine."

"I know."

"What the fuck? Does the whole world know?"

"I just figured it out." She squeezed his shoulder. "Wish you'd told me sooner. Could've helped."

"Nobody could've helped. It was done. It was stupid … it'll be what it'll be."

Who knows other than us, your ol'man and Neef?" Anybody?

"Goodall might even know."

"You're joking? Geez, can it get worse?"

"It is." He gazed at her, his pain was obvious. He related the Hawkin's conversation and emphasized how he'd used the word "policeman," nothing specific. But he knew it was only a matter of time and if Goodall's lawyers got this, the case was lost. So was he. But he didn't give a shit about that. He just wanted Goodall. And Gritt … wanted her to understand, to accept him, warts and all.

"How'd your ol'man find out?"

"He tailed me. Or had me tailed. But I went to him and – "

"You what?"

"What, what?"

"You went to him in the middle of your biggest screw up and told him?" Did you also hand him the bat to hit you with? You crazy man. He's your worst enemy at a time like this. He's going to flog you with this, until the day he dies.

"Hey!" He snapped off the Mets. "He already knew. Had me tailed. Probably hired Neef. Probably knows everything."

"Everything?"

He pulled her onto his lap and she wrapped herself around him, kissing his forehead.

He held her tight and opened up, beginning with the first phone call from Chrystine. It was good to talk. He said he hadn't confided in her earlier because of fear and shame. He talked, she listened.

She saw the gentle boy inside the strong man, and she liked the kid. And she'd be there for the kid, and the man, no matter what.

By the time he'd run through everything, he not only sounded better, his fighting spirit was rekindling, the indomitable Michael Cougar was rising. She'd never been closer to him. "So boss, what're we doing first?"

"First? You really have to ask?"

"I'm asking."

"Before solving the case? Before cleaning up my mess? Before trying to – "

"Michael …"

In one motion, he tipped the recliner back and rolled her onto him, kissing her lightly. "First, I want to try and tell you something, something I've never tried to say before … maybe don't know how to say."

She sank into his powerful arms as his entire body rose into her. "Michael … you don't have to say anything. Nothing. I know you … I want you … as you are, who you are." She took his mouth.

She wanted to devour him, extract every ounce of pain, fill him with joyous pleasure.

He wanted to yell her name and give into her sexual wonders, but all he could manage was a guttural whisper, "My beautiful Gritt." His physical strength knew no bounds.

The chair was cramped and awkward, heightening the desperation. He was forceful, taking her mouth, entangling her tongue, pulling her in, one hand on her buttock, the other, full of hunger, pressing into the small of her back. She raised herself over him, pushing her hands into his chest … the recliner sprung up, almost dumping her on the floor. They burst into laughter. But never let go of each other. He stood, holding her long legs around him. She squeezed – straining every muscle – "Here Michael … here."

Ripping clothes off, they rolled onto the floor, her buttocks pressed into the rough carpet, inflaming her arousal, as his hunger, pain and potency released. His freedom was her ecstasy.

The floor was cool and soothing as they lay silent. She nuzzled into his rock-hard chest.

He rolled her on top and kissed her gently. "Well Deputy Hansen, you solved one problem."

"The most important one, you."

"You've given me a place to go whenever I can't figure me out. Whenever – "

"Remember what we said. Always trust."

"You know Deputy Hansen, you're much more than a professional partner, more than a deputy."

"I do."

He chuckled. "You're the sheriff of Cougar country."

She nudged closer. "To serve and protect." Then she propped up on an elbow. "Just one thing … Cougar country doesn't include any other Cougars, right? As in, no Jackhammer, no Grampa Jackhammer. Only Michael."

They laughed, kissed and hugged.

She said, "As sheriff of Cougar country, I think it's time to go to work and solve this goddamn Goodall case, once and for all." She jumped up, stood over him in all her nakedness. "Let's go."

From his prone position, he saluted. "Yes boss. At your service."

She flashed a wicked grin, "If you're at my service, then I'll have to come back down there and let you do your job."

She did. And he did.

After showering, they brewed coffee and sat at the kitchen table. She took his hand. "Let's start with you. Then put the case together on Goodall. That way we can solve it before anyone knows." *Maybe.* "After you left the hotel, you drove around all night, right? We'll check dispatch … tell me you radioed in, at least once, and – "

"No."

"Anybody see you?"

"Probably the old man."

"Hope not."

"Got a coffee at Dip & Sip – drive through."

"Good. I'll talk to their night shift. What time?"

"Can't figure my old man. What the hell he's thinking. Makes no sense. Him knowing, not saying anything."

She repeated. "What time?"

"Two, two-thirty."

"You in uniform?"

"No."

"Which Dip & Sip?"

"Out on Forty-three, next to Ford dealership."

"Good. That puts you at least twenty, twenty-five minutes from Goodall's."

"You constructing my alibi?"

"Yep."

"You think we can get through this?"

"Mike! This is police business. In case you forgot what your job is. Can you be more specific about the time at the Dip?"

"Only way we're gonna get through this is together. Like that quote from Robert Frost, "The only way out is through."

"I hear you. Isn't gonna be easy – for you."

"You too. Fuck. I haven't made it easy. One-minute I'm good, next I'm not. One-minute I'm crazy about you, next I'm brooding. Brooding about my ol'man – "

She smiled. "It's the 'crazy about me' part that gets me brooding … well, thinking … you know, about us and – "

He touched her arm. "I never want to be a problem for you. Or for my problems to be yours. I respect you … care – "

"I know you care. Just think you're on overload … Goodall … Chrystine, your old man."

"And you." He touched his forehead to hers. "You're my rock."

"I don't want to be one more thing to worry about."

He pulled back. "Sweet Gritt, you're so much more than you realize. You're all I think about, worry about … care about." He brushed her cheek with his finger. "And you are not a rebound. You've been with me long before I met her. She was only – "

She placed a finger on his lips. "Shhhh … I'm here now. And will be. We'll see this through, together."

"Partners." He kissed her.

She ran her hand through his hair. "Always trust each other."

He kissed her again. Longer. "When we get through this I am taking you away, far away from this mess. Not as sheriff and deputy chief, as you and me."

"Michael and Gritt." I like that.

He kissed her again.

She lingered on the edge of fantasy for a moment and then did what she – one of them – had to do. "First things last."

He grinned. "You mean first things first?"

"No. First come my uncontrollable feelings and need for you. But I have to put them last. And put the case first."

"The last thing I want to do right now is talk about this case." He sat up straight. "I might have to delegate control to my Chief Deputy." He winked and sipped his coffee. "Isn't that what a good deputy does?"

"Yes, a good deputy would. But what would a not-so-good deputy do? Maybe she'd – "

"You mean you're a 'bad deputy,' as in bad girl." He smirked.

"I think she'd pull out her cuffs, cuff you, and have her way with you."

He placed his arms on the table, wrists together.

"Like I said, first things last. Let's cuff Goodall … then you."

He went for more coffee. Had to think more clearly. She was a dilemma, a wonderful dilemma.

"You haven't done yourself any favors by going back to your old man, again. Hell, if he was the guy next door you wouldn't give him the time of day. If he was your deputy you'd fire him. So fire him. He's an angry man. And he takes it out on you. Your sister got smart and moved away."

He said. "As soon as we clean this mess up." He spoke as if he was about to try and land a 747 with only one working engine. "What do we know that's new?"

"I found an odd marking on the bureau in room 717. Funny indentation. Tech said it could be from something about two pounds. I was wondering if – "

"Saw it. That night. Was my gun, the metal snap on the pancake holster." He looked guilty. "How the hell did you figure that out?"

She smiled.

They reviewed next best steps. She wasn't too concerned about his alibi, although chances were slim that a Dip & Sip attendant would remember him. They'd meet with Waggs and Gibson, go to the DA and maybe get Goodall back in jail. Ryder was a problem in that they were at a dead end; he'd disappeared. Their best shot was getting Goodall for his wife's murder and continuing to keep Ryder as the main suspect in the Douglas shooting and the Leigerman assault with possible ties to Trott and Riggins. It was loose, but the best they had.

He flopped on the sofa. "Let me try something on you."

She stayed away, sitting in the recliner, in the up position. "Fire away."

"Thought of this a few times but haven't mentioned it. It's either too crazy or too scary. Could make us look like complete idiots." He set his mug on the coffee table. "Suppose some psychopath killed all of them. Some guy, smart enough to pull off all these murders and purposely make them appear disconnected. To mislead us. To taunt us. Chrystine doesn't fit the scenario, unless Goodall was the target. Because this guy is out to get CEOs. All fits. Douglas, Goodall, Trott, Riggins."

She added. "Maybe it's Ignagni. That's why he disappeared. Maybe somebody hired him to do them."

"It's a stretch. And what's the motive?" He shrugged. "At one point I checked backgrounds of the victims and sure enough all of them were serious downsizers; laid-off tens-of-thousands. I thought if it was a serial killer doing CEOs then his motive could be to frighten them or frighten those who were contemplating layoffs so they might think twice if their life was on the line. But, and it's a big but, the pattern is too random to fit that motive."

The phone rang. "Cougar …" He listened. "When? … Be right in."

She was already buckling on her gun.

He headed for the front hall. "Waggs. Call from Bill Edwards, he's on his way to Syracuse." He grabbed his gun belt. "There's been another shooting, last night, about ten. A CEO."

CHAPTER FIFTY-SIX

Mike dispatched Waggs to Syracuse, asked Gritt to follow up with Neef and he went to see the DA, Matt Morten.

Morten was good. An ex-navy seal with ice in his veins. Never backed down from a challenge, but today he seemed less combative. Since Goodall's arrest the media were snapping and yapping at his front door, it was all on incessant radio and TV-talk shows and the front page. The mayor was demanding a press conference, '… with or without you and the sheriff.' Morton wanted one more review of the facts before stepping into the media scrum. "Two o'clock. Come hell or high water. We're doing the press conference."

Mike asked. "What if we pick-up Goodall before that?"

"Don't play with me Mike. Christ knows, everybody else is."

"I'm serious."

Morten held up a blue folder. "Before you do, know that Goodall's lawyers are suing us, the city, and you. And I have two motions to dismiss the case. Not to mention calls from Senator Rodder, the mayor and some jerk at the Chamber of Commerce. All beseeching me to rethink the case, see Goodall as a savior, not a murder, etc. etc. It's bullshit. Unfortunately, it's also my job."

"Suing? On what grounds?"

"Doesn't matter. It's smoke. But I can't have you bring him back in unless we have a slam-dunk to take to the grand jury."

Mike outlined the new facts.

Morten asked. "How reliable are the two McDonald's kids? And if we can't get Pomante in front of a grand jury, we got a problem. Has Philly confirmed the match with ID on Ignagni?"

"You need a grand jury, I don't. I can get another warrant and do this immediately. It doesn't have to go to the grand jury, yet. It'll isolate you a bit and you can always blame it on me. I'm prepared to take the heat just to get this bastard in my nine-by-nine room again. I'll make him eat every lie he's told us."

"Bring him in. This time with less pomp and ceremony. Think you can do it before the press conference?"

"If I can find him."

• • •

Gritt figured the creep Neef had been around the Goodall woman a few hours before she was killed and maybe inadvertently saw something or put her in harm's way. They were pretty sure the sleaze hadn't killed her. Wasn't smart enough to get past the alarm system, and the scene was too clean to be his M.O. Guys like him never used one shot; they're maniacal in these situations, pumping multiple shots into a victim. Even if his alibi was weak, it was probably to cover up some other crime, not murder. Although she didn't get anything new from Neef, she wanted to box him into a corner, just in case they needed a witness to establish Michael's timeline and exit from the hotel.

CHAPTER FIFTY-SEVEN

Mike could only handle a couple more questions and then he was done. The media were relentless, asking the same idiotic questions a dozen different ways. Over and over he would say, "I'm not going to answer any questions about evidence," but, over and over, the next headline-hunting ass would ask something about evidence. He was sure the media's hiring policy placed a priority on high school dropouts. He pointed into the scrum and said. "Just two more questions." He took the first one then heard a shout from the back.

"Sheriff." It was his old man. "If this is a murder-for-hire, have ya' found evidence of payoff money … know what I mean? If ya' haven't, how come? Know what I mean?"

Mike was between dumbfounded and boiling. The old man sounded half-bagged. How dare he show up and open his big mouth. He heard the wavering in his reply. "This is a press conference. Questions from the media only. Thank you everyone." He turned and walked away with a cacophony of questions following him.

Gritt and Matt Morten were on his heels. Matt closed the door to Mike's office. "What the hell was that?"

"He was drunk," said Gritt.

"I don't give a shit if he was dead," said Matt. "You don't ask a question like that."

She said. "He's still trying to play cops and robbers. Nothing better to do. Still harassing Mike."

"At a press conference? In public?" Matt was furious.

"He's an idiot," she said. "If he – "

"No. He's not," said Mike. "He had a reason. May have been drunk but he knew what he was doing. Showed up at the last minute. Fired off his question – to embarrass me for sure – but that wasn't his only reason."

She said. "Mike. When it comes to you and this case, your old man can't control himself. He has to humiliate you. In public. A few drinks and his emotions got the better of him. He may have been a cool calculating cop, but that was yesterday. I've watched him around you. Won't give you an inch. Has to upstage you. There may have been a message in his question, but I think his deranged ego got the better of him."

Mike headed for the door. "I'll be back."

Matt turned to Gritt. "Is he really that bad?"

"Worse."

Mike found the taxi in the driveway and his father in the kitchen. "First, I should arrest you for DUI. It's three o'clock in the afternoon for christsake!"

"Well hello St. Peter. Have a drink. Pretend it's communion, I'll break some bread."

Mike rattled around in the cupboard looking for the coffee pot. His father detested drip coffee, always used a percolator, an old aluminum one his mother had bought thirty years ago. Mike had warned him about aluminum, but he'd ignored him. While the coffee brewed, his father brooded. Then he went to the living room to fetch his bourbon.

"That's the last thing you need," said Mike. He pointed at the coffee. "What the hell do you think that's for?"

"So ya' think ya' got Goodall, uh?"

"Stop with the Jack Daniels and I'll talk to you."

"You'll talk to me? Thank you, Wyatt Earp. I think ya' need to talk to yerself. And that asshole DA. You guys are gonna blow this. Ya' can't close it. I'm tellin' ya'. His defense team'll tear ya' apart if ya' leave one tiny hole. And ya' got a big one. The money. Ya' can't connect Goodall and Ignagni unless ya' can connect the money."

"We've got them together in a McDonald's shortly before the

crime. Two witnesses. And Pomante and Hawkins – ”

"Ain't enough. Reasonable doubt. That slippery slope begins and ends with the money."

"Perk Allen made the connection. Records show Goodall made a withdrawal for twenty-five thousand. After that it's a cash transaction and no way we can trace that. It's gone wherever Ignagni is gone. DA is prepared to – ”

"Bullshit! He's gonna lose this one. And it'll be on you. What with all the pressure. Those mucky-mucks don't want someone like Goodall going to jail. He's one of them, climbing the ladder on the backs of us lesser-lights. The politicians, the business elite, they're all crooked in one-way or another. They want to be heroes without doing what heroes have to do. They know if he's guilty, they're all guilty. I'm tellin' ya', he ain't going down. Not unless ya' tie off the last loophole. The money." His alcohol-burning eyes half commanded, half begged. "Did ya' ever think that maybe the twenty-five thousand was an advance payment and just maybe Ignagni might put it somewheres safe for a few days while he cased the joint? Maybe in a bank account? Did ya', uh?"

Mike poured coffee and moved the Jack Daniels. "You're repeating yourself."

"'Cause yer not gettin' it. Why the fuck do ya' think I came to your bullshit talk show. So I could be proud of my son? I don't think so. So I could learn something new? Don't think so. So I could maybe embarrass you into doing some real cop work?"

"Screw you. I'm sick and tired of you shoving it up my ass every time I get close to solving it. And in public. That's unforgivable. You – ”

"Unforgivable? What the fuck do you know about forgiving? Yer mother was the only one in this family who knew the meaning of the word. Not your sister, not you."

"What about Don? Does he forgive you?"

"What about him? Least he shows me some respect and – ”

"Respect. Now there's a word you might want to look up in the dictionary. You'll find it doesn't mean, if you're nice to me I'll be nice to you, and we'll pretend we're okay, and we'll call it respect. You and Don have been working from the same dictionary for years."

Jack remained hunched over his coffee. "You and your smart-ass college talk. Don never talks to me like that. Shows respect. I'm his father. He was doing fine 'till that asshole Goodall let him go. Never shoulda' done that. He's a good kid. You and yer sister are just a little misdirected. Immature. Never want to listen. Know-it-alls."

"Know-it-all? If Emily and I are like that it must be in the genes. Problem is sometimes we know something you don't, but you can't admit it. There's no give. You wouldn't admit you were wrong if someone held a gun to your head. Not sure a bullet could penetrate it anyway."

"Go ahead. Put a gun to my head. Ya' think I deserve it? Do it." He held his forefinger to his temple. "Is that what ya' want? Me dead and yer mother alive. Right? Always have. Never forgave me for – "

Mike yelled. "It's a fucking metaphor. For your stubbornness. Nothing to do with mom."

"Oh yeah. Let the truth be out. I killed her. I was driving. I made sure that stupid Syntex truck was good and close before I hit the brakes. I caused the snowstorm. I insisted on going to the stupid convention. I – "

"Enough!" Mike turned away. "Grumpa insisted you go. And when he said go, you jumped. He had your number and played it over and over again. And you danced to his tune one too many times."

"He's an asshole. What can I say. But he was a good cop. Tough. Strict. Taught me a lot."

"And that's enough, right? That's what fathers are all about? Go ahead, keep rationalizing. Lie to yourself. Whatever you do, don't admit he was, still is, a fucking bully."

"See what I mean about respect. Ya' don't even respect your grandfather. And he's dying in a decrepit home where they don't give a shit about life or death, don't even change his fuckin' diapers after eleven at night. You don't know what respect means."

Mike went to the door. "You're impossible!" He walked out, slammed the screen and it bounced back, tearing two screws out of the hinge.

Jack reached for the Jack Daniels.

CHAPTER FIFTY-EIGHT

They had Goodall back in custody. Gibson had picked him up before the press conference and booked him into county jail. The judge had revoked his bail and upon learning he had taken a trip to Bermuda, took his passport.

Mike was watering his plants, thinking about his mother and trying to forget about his father when the phone rang. He ignored it, but after six rings he knew Hong was away from her desk so did what he shouldn't have, picked it up.

"Cougar."

"Sheriff, this is Judy Spade, Westhaven Chronicle. Is there any truth to the rumor that Chrystine Goodall was having an affair before she was murdered?

He didn't reply.

"Would you care to comment?"

"No comment."

"A source says it involved a policeman."

He collected himself. "We are not commenting any further than we did at the press conference on any aspect of the case, especially rumors. There'll be another press conference soon." He hung up. The rest of the flowers went thirsty. His mind was trapped between the bricks, void of thought.

Gritt walked in. "Guess what? The Fibbies may actually be doing something worthwhile. Waggs spoke to Briefcase Bill in Syracuse. Good news, bad news. The good news: They're bringing divers into Cattarugus Park. Apparently, someone found an odd-looking yardstick floating in the quarry. Had a funny cut made in one end and was covered in blood. Man who found it didn't know it was blood, but the deputy did."

"Yardstick?"

"You know. Wooden one. I got one in my kitchen. Never use it. Says Mancari's Hardware on it.

"So what?"

"Well, when I was in the FBI, I saw something similar. It can be a deadly tool. Some nuts use it to commit suicide."

"With a yardstick?"

"They cut a notch in one end. Put a shotgun in their mouth. Put the notched end on the trigger – which is too far away to reach – and boom."

"You thinking Ryder?"

"Yep."

"When do the divers go down?"

"He was in that area and spotted once at the park and maybe twice. Suicide after you've murdered a few people is not unusual for nutcases."

"What's the bad news?"

"Syracuse. Waggs said the M.O. is looking a lot like others. .30-30, one shot, CEO. Guy was getting in his car. Reserved parking spot with his name large as life on it. Like a bullseye."

"Was he a big downsizer?"

"Don't know."

"Find out."

She reached for his desk phone.

"Use your own. Gotta talk to Gibson."

She smiled warmly, he smiled coolly.

Something's bugging him. She left talking on her mobile.

He called Gibson. "Hodge, want you to do a little checking on banks. It's possible that Ignagni may have deposited the twenty-five thousand if he got it from Goodall that night at McDonalds. You know, he might not like carrying all that cash around if he was going to be busy. Check ATMs for deposits or transfers. Start with banks here, if nothing, try some in Rochester around the McDonalds. Or between

McDonalds and any rental car agency in the area." He paused. "Did we ever check rentals at the airport with a photo of Ignagni? … Shit. Do it. But do the deposits first."

Gritt was back. "Andover Wire and Cable. Employs sixteen-thousand people. Used to employ twenty-two thousand. That's a lot of bitter people. What are the odds that one could be a copycat?"

"One in nine thousand," said Mike.

"I flunked math. Maybe that's why I never win much at the ponies."

"I'd like to come up with something before Briefcase Bill rolls in." He put his feet on the desk, looked out the window. "If we take Chrystine's murder out of the mix…."

She noticed he'd dropped her surname.

"We have four dead CEOs and Leigerman the scared-shitless number cruncher. And it all started here. Somehow a serial killer doesn't make sense. The way it's done, the execution – pun intended – is too inconsistent. Douglas was up close and personal. Leigerman a bad miss. Trott from long distance, with misses. Riggins, up close and personal. Syracuse … what's the guys name?"

"Evans. Bob Evans."

"Not the restaurant guy?"

"No relation."

"Syracuse … was it a good shot, long distance?"

"Great shot," she said. "Came from a ravine three-hundred yards away."

Mike rolled out a white-board and started writing. "Maybe Douglas was a one-off hit – for reasons we haven't yet figured out. Ryder, being a bitter nut got the idea and did Leigerman and Trott."

"Why Trott. He didn't work for her?"

"Don't know. Maybe Trott was a copycat. Then Pittsburgh was a copycat. Syracuse a copycat.

She said. "Or … maybe Ignagni is doing all of them. That's why he isn't showing up. He's not finished. Somebody with deep pockets and a deep hatred of downsizing CEOs hired him. Maybe a union? They got money. They did Hoffa. And he's clever enough to mix the pattern so we'd never figure him for it."

"Except we have him doing Chrystine for Goodall," said Mike.

"Unless she was a mistake. And the husband was the target all along and Ignagni had to take her out because – "

"Don't start down that road again. We got Goodall for it. Besides he met with Ignagni. Evidence is there. If Gibson can find the deposited cash, we'll deposit him in a prison for the rest of his life."

They worked through a pizza and Coke dinner and kept coming back to the copycat theory.

She mused. "You think it's the same copycat working different cities? Or different guys in each city?"

He went back to the board. "Different guys. One a good shot. One a lousy shot. Maybe another one who's good close up. That takes guts – ex-military. Or maybe the close ups and crack shots are one guy and the sloppy ones another." He circled the names with a red marker That would make Douglas, Riggins and Evans the same … in Westhaven, Pittsburgh, Syracuse. Then Leigerman and Trott the same … in Westhaven and Rochester. Shit! There's no pattern." He sat down, cracked his knuckles and ate another slice of pizza.

By nine o'clock the white board looked like a multicolored pasta dish and she was doodling while he counted bricks. He dropped his feet to the floor. "Let's go to Frankie's. I'm buying."

He ate again – steak, mashed potatoes, tapioca pudding and coffee. She had a couple of beers, enough to loosen her tongue.

"Mike, I think you might have a bit of a blind spot. You know what I'm saying? You're so focused on getting Goodall you might be ignoring some pieces."

"Shit. I forgot to tell you. I had a call from a reporter this afternoon. Asked me to comment on a rumor that Chrystine Goodall was having an affair … with a policeman."

In mid-slurp, she looked down the length of the glass. There was nothing to say.

He scowled. "Getting too close. I'm going to have to come clean."

"Wait a minute, wait a minute. Slow down a sec. You're not going anywhere, to anybody, until we got this figured out. Silence is a value. Right?"

"Virtue."

"You said he said it was a rumor – "

"She."

"What?"

"She. The reporter was a she."

"Since when do we react to rumors?"

"Since when has the sheriff had sex with a murder victim a few hours before she's killed?"

"Good." She was staring into his eyes. With compassion. "Do you feel better? You've said it out loud. You know, and I know, it's irrelevant. So, let's keep it there. Don't comment, don't tell anybody. And if you have to deny it. Lie. This is about a lot more than a one-night stand. Or your feelings of guilt. We've agreed. First, we solve the murder, then it goes away." She leaned across the table. "Michael, I know you're an honest guy and you need to do what's right. Well, I'm telling you, coming out on this is not right. Would do *no* good. And would let Goodall off for a murder we know he had done. And it's the end of your career."

"That's not necessarily a bad thing. End my career. Move on. Maybe there's something over the horizon for me."

"Yeah, prison." Her eyes delivered her feelings. "Michael, please. Cop is in your blood – a good cop. There's plenty of good things over the horizon for you."

She's right – god she's beautiful when she's serious. "Maybe a PI? Thought about it before. Same stuff, no bureaucracy, no political bullshit, less work – "

"Less money."

"But there's just me to support."

She waved to Helen for more coffee. "That's another discussion for another day. Right now, let's stay away from the media rumor machine."

"Goodall must have leaked it. Hawkins didn't like my response and went to him. He paid him and got what he needed."

"And that, my friend, is our hook. That's witness tampering. Or can be construed that way. Let me pay a little visit to Goodall's lawyers tomorrow."

• • •

The next day Gritt came back to the office about noon and said Goodall's lawyers had pleaded ignorance and stonewalled, but she was sure they got the message. She'd also called Hawkins and informed him likewise. But it didn't make Mike feel any better.

Just after lunch, she came into the office with a healthy salad dish in her hand and shit written all over her face. She walked to the white board and slashed a red marker through Dick Ryder's name. "Found him at the bottom of the quarry. In his car. Dead for days. Shot himself in the head with a .30-30. Still a mystery as to how he did that and drove the car off the cliff. How's a guy shoot himself and drive? Why?"

"Could have put the car in gear, pointed it toward the quarry, hit the gas – like Thelma and Louise – and pushed the trigger with that yardstick gadget as he went off the cliff."

They talked through the impact Ryder's death had on their theories and how it would change their tactics. "There's still some loose ends on Ryder," said Mike. "I want you to tie them up ASAP."

"Means I'll have to go to Oleans. Shouldn't I be here right now?"

"I'm fine."

Hong called out. "Your sister on line two."

Gritt got up to leave but he motioned her to stay. "Hi Em." He listened. "When…? Do they know how…? I'll find him. Call as soon as you know more … Take care." He hung up. "My grandfather died. Under suspicious circumstances."

"How's that?"

"Don't know much. Someone found him in the bathtub. Suspect he fell, but police say a few things don't add up. Emily will stay on top of it and let me know. Have to tell Pops…. Hope he's sober."

"I'm sorry Mike."

"Maybe you can hang here while I tell the ol'man."

"You got it."

CHAPTER FIFTY-NINE

Three knocks on the back door and no answer. The taxi in the drive meant he was sleeping or drunk. Mike opened the door. His father was sitting at the kitchen table with Jack Daniels. It was lunchtime, the bottle was half-empty.

"Pops, you okay?"

His father did a slow turn toward him. It was as if he was staring down a vacant tunnel. He looked exhausted, hollow. His eyelids hung like wet burlap sacks, his jaw drooped as if his mouth was full of marbles. His face was flush with booze.

"The prodigal son. Mr. smart-ass. College know-it-all. Guessin' ya' don't know it all this time."

He didn't sound too drunk. No slurring. But that wouldn't last long, not when he heard about his father. Mike decided to get right to it. "Pops. I have something to tell you." He sat down. "It's not good."

"Never is with you?"

"Grumpa died…. Last night. I had a call from Em."

"I know."

"You know what?"

"I know. What part of 'I know' don't you get?" Below hanging eyelids his eyes were in pain."

"You know he died?"

"What did you study in college, pig Latin? Ya' don't even fuckin' understand English."

"How'd you know?"

"A picture fell off the wall. The one of him and me and you. Thought maybe you was dead too. Just my luck. I was sittin' in the livin' room watching TV and bang, the fuckin' thing fell. I knew then…. Satisfied?" He drained and refilled his glass.

Mike had heard the old wives' tale about pictures falling off the wall when someone died so didn't raise the obvious question about cops never believing in coincidences. He didn't know what to say so made coffee and sat down with a bag of chocolate chips.

Jack said. "He was a good cop, too bad he went bad. Not dirty bad, just mental bad. Began to lose it in last few years on the job. Hated the desk job, drove him nuts. I think he was senile, goin' on about crazy stuff. But it was those bastards that tied him to a desk that killed him. His mind was never the same. Angry all the time. Used to be sharp as a whip. Tough. Gave no quarter. Good cop. Cleaned up a lot of scum. Then died at his desk." The eyelids had doused the fire in his eyes and he was talking to the tabletop.

Mike didn't interrupt even though he was tempted to correct the story. Jack Senior had never been assigned a desk job, it was Jack Junior who got chained to a desk the last two years of his career. Jack Senior had walked the beat until his last day. And he never let his son forget it, 'Was at my post to the end.'

Jack looked at him. "Don't let them do that to you son. Do what you want but don't get tied to a desk. Quit. Get fired. Get downsized – like Don or Archie – even that ain't as bad. I hope you fry that bastard Goodall. Can you get that billionaire asshole on his board too? These guys are killers. Serial killers. Goin' from one company to another and ruining hard working Americans' lives. If you put Goodall away for life, it's a start. Hey, what 'da 'ya hear about the guy in Syracuse?

Mike didn't respond and left him to swirl the bourbon around the glass.

"How'd he die?"

".30 -30."

"My ol'man. Not the corporate rapist…. That's what they are ya' know. Raping people of their life's earnings in order to cash-in bigger stock options. Bastard deserved to die."

"Em didn't have much information. Apparently, he fell in the bathtub."

"Apparently? What kind of answer is that. Have they got rookies on the case? Wouldn't surprise me. They don't give a shit about old people. Leave 'em to die whenever and wherever. Your sister on the case?"

"No. But she'll stay close to it."

"She better. Especially if they suspect something."

"They're not saying that. Just said a few things didn't add up."

"What's she know? Practically a rookie."

"Ten years is not a rookie Pops. But she couldn't get much; it's early. His door was locked. So they didn't find him until this morning. And they can't find his room key. Appears as if he fell. Wasn't very steady on his feet. Should never have been taking a bath alone."

"Why not? Old bastard did everything alone all his life, why quit now." He finished another bourbon. "Ya' know they only change diapers two times a day in that shithole. Who pisses only twice a day? Specially at his age. Poor bastard. No wonder he was taking a bath." He poured the bourbon and when he set the bottle down Mike picked it up and put it on the counter. The lids rolled back, and the eyes ignited. "What…. My ol'man dies and now ya' think yer my father." He grabbed the bottle and slammed it back on the table. "I don't need a father. I don't have a father." He drank. "Never had a father. Never was a father. Just a solider and a cop. A good solider and a good cop. It's all I ever learned. How the hell do' ya' learn to be a father. Nobody teaches ya'. Nobody tells ya'. Ya' either get it or ya' don't. I didn't." He drank. "Neither did he. Never got it. And ya' can't teach what ya' don't know. Just keep making the same fuckin' mistakes over and over. It's a plague. Once it's in a family ya' can't stop it. Just like them fuckin' downsizers. They can't stop. It's in their blood." He grabbed the bottle.

Mike clamped a hand on top of his father's hand. "Pops. That's enough."

Jack rose like the Loch Ness monster. "Ya' can't stop it. Nobody can stop it. But somebodys gotta stop it. Ya' don't get it do ya'? Yer not cut out to be a cop. It's not in yer blood. Maybe you'll quit when this is over. Should. 'Cause I won't be able to help ya' anymore." He walked into the bedroom and came back carrying his Smith and Wesson .38. "This is the last time I'm gonna help?"

"What the fuck is that for?"

Jack sat at the table and put the gun next to the bottle. "Man's best friends, Jack Daniels and his buddies Smith and Wesson. They'll get ya' more respect than any weak-assed human ever will."

Mike knew he had to stop the roiling mix of anger, regret and booze. "Grumpa was eighty-three wasn't he?"

Nothing.

"Had a pretty good life until – "

"Until he died. Right. Until he died. We all have a pretty good life until we die. Some just don't die soon enough."

The phone rang. And rang and rang. Jack said. "Fuck'em. Don't answer it."

Mike picked it up. "Hello." He listened for the longest time only giving muted sounds of acknowledgement. "You're sure?" He leaned back against the wall and looked like he was going to slide to the floor. He glanced at his father who was holding onto both of his good friends. "I will. Don't worry…. Call you back." It was no more than four paces from the phone to the table, but it was a Grand Canyon.

CHAPTER SIXTY

Matt Morten scanned the spectators from his table at the front of Room III in the Adam Thomas Smith County Courthouse. Thirty people, but no Mike. He figured Mike would have been there for the second-degree murder indictment against Alexander Goodall. They'd put together a solid case, and with a good jury they should send him away for life. Chief Deputy Hansen was absent too.

CHAPTER SIXTY-ONE

Mike hung up and sat next to his father. "Pops. When we were talking earlier you mentioned how upset you were with the care they were giving Grumpa. Mentioned something about never changing his diapers at night. Remember that?"

No response.

"When you and I went to Syracuse that was the first time you'd visited him in … what, two, three years?"

Nothing.

"So how do you know they don't change diapers at night?" Mike's pulse pounded inside of his temples – anger, and perhaps sadness. He saw the fists tighten around the two friends. "Em didn't tell you."

"Nobody told me." He stood up, gun in one hand and the glass – spilling bourbon – in the other. "I found out for myself. What else is new? Nobody tells me anything. Never has. That's okay. I can take care of myself. Sure as hell nobody was taking care of my father. Poor bastard. Stunk like a steer pen. Fuckin' awful."

Mike almost whispered. "Pops. Put the gun on the table."

"He deserved better. Was a good cop. Shouldn't be humiliated like that. Nobody cared. I didn't care."

"You cared. That's why you went to him. Right? Last night? Of course, you cared." Mike slowly stood, hoping to get close enough to ease the gun out of his father's grasp. They were like two bull moose, sizing up the situation. Emily said the staff confirmed their father visited last night, signed in at 10:07 p.m. But never signed out. They also said Jack Senior could never have gotten into the bathtub on his own, someone must have helped him. The police were following up on it.

Jack bellowed. "There ya' go again. Thinkin' ya' know it all. Ya' still don't know shit. College-ass education didn't do ya' no fuckin' good. Ya' think ya' know me? Well, ya' don't. Never have. Never will. My ol'man didn't know me either. Here I go to help him and what the fuck does he do. Same old shit. Starts beatin' on me. He mighta been crazy but not when it came to remembering my shortcomings. He stunk so bad I said I was goin' help him take a bath. First, he says okay. Then I get him in there and he starts telling me how to do it. Tells me I never could do nothing without him. I just up and let go. He dropped like a sack of potatoes." He looked at Mike with empty eyes. "Didn't even sound bad. Maybe the water broke his fall. Hit his head and slipped under the water. I just watched…. He drowned." He leaned against the kitchen counter as Mike stepped a few inches closer. "It was as if I was looking at a crime scene. Not mine. I saw it, took stock and left it untouched. Took his key off the nightstand, locked the door and left. Knew none of those lazy fuckin' bitches would be looking in on him 'til morning. I was right."

Mike reached for the gun, felt the cold barrel, squeezed gently. "Pops – "

"Fuck you!" He yanked the gun away and pointed it at Mike. "Don't play cop with me. I'm in charge here, not you."

Fear flooded through Mike. He stepped back. Booze and guns were at the top of the situation-risk list and his father's anger was unpredictable. "Pops, put the gun down. This is Mike."

"I know who the fuck ya' are. Yer the kid who doesn't listen. Who doesn't get it. Who doesn't want his father's help, even when ya' need it. And ya' need it bad now. Well, I'm gonna help you this one last time. So listen up." He waggled the gun and pointed at the chair. "Sit." He sat on the other side of the table, out of reach.

"Pops – "

"Just listen. For once!" He gulped half a glass of bourbon. "I did it. I – "

"It was an accident," said Mike.

He pointed the gun. "Shut up."

Mike folded his arms across his chest trying to look relaxed and unthreatening while calming his nerves. He hoped the fear wasn't too obvious.

"I killed him. I dropped him. He pissed me off one time too many. I didn't even feel bad. Still don't. But the killing has to stop. It hasn't solved anything. The fuckin' world goes on, passing by the dead bodies like they're roadkill on an expressway to economic progress. They do nothing until the body count is so fuckin' high they can't ignore it. Money keeps running everything. I thought I could help, you know, make a difference. Start a movement, like Jimmy Hoffa did with the Teamsters. Ya' know they killed more than a few poor bastards. Jimmy took one to the head. That's the price ya' pay. So I thought, what the hell. Even thought it might make my ol'man proud. He liked Jimmy Hoffa ya' know. But I fucked up somewheres. Didn't plan it good enough. Got off the rails with that Goodall woman. If – "

Mike's voice ripped out of his throat. "What the fuck?"

Jack pointed the gun. "Shut the fuck up. 'Til I'm done."

Mike's emotions raged as he tried to maintain control. His father was in a dark place, a depressed state. But the anger was receding. *Keep him talking 'til the gun is eliminated.*

Jack rattled on. "You don't know the half of it. Never did. But that's okay because now yer gonna know it all. And be the hometown hero. I'll make you the hero. You know in the end, we all just want to be heroes to somebody. Just remember, when yer in the big parade, give the old, street-wise cop some credit for a little help. A little respect." He drank. "I started with Douglas. Right after Archie committed suicide. Douglas as good as took Arch's life. So I took his. Like the Bible says, An eye for an eye."

Mike felt the *no* form somewhere in his bowel, a desperate cry of denial, a screaming leap to try and avoid the black reality that was enveloping him.

"I thought when Weiss died it was our town's lucky day. Then Douglas showed up and sacked three thousand people, including

Archie. I figured he was all I'd have to do. But no, next they send in asshole Goodall. Twenty-five hundred more innocent lives. The town, our town, my town was dying. Decent people being prevented from making a decent living, asking nothing more than to do what they'd always been doing, workin' hard. I had to do something. And it wasn't just here; it was everywhere. That's when I figured it out. Knock a few of these fuckers off and pretty soon the rest of them would get the idea. If you keep downsizing innocent workers, you could be next. Figured it would put a stop to the carnage … right across the country. If it worked, they'd stop the downsizing. I call it deadsizing. Killin' towns like ours – dead – one after the other. After those office shootings in Ohio, Pennsylvania, San Francisco, I thought yeah … Posties do it too. But they're shootin' the wrong people. Gotta go to the top. Cut the head of the beast off and you stop 'em." He stopped for breath, and a swig. "That's why I woulda like to have gotten that bastard Schodenhauer – and a few more greedy-ass shareholders … maybe somebody else will. See, I figured if I did a few then the idea would catch on. Ya' know, copycat."

Mike's mind was red-lining. Emotion seared his brain, his heart was beyond pumping capacity. He tried to shut down. He was in the kitchen of his family home where his mother had baked chocolate-chip cookies and made oatmeal porridge, where life had had so much promise. And where so many of the verbal battles with his father had begun. Now … he fought to detach himself, to find the cop in him. He was being confronted by a blathering drunk, an angry, depressed, psychotic madman, reciting some farcical fiction that was, in fact, a confession. It was his father. It was real. *You're a cop. Handle it.*

Jack continued. "I was following Goodall. Getting his habits. Bastard never stopped traveling. In town he was pretty predictable. I staked out his house. Got his routine. One night I followed him to Rochester. He meets up with a guy I recognize, Sal Ignagni. Big time bopper from Philly. I knew I was onto something. It wasn't that first meeting at McDonalds, was a couple weeks later. After that Goodall goes in the direction of the airport and I follows Ignagni. He hangs around Rochester for a few hours then drives to Westhaven. Drives out to The Hill and past Goodall house, cases the joint. Parks his car at the bottom of the hill behind Goodall's and walks up through the woods. I follow him. He broke a window, was in and alarm off in no time. Obviously had the code. I sat tight then went up for a look-see. That's my footprint you got." He leaned back and tried to lift his foot and damn near fell off the chair. "These shoes right here, walked the beat for years. The lady showed up little before two. I decided it was time for me to get outta there. I knew what was next. Before I made the edge of the woods I heard the shot. Got to my car and waited. Ignagni was back in minutes. I followed him. Pulled him over out on Cross County Road. Used ID, said I was undercover. Walked him down to the river. He was cool as a cadaver, even belligerent. Fuckin' Wop. Gave him an alternative, spill his guts or I spill his brains. Told me to 'fuck off.' I blew out his kneecap. Then the big shot talked like a canary. I got the whole scheme. Goodall had the hit on his wife. Fifty-thousand. I knew right then I had a perfect scheme for getting the bastard put away. Better he rot in a fuckin' prison than go quick and simple. In there, instead of being the screwer he'd be the screwee. I capped Ignagni. He had the twenty-five thou' on him. I took it. Opened an account in his name over in Rochester, deposited it to complete the frame. You, and the professor, never found it – pretty lousy police work."

Mike realized Jack was talking pretty well through the booze. *Maybe not as drunk as he seems.*

"Her dead didn't fit the fear pattern I was tryin' to create but it still got me Goodall. And it was a good challenge for you. Ryder was an added bonus, and added to your test. After I did the shooting at Syntex – scaring Leigerman was good but it was really to set up Ryder. Got his prints on the quarters and left'em there for you. Simple. I set him – actually you – up. Gave me more time to do what I had to do for this godforsaken town. You shoulda heard the talk around town. People were sorry I missed Leigerman. I don't know what the fuck you and those jerk-off Fibbies were thinking about Ryder. Any idiot should've seen he couldn't do it. I told ya' those Fibbie profilers are no better than reading Tarot cards. The fact that he was a wingnut helped my cause. Anyways, from there the mission was straight ahead – "

"Anyways?" Mike tasted the bile in the back of his mouth. "Anyways? That's all you can say?" He slammed his hand down and pushed up from the table. "It's not even a fuckin' word. It's *anyway*, you … fuckin' moron." He didn't see the gun. He didn't see the drunk. He didn't see his father. He saw the man who walked away knowing Chrystine was about to be killed. The man who could have saved her. In one ferocious, move he was around the table and twisting Jack's arm behind his back. The cold-blooded killer was yanked to his feet, the bottle crashed to the floor and the gun dropped on the table. He ripped the second arm around in its socket. There was only a drunken stupor of resistance. He snapped on the cuffs. "Jack Cougar, you are under arrest for the murder of Chrystine Gallagher-Goodall, you have the right to remain silent, anything you say may be used against you. You have – "

"Heard it before."

Mike was about to pull his gun and stick it against the back of his skull. He had to get control – of himself.

Father and son sat three feet apart with a lifetime between them. Jack's bloated eyelids had collapsed to slits and Mike stared at the pigeon-shit floor. The box-like kitchen was saturated with anger, regret, despair, disbelief, even relief. He had re-cuffed his father's hands in front and planted him in a chair at the table and put the gun in a drawer. He stared at the slouching form that used to be his father, looking for some trace of sanity, some semblance of understanding. Gravity gradually pulled the liquor-laden body into a slump and he made noises that were a series of grunts, snorts and snoring. At one point, his own disgusting snort startled him and he damn near fell off the chair. He lifted an eyelid, glowered, then went comatose again. He obviously preferred it there.

They'd been sitting for twenty minutes and he still had no idea what to do. Nothing made sense. It was as if the billions of cells in his brain had died. His body felt like it had been drained of bodily fluids, embalmed and replaced with toxic chemicals. He was in no hurry to confront the destructive emotions swirling around the tiny kitchen, and his father was not about to return any time soon.

He went to the bathroom and buried his face in a cold washcloth. He didn't feel the cold. He tried hot. No relief. He tried peeing.

It sounded like thunder does when lightning strikes a tree outside your house. Deafening. Lifting the body off the floor, not from the sound but from the entire nervous system firing shock waves through the body – from instantaneous fear. Knowing in that moment that life and death were shaking hands.

He saw his pee spray across the toilet seat, across the floor, felt it on his hand and down his leg. He was through the door before his zipper was up. Somewhere in the hall he heard his voice exploding … "Nooo."

He dropped to one knee on the floor and watched the life-giving blood ooze across the pigeon-shit spots. Never did the brutality of death get past his shield – the emotional shield cops erect to compartmentalize reality. But this could not be compartmentalized. It was brutal in its simplicity – one minute, one lapse, one bullet, one father. The tears screamed to be released but years of building defensive mechanisms – from the first day his father had picked him up off this floor and spanked him – protected him from having to be the real son. He could be the cop his father wanted: tough, stoic, false. False had been the cornerstone of their false relationship, built on false expectations. And now the father was dead. Of his own hand. The same hand that had killed half a dozen people, including his own father.

He could not make sense of his feelings. Anger. Sadness. Abandonment. He called Gritt.

CHAPTER SIXTY-TWO

They were all waiting to go to John "Jack" Orville Cougar Junior's funeral. Yesterday, they had buried John "Jack" Orville Cougar Senior in the same plot. Mike had stood over the freshly dug graves and commented that his father and grandfather would be closer in death than they'd ever been in life. Today's funeral would be a small affair, as was yesterday's. The police department had distanced themselves from everything, despite Jack's decorated career. After all, there weren't many serial killers who got a parade and twenty-one-gun salute.

Mike and Gritt were at his place, still in their civvies, procrastinating, not looking forward to the day's events. He was ambivalent, she uncertain.

She said, not sure it was the right thing. "As bad as he was, he was still your father. I think you need to do it for you. Closure ... or something like that."

He straightened out of his slouch. "You're right. Need to put it behind me." He went to get into his uniform.

She was exhausted. They'd spent the last four days grinding through swirling emotions, holding onto each other when they could find a private moment – being closer than they'd ever been – and acting stoic amid the tedious process of starting to wrap up the case. They got to sleep together two of the nights – she had to be on duty the others – and holding each other helped. But it was the most bizarre clash of emotions for him, and for her an unimaginable ride of feelings, from attending to his pain to reprimanding him for lame rationalizations of his father's vigilante action.

They'd solved Westhaven's biggest murders, but they were burying the sheriff's father, the killer. It was wrenching for him and she could only stand by him during the day and hold him tight at night. They worked through the media circus by focusing on filling out reams of paper: evidence submission slips, incident reports, body custody forms and going through a battery of interrogations. Mike had violated procedure in leaving a prisoner with access to a loaded gun. There would be an internal investigation. What was happening was at odds with what she'd always imagined would happen when they closed these infamous cases. She assumed they would be drinking champagne, instead it had been a couple of quiet beers at Mike's place, just the two of them. And they had opened a file tagged, *S959 Cougar* and it wouldn't be closed until the investigation was complete. She'd thought how weird it looked to have an "S" (for suicide) file named Cougar. They'd pieced everything together based on what Jackhammer had admitted and the evidence now made sense.

Richard Roger Ryder had obviously been suffering from severe depression and fit, in part, the profile of a potential killer. Of course, profiles are guesses at best and in hindsight they had put too much weight in the profile. But there'd been evidence, as well as pressure, to have an alternative suspect to Goodall. Jack purposely set it up to create the illusion of a disgruntled ex-employee. Jack was a crack shot and he had missed deliberately that night. And he made the Trott shooting similar, except he killed her. He'd planned to expand his killing to other cities like Pittsburgh so when Ryder ran in that direction he moved up his schedule. He gained close access to victims like Riggins and Douglas with police identification, easily obtained by an ex-cop. He acknowledged the killing of Mrs. Goodall by Ignagni was a mistake, but in his twisted mind he couldn't resist the thought of Goodall spending life in prison, and watching his son put him away.

CHAPTER SIXTY-THREE

Mike had attended more funerals than he wanted to because the department always tried to send someone to victims' funerals. As he stood next to Gritt and the fake, green-grass carpet that covered the dirt that would soon cover his father, he wondered who the victim was in this case. If his father was the victim, then he was the victim's family. But how could a serial killer be a victim. If his father wasn't a victim, then he wasn't the victim's family, he was the killer's family. What was he doing here? The pain burnt through him. He wished it was over. He wanted to shout, *bury the bastard.*

It seemed like an eternity before they lowered his father into eternity and, in that moment, eternity was more than just a hole in the ground, it was a place where latent anger might get transformed into acceptance and understanding, and maybe even love, someday. His capacity for love had been absent since his mother had left … until now, until Gritt.

Side-by-side, they stood at attention as the bugler played Taps, and as the last, forlorn note faded, he touched her hand.

She took it. *Give a damn what anyone thinks, I'm here for him.*

The past dropped away, and the future was before him – and next to him. He turned to her, "Thank you." His eyes said everything.

EPILOGUE

Two months after his father's funeral, Mike Cougar resigned as Sheriff of Haven County. Chief Deputy, Gritt Hansen, remained on staff and was appointed 'Acting Sheriff' until a new sheriff could be elected.

Before retiring, Mike and Gritt delivered a solid case to the DA and the grand jury indicted Alexander Goodall for murder. They had Jackhammer's confession and his shoeprint helped corroborate his story. Gibson tracked the twenty-five-thousand dollars that Jackhammer had deposited, and Perk Allen found a second, twenty-five-thousand withdrawal made by Goodall and redeposited by him two days later. The DA pointed out the obvious. Ignagni had never showed up to collect – they never found Ignagni's body, but they had his rental car records. The McDonald's kids and Grant Hawkins were good witnesses, and the clincher, Special Agent Edwards found Vincenzo Pomante in Florida and dragged his ass back for the trial. Goodall got life, eligible for parole in fifteen years. Mike and Gritt had a small celebration over Goodall getting the publicity he so craved – Wall Street Journal, Forbes, Fortune, Business Week, CNN – just not the kind he wanted. Mike called it 'one huge downsizing of a reputation.' Perk Allen earned his stipend and Goodall earned a spot on his wall of rogues.

The new CEO at Syntex laid-off another two thousand workers and Andover Manufacturing of Syracuse moved their operations to Juárez, Mexico. Frankie and Helen had to close the diner and Sid Leavens died of a heart attack. In his will, he left Irene Ryder fifty-thousand dollars.

So far, the best part of Mike's retirement had been that he and Gritt no longer had to hide their relationship. But they were discreet, wanting to maintain a degree of separation until Goodall's trial was over. But they couldn't. The trial had kept getting delayed and they kept needing to be together.

Mike had taken time off and was now dabbling in private investigation work. His reputation as a skilled investigator brought him assignments from Ethan Solomon and Wyatt Jones. It was boring; but paid the mortgage. He spent most evenings at home, watching the Mets, keeping his cat Mercedes company and welcoming Gritt into his home and bed. She was up to her pretty little ass in work – another homicide – and was putting in long hours, but there were lots of sleepovers. He was happy, she was happy – mostly.

It was after midnight when she came through the door – she had her own key. "You can't still be watching the Mets?"

"Fifteenth inning. Six-six tie. Good game." He flipped out of the recliner and kissed her. She unbuckled her gun belt, threw it on a chair and flung herself against his granite physique. They tumbled onto the sofa.

"I'm exhausted. Need my Michael fix."

"Not too exhausted to escape to our sanctuary of – "

"Never." She kissed him. "Maybe the quiet sanctuary tonight, instead of the wild one."

He slipped his powerful arms under her. "Your wish is my command."

She let her fantasies replace the fatigue. "And your command is my wish."

"Is that another of your twisted clichés or more of your deep desire?"

"Find out." She remembered him unbuttoning her shirt, standing up, pulling her pants off, lifting her over his shoulder, bumping her feet on the bedroom door, and then absorbing the demanding weight of his body and the glorious desperation of his arousal. Submission. Then sleep.

"Coffee … for my beautiful, Olympic whore."

"You sure know how to charm a girl." She sat up in bed as he put the coffee on the side table. "Love it when you yank me out of my exhausting, law-enforcing good life and turn me into a prostituting, fantasy-filled, bad girl. Except, it's exhausting."

"I'll never believe you. If you can run a mile in four-minutes, then – "

"Not quite four-minutes."

"Helluva lot faster than any other woman. And to have the woman who is faster than all others, better in bed than all others, stronger than all others, more loving than all others, and – "

"And your whore."

He grinned. "Yes, that too."

"I love it …" She looked up at him. "I love you Michael."

He hesitated. His eyes softened. She saw them connect to something, something deep inside.

"I love you too."

She pulled him onto the bed. They folded into each other, lying perfectly still for the longest moment. Close. Alone. Complete.

• • •

Shortly after the new sheriff was elected, Gritt resigned – for two reasons. One, she didn't see eye-to-eye with the new guy, and more importantly, she wanted more time with Michael. He was now busy as hell with his PI business and who better to help than her. They took a four-day, get-away to the Bahamas and came up with a plan. Michael said, "We'll be partners-in-crime, solving the crime of being apart, making money solving other people's crimes, and making sure we never get caught for our own sexual crimes of passion. They became partners in Cougar-Hansen, Private Investigations Inc.

Then one day, they got a call from Grant Hawkins in Manhattan, Justine, Chrystine's daughter was missing, vanished. NYPD were doing nothing, saying, 'Probably a runaway.' Hawkins was desperate. Mike's heart accepted the case before his mind considered the facts. He asked

Gritt what she thought, and that night they were on a flight to New York to take on a case that would immerse them in one of the most twisted and unspeakable crimes imaginable.